Currency of Souls

Currency of Souls

KEALAN PATRICK BURKE

SUBTERRANEAN PRESS 2007

First Edition

ISBN-10
1-59606-069-7

ISBN-13
978-1-59606-069-2

Subterranean Press
PO Box 190106
Burton, MI 48503

www.subterraneanpress.com

To Bill Schafer,

For the faith

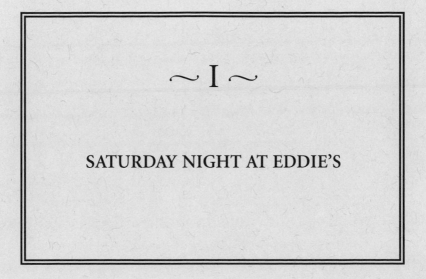

~ I ~

SATURDAY NIGHT AT EDDIE'S

1

Eddie's Tavern.

    This is where I come to try to forget my pain. There's so much of it here that isn't mine, it should make me feel better, but it doesn't.

And yet here I am, same as always. Saturday night at Eddie's. There's no neon sign out front, nothing to advertise this as a place to come drown your sorrows, and that makes sense because sorrows aren't drowned here, not all the way, only pushed under and held for a while.

The moon is a nicotine-stained fingernail as I step out of my truck, ponder the feel of my gut straining against my belt, and ease the door shut behind me. I'm getting fat, and I suppose as they say, like death and taxes, I'm shit out of luck if I expect to be surprised by it. Man eats as much chili as I do without chasing it down with a few laps around the barn, well…weight doesn't evict itself.

I start on the path to the tavern door and see pale orbs behind the smoked glass turn in my direction. Nothing slips past these people, quiet or not. The door doesn't creak, though it's old enough to have earned that luxury. Instead it sighs. I sigh too, but I don't share the door's regret. For me, I'm just glad to be out of the cold and among friends, even if they mightn't look at me the same way. Even if, in the dark of night when sleep's a distant memory, I really don't think of them the same way either.

All the usual folks are here.

The pale willowy woman with the figure that could have been carved from soap, that's Gracie. She inherited this place from her Daddy, and considers it less a gift than another in a long line of curses from a man who dedicated his life to making hers a living hell. Leaving her the bar was his way of ensuring she'd stay right where he wanted her, in a run-down hole with no prospects and surrounded by friends not her own.

Gracie has no love for anyone, least of all herself. She's still got her looks, though they fade a little every day, and she'd get out of this place in a second if she thought the city would take her. I'm sure it probably would. Take her, grind her up, and spit her out to die on some dogshit-encrusted sidewalk a thousand miles from home. Chances are a pretty girl like that with little world experience would end up missing, or turning tricks in the back office of some sleazy strip-joint to keep her in heroin. No, a girl like Gracie is better off right where she is, polishing glasses that stay so milky with grime you almost expect to see smoke drift out of them when she picks them up. She might be miserable, but I figure that's her own doing. Her overbearing father's influence is just an excuse. He's dead, after all, and buried out back. There's nothing to stop her selling this dive, except maybe a burning need to prove herself to his ghost.

At the bar sits a naked man. That's Cobb. Cobb says he's a nudist, and is waiting for the rest of the colony to come apologize for treating him so poorly. What they did to him is unclear, but he's been waiting almost three years now so most of us expect he's going to die disappointed. Cobb has big ears, a wide mouth and a line of coarse gray hair from the nape of his neck to the crack of his bony ass. He looks like a hungover werewolf caught in mid-transformation, and knows only four jokes. His enthusiasm doesn't diminish no matter how many times he tells them.

"Sheriff…" he says with a wide grin.

Here comes the first of them.

"A sailor and a penguin walk into a bar…"

"You'll have to take the back door," I respond, feeding him his own punch line.

"Shit…I told you that one?"

"Once or twice."

Two stools down, sits Wintry McCabe, a six foot six giant of a man who could probably blow the whole place clear into the next state if he sneezed. He's mute though, so you're shit out of luck if you're waiting for a warning. Gracie asked him once how he'd lost his voice and that's how we all found out that even if he could talk, chances are he wouldn't say very much. Near the top of the *Milestone Messenger* (our weekly rag), in the tight white space beneath the headline, he wrote, in blue ink and childish handwriting: WENT UP THE RIVER. COST ME MY WORDS.

Then he smiled, finished his drink and left. After he'd gone, we speculated what the *Messenger*'s new and intriguing sub-header might mean. Cobb reckons Wintry lost his tongue in a fishing or boating incident. Florence thinks he did something that affected him spiritually, something that forced him to take a vow of silence as repentance. Cadaver believes Wintry's done hard time, was "sent up the river" and someone in there relieved him of his tongue. I favor this theory. He looks like a man with secrets, none of them good. But Wintry has never volunteered any clarification on the subject; he hasn't written a message since, and he seldom opens his mouth long enough or wide enough for us to see if that tongue's still attached. If he can't communicate what he wants with gestures, he goes without. That's the kind of guy he is. But while it remains a mystery why he's mute, we at least know why he's called "Wintry". He got the name on account of how he lives in an old tarpaper shack on the peak of Grable Mountain, the only mountain within 100 miles that has snow on the top of it no matter what the season. As a result, even when there's suffocating heat down here in the valley, Wintry's always dressed in thick boots, gloves, and a fur-lined parka, out of which his large black hairless head pokes like a turtle testing the air. Tonight, he's testing a Scotch, neat. And while may not be able to talk, he sure likes to listen.

He's listening to Florence Bright now. She's sitting sideways on her stool, her pretty ankle-length dress covering up a pair of legs every guy in town dreams about. She's wearing a halter-top to match, the flimsy cotton material hiding another pair of attributes every guy in town dreams about. Flo is the prettiest gal I know. Reminds me a little of Veronica Lake in her heyday, right down to the wavy blonde hair and dark, perfectly plucked eyebrows. Florence has the dubious honor in this town of being both a woman in high demand, and a woman feared, but guys get drunk enough they forget they're afraid of her. Everyone thinks she murdered her husband, see, and while I don't know for sure whether she did or not, it's enough to keep me from sidling up to her in my sad little lovelorn boots. Wasn't much of a justice system here at the time, and I did what I could investigation-wise but wasn't a badge inside the city limits or out that could pin the blame on Flo. Nothing added up, and I have to wonder how many male—hell, maybe even *female*—cops were just fine with that. Wonder how many she sweet-talked into forgetting themselves. After all, we had a woman obviously abused by her husband, then said abuser turns up not only dead but so dead even the coroner coughed up the last bit of grub he'd poked into his mouth when he saw the body. Something wasn't right. That, or someone didn't do something they should've. More than once I've put myself under that particularly hot spotlight but quit before I get too close to things I'd rather not see.

So that's Flo, and looking at her there, the last thing you'd ever call her is a murderer. Of course that might just mean she's cold-hearted. But whether or not she knifed Henry Bright to death, doused his body in kerosene and lit the match, I have to admit I get a stab of envy every time she laughs and touches Wintry's elbow. Long time since I made a woman laugh. Long time since I did anything to a woman but make her weep.

I take a seat at one of three round tables spread out between the bar and the door. The abundance of space and lack of furniture make the place seem desolate and empty no matter how many customers it has, though the seven people here now, myself included, is about as busy as it gets. Except on Saturday nights, of course, when we expect one more. The poor lighting, courtesy of two plain bulbs hooded by cracked green shades, does nothing but spotlight dust and crowd everybody's table with shadows.

At the table across from me, a young man in a plaid shirt sits sweating and scowling at me through his dark hair. One hand holds his bottle of beer in a white-knuckle grip; the other is under the table. Probably on a gun. That's Kyle Turner, and he's wanted me dead since the night I murdered his parents. That was last summer. Every Saturday night since, the kid's been in here, trying to talk himself into using that Magnum .357 of his to ventilate my skull, but so far he hasn't been able to draw it out from under the table. So he just sits there glaring, and has Gracie drop the beer down to him at his table so he doesn't have to get up and reveal the piece he thinks I don't know about.

Someday he might get the guts to do it, and they'll probably kick him out of here, but only for disturbing the peace, not because he'll have disturbed my brain with a few warm rounds of the kind not meant to be served in bars. I admit I get a bit of a kick out of seeing him though, and if he weren't there I'd surely miss him. His hatred of me makes me feel a little like Wild Bill Hickock.

I know nodding a greeting at him will only aggravate him further, so instead I look the other way, away from the bar, back toward the door and the table shoved right up against the wall to the right of it. Cadaver is sitting there, lost in the shadows, though I smelled him as soon as I came in. I didn't offer him a greeting because you're not supposed to unless he offers you one first. It's a tradition that precedes my patronage here, so I honor it without knowing why.

"Evenin', Tom," he says, in that voice of his that sounds like someone dragging a guitar pick over a bass string. He's got a box where his larynx would be, which I guess is the cost of sixty years of smoking, and his face has sunken so deep you can almost see the contours of his chipped fillings beneath the skin. He's got a cataract in one eye, the lid is pulled halfway down over the other, and an impressively wide scar bisects his face from forehead to cleft of chin. He's a sight, and knows it, which is why he favors the dark, where he counts the pennies from his pocket and places them in rows, over and over and over again, until the sound of those coins meeting each other starts to feel like a measurement of time.

An ugly man, for sure, but damn he smells so good he makes me ashamed of my cheap cologne. Makes me wish I'd remembered to buy a nice bottle of Calvin Klein or some such fragrance. Something expensive. You can tell a lot by the way someone smells. Cadaver uses his to hide the smell of death.

"Evening," I tell him back, and feel more than see his twisted smile.

"Wonder who's drivin' tonight," he says, each word separated by a crackling swallow. It's wrong of me to say it, but I wish he wouldn't talk. Man without a human voice is better staying quiet, and I know that grinding electro-speak gives everyone else the creeps too.

"Wish I knew," I say, and turn to the bar. "Gracie?"

"Comin' up." She tosses on the bar the soiled rag she's been using to wipe the counter. "Hot or cold?" This is her way of asking if I want beer or whiskey. A strand of her auburn hair falls across her eyes as she waits for my reply, and she whips it back with such irritation, I'm suddenly glad she doesn't have a kid to use as a piñata for her misery.

"Both," I answer, because it's that kind of night.

As if I've asked her to wash my damn car, she sighs and sets about getting my drinks.

I drop my gaze to the mirror behind the bar and see Wintry raise a hand. His reflection waggles its fingers, keeps waggling them like a spider descending a strand of silk, until the hand is out of sight, then he nods twice and goes back to his drink.

"I heard," I say to his broad expanse of back. "We could do with it." I glance over at the kid, see his puzzled expression surface through the anger before he catches me looking and quickly goes back to scowling. His arm tenses, and I wonder briefly if I'm going to feel a bullet rip through my crotch, or my knee. The way that gun is angled makes me wish he'd just take the damn thing out and go for a headshot. But I guess he wants to make me suffer as much as possible.

"Wintry says rain's coming," I explain, careful to make it seem like a general announcement so the kid doesn't decide I'm trying to make a fool out of him by implying he didn't get it.

"Started already," Cadaver drones from the shadows.

"Weatherman says it's goin' to be a storm," Cobb intones, his buttocks wriggling as a shudder passes through him. "Hope I can bed down in here if it does." This last is directed at Gracie as she rounds the bar, a bottle of Bud in one hand, a bottle of whiskey in the other.

"This ain't a boardin' house, Cobb," she says over her shoulder, puffing air up to get the errant lock of hair out of her eyes. I'm struck by the sudden urge to brush it out of her face for her, but she'd likely jerk away and tell me to mind myself, and she'd be right of course. Long ago I learned that men and women's ideas of polite isn't always the same, and never will be as long as we guys feel compelled to consult our dicks every time a woman walks into the room. "But there are plenty of empty places on Winter Street. I'm sure Horace and Maggie'd show you someplace to lay your bones. Hell, if you dog Kirk Vess's heels, I bet he'll lead you to shelter."

Vess is our town lunatic, a card Gracie has played in the past just to get on Cobb's nerves.

"I'm sure." Cobb's repulsion at the idea is clear, but everyone here knows he's fighting a losing battle if he thinks he'll get Gracie to cave. "I can pay you though."

Gracie puts down my drinks, brushes dust off my table and looks into my eyes for the tiniest of seconds, enough to let me know that the superhuman precognitive sense unique to women has alerted her to what I'd just a moment ago been considering. And the message is: *Lucky you didn't.*

She heads back to the bar, a lithe woman dressed in drab clothes designed to make her look less attractive. I'll never understand that, but then again, the day men understand women is the day we may as well go sit on our plots and wait to be planted.

Or maybe I'm just not that bright at the back of it all.

"You can pay me by puttin' some clothes on," she tells Cobb. "Maybe if you were covered up, you wouldn't need to fret about the rain."

"I'll put you up," Cadaver offers in his robot voice, and Cobb turns slowly around, his bare ass making squeaking sounds against the top of the stool. I wonder how much Pine-Sol Gracie uses in any given month on that chair alone. It's the only one she allows him use. Just that chair, or his squeaky ass goes on the floor.

There's a look of consternation on Cobb's heavily bearded face when he turns fully around, his small blue eyes squinting into the shadows, as if seeing Cadaver will lessen his distaste at the idea of spending the night with the man. His chest is a mass of silvery curls, thickest along his sternum where it leads down over a swollen belly to a frenzied explosion of pubic hair, from which a small stubby penis pokes out. We've been seeing Cobb and his tackle for three years now. We should be used to it, and I guess for the most part we are, but every time his dick eyeballs me, I want to ask him if chestnut leaves are considered clothing by whatever governing body inflicted his nakedness on us in the first place. But I keep my mouth shut and avert my eyes, to the kid, who's doing a good job of looking like he may rupture something at any minute, and finally focus on my drink.

There's a thumbprint on the shot glass too large to be mine.

"That's mighty decent of you," Cobb says eventually.

"Don't mention it."

Over Cadaver's pennies, I can almost hear the hamster wheel spinning in the nudist's head. Then he says, "But you know what…? I'll just call my wife. She won't mind comin' to get me. Not at this hour. Not at night." He claps his hands as if he's just stumbled upon the cure for world hunger. "Hell, she'll have heard there's goin' to be a storm, so she'll have to come get me, right? No woman would make her man walk in this kinda weather." He's looking for support now, and not for the first time I envy Wintry's muteness, because everyone here knows that getting Mrs. Cobb to come get her husband isn't going to be as easy as he seems to think. The day he abandoned clothes was the last time anyone saw Eleanor Cobb in town. Naturally, we worried, but a few weeks after her husband's 'unveiling' I checked on her. She's fine, just laid up with a terminal case of mortification that I don't see ending until Cobb starts wearing shorts, or that chestnut leaf. Why she stays with him at all is another one of those mysteries.

"You could always start walkin' now before the worst of it hits," Flo chimes in. Her voice is husky, perfectly befitting a crime noir femme fatale. It makes my hair stand on end in a good way. "No one ever drowned in the rain."

Cobb ignores her. He's got a drink before him and intends to finish it. He squeaks back around to face the bar. "Can I use the phone?" he asks Gracie, and this at least she's willing to allow, even though it's a payphone and no one should need permission. But this is Gracie's place, and things run differently here. Stone-faced, she scoops one of the nudist's dollars off the bar, feeds it into the till, and drops four quarters into his outstretched palm. With a grin of gratitude, Cobb hops off his stool and heads out to the small hallway that leads to the payphone, and the restrooms beyond.

No one says anything.

There is silence except for the clink of Cadaver's pennies.

A few moments later, Cobb starts swearing into the phone.

No one is surprised.

I raise my glass with a muttered: "To Blue Moon," in honor of the man who can't be here, and take the first sip of whiskey. It cauterizes my throat. I hiss air through my teeth. Flo goes back to talking to Wintry, leans in a little closer, one leg crossed over the other, one shoe awful close to brushing against the big black man's ankle, and there's that envy again. But I remind myself that she's probably only cozying up to him because he's mute, and therefore unlikely to ever ask her about her past. For the second time in a handful of minutes, I'm covetous of Wintry's condition.

Cobb slams down the phone, curses and stalks back to the bar, his flaccid tool whacking against his thigh. I close my eyes, pray my gorge can handle another night of the old man's exhibitionism and concentrate on refilling my glass.

"She weren't there," he mutters before anyone has a chance to ask, and slaps a hand on the counter. "Fill me up, Gracie," he says. "And make it same as Tom's. It'll keep me warm on the walk home."

I almost expect Cadaver to remind Cobb of his offer, but Cadaver is ill, not dumb. He says nothing, just keeps on counting those pennies.

"You make it sound like you can just walk outta here as you please," Gracie says scornfully. "You take a blow to the head, or is all the drink just makin' you dumber?"

"He ain't the boss of me," Cobb says, scowling like a sulky teen. There's no passion in his voice, no truth to his words. Everyone here knows that, just like we know a little brave talk never hurts, as long as you only do it among friends.

"You reckon he'll show up tonight, Tom?" Flo asks, twirling a lock of her hair around a fingernail the color of blood.

"I reckon so."

She sighs, and turns her back on me. Flo wants hope, wants me to tell her that maybe tonight will be special, that maybe for the first Saturday night in years, Reverend Hill isn't going to come strolling in that door at eleven o' clock, but I can't. I realized a long time ago that I'm a poor liar, and despite the gold badge on my shirt, no one should look to me for hope, or anything else.

From the corner comes a sound like a dead branch snapping. It's Cadaver clucking his tongue. Seems a coin slipped off the top of one of his miniature copper towers.

Gracie goes back to pretending she's cleaning the bar.

Cobb grumbles over his beer.

Occasionally I catch Wintry looking at my reflection in the mirror. What I see in his dark eyes might be concern, even pity, but if I was him, I wouldn't be bothering with the mirror, or me, not when Flo's breathing in his ear. Besides, I'm not looking for sympathy, only solutions, and I don't reckon there's any to be had here tonight or any other.

The heat from the kid's glare is reliable as any fire on a winter's night.

These are my friends.

2

The clock draws out the seconds, the slow sweep of the narrow black minute hand unable to clear the face of a decade's worth of dust. When at last it reaches eleven, with no sign among us patrons that any time has passed at all, there comes the sound of shoes crunching gravel.

Everyone tries real hard not to watch the door, but there's tension in the air so tight you could hang your washing off it.

Reverend Hill enters, and with him comes the rain, and not the spatters Cadaver announced, but a full-on tacks-poured-on-a-metal-roof downpour. Bastard couldn't have timed it better, though if it inspires an impromptu sermon from him, he'll have trouble getting anyone to believe God is responsible, no more than we'd buy that the silvery threads of rain over his shoulder are strings leading to the hand of a divine puppeteer.

For him, the door groans as he shuts out the storm.

He doesn't pause to regard each of us in turn like any other man would, gauging the company he has to keep, or counting the sinners. Instead, that confident stride carries his lean black-clad self right on up to the bar, where Gracie's stopped cleaning and watches him much the same way the kid at the next table is watching me. Except, of course, Kyle's not looking at me right now. All eyes are on the holy man.

The town of Milestone has rotten luck, much like the people who call it home, though to be fair, over time we may have grown too fond of blaming the things we bring upon ourselves on chance, or fate. It's more likely that bad people, or folks with more to hide than their own towns can tolerate gravitate here, where no one asks questions and they carry their opinion of you in their eyes, never on their tongues.

When Reverend Hill came to town, filling a vacancy that had been there for three years, he brought with him the hope that spiritual guidance might chase away the dark clouds that have hung over the people of Milestone since Reverend Lewis used his belt, a rickety old chair, and a low beam in his bedroom to hasten his rendezvous with his maker.

But in keeping with the town's history of misfortune—or whatever you want to call it—what Hill brought to Milestone wasn't hope, but fear.

"Rum, child," he tells Gracie, and leans against the counter right next to Cobb. He makes no attempt to conceal his disgust for the naked man.

Hill has beady eyes, too focused, self-righteous, and intense, to bother with color of any determinate hue. I'm convinced those eyes can see through walls, which may explain why no one in Milestone goes to confession anymore. He has eyebrows a woman would kill for, plucked and arched like chapel naves, a long thin nose that spreads out at the end to allow him the required amount of air with which to fuel his bluster, and a thin pale-lipped mouth that sits like a scar above a pointed chin. At a guess I'd say he's about sixty, but his age seems to change with his mood. The dim light shuns his greased back hair, which is artificially black. Everything about the guy is artificial, as we discovered not long after he came to town.

Some folks think he's the devil.

I don't, but I'm sure they've met.

"Evenin', Reverend," Cobb says, without looking at the man. Cobb's afraid of Hill. We all are, but the nudist's the only one who greets him.

"What do the young children of Milestone think when they see you walking the streets with your tool of sin flapping in front of their faces, Cobb?" the Reverend asks, louder than is necessary. "Immodesty is a flagstone on the path to Hell, or were you operating under the false assumption that nakedness is next to Godliness? Think your 'gift' gives you the freedom to disregard common decency?"

Cobb turns pink all over, and doesn't reply.

The Reverend grins. His large piano key teeth gleam. Gracie sets his drink down in front of him. She doesn't wait for payment.

I'm alarmed to find myself choked up, gut jiggling, trying to contain a laugh. "Tool of sin" is bad, even for Hill. Sure, he makes my skin crawl every time I see him, but even though I know there's nothing funny about this situation, nothing funny about what goes down here in Milestone's only functioning bar at this same time every Saturday night. As it turns out, the humor must already have been on my face, because those coal-dark eyes of his move from Cobb's pink mass to me, and his grin drops as if someone smacked him across the face.

"Something funny, Tom?"

"Nope."

"Are you sure?"

"Yep."

"Your smile says different."

"Who can trust a smile these days, Reverend? I sure don't trust yours."

That's enough to give him his grin back. He scoops his rum off the counter and saunters over to my table with all the confidence of a man who enjoys his work, who's going to enjoy knocking the town sheriff down a few pegs. He drags back the empty chair opposite me, sits, and studies me for a second. I feel like carrion being appraised by a vulture.

His face is only a shade darker than the little rectangle of white at his collar.

"Tell me something, Tom."

"Shoot."

At this, Hill looks over his shoulder, to where the kid is still sweating, but I'm willing to bet that sweat's turned cold now. The Reverend turns back and winks. "Better not say that too loud. Someone might take you up on it."

"He's confused," I tell him, and take a sip of my whiskey. Beer's a pleasant drink, and requires patience; whiskey's a straight shot to the brain, and I need that now if I'm going to act tough in front of the only man in Milestone who scares me. "He should be gunning for *you*."

Thunder rattles the rafters; the smoked glass flickers with light, illuminating the rain pebbled across its surface.

"Maybe so," the Reverend says, "But he knows better than to shoot a man of the cloth. He's a God-fearing soul. He wants vengeance without damnation."

"Bit late for that isn't it?"

His lips crease in amusement. "I'm not sure I know what you mean."

I decide not to humor him. "Who is it tonight?"

Cadaver has stopped counting his pennies.

"Straight to it, eh? I like that."

"Cut the bullshit."

He clucks his tongue. "Profanity. The mark of an ignorant man."

I wish that were true. I'd love to be ignorant, sitting here with my drink, trading barbs with a priest who may or may not be the devil himself. At least then I wouldn't see what's coming.

"So who's driving?" I ask, and everyone but Wintry turns to look. He's watching the mirror.

The Reverend reaches into his pocket and tosses a pair of car keys on the table between us. "You are," he says, and every hard-earned ounce of my defiance is obliterated. He might as well have shoved a grenade down my throat and locked me in iron skin. I release a breath that shudders at the end. No one in the bar sighs their relief but I see shoulders relax, just a little, and hear the clink of Cadaver's pennies as he goes back to counting.

On the table, there's a ring of six keys. Three of them are for the pre-fabricated hut that passes as my office. Two are for the front and back doors of the prefabricated hut that passes as my house. The last one's for my truck, and the keys have fallen so that one is sticking straight up, toward the Reverend. It's not a coincidence.

"You know how it goes," he says, and sits back in his chair. "And if I were you, I wouldn't be all that surprised. You've dodged the bullet for quite a while, haven't you?"

His face swells with glee. I imagine if I punch him right now, which is exactly what every cell in my body is telling me to do, his head would pop like a balloon. But no matter how satisfying that might be it won't change the fact that tonight my number's come up. I get to drive. Hill, son of a bitch that he is, is still only a messenger, a courier boy. Putting a hurting on him wouldn't make a difference.

Cobb speaks up, "Hell, Tom, I'll drive for you. It'd keep me out of the rain. Besides, I told 'ol Blue Moon I'd take him up a bottle of somethin'. Kill two birds with one stone, right?" His nervous grin is flashed for everyone's approval, but he doesn't get it. No one even looks at him, except me, and though I don't say it, I'm grateful. I know Cobb walks around in the nip for one reason only—he wants to be noticed, remembered for something other than his gift, or maybe he does it to draw attention away from it. A *hey look everybody! Underneath my clothes I'm just the same as you!* kind of gesture. It doesn't work, and I guess, like the rest of us, he's tired of trying, tired of waiting here every Saturday night to find out if he's going to have to murder someone else. Considering what he can do, and what he's had to do in the past, it's got to be tougher on him than most of us. Like being God and the Devil's ping-pong ball. I also know, even if the Reverend allowed it, Cobb wouldn't follow the rules tonight. Chances are, he'd drive my battered old truck right off the Willow Creek Bridge, be smiling while he drowned and poor old Blue

Moon Running Bear would have to go without his whiskey for a little while longer.

"Very noble of you," Hill says, sounding bored. "But this isn't a shift at the sawmill. There's no trading." He looks Cobb up and down. "But don't worry. You'll get your turn. You get that car yet?"

"Wife doesn't let me drive it. Not here. Not when I'll be drinkin'."

"Then either lie or quit drinking. But get it."

"All right."

Cobb offers me a sympathetic glance. I wave it away and look hard at the priest. "Who is it?"

From the breast pocket of his jacket, he produces a pack of Sonoma Lights. "Anyone got a light?"

When no one obliges, Gracie tosses him a box of matches, which he grabs from the air without looking—an impressive trick that leaves me wishing like hell he'd fumbled it. He lights his cigarette and squints at me through a plume of blue smoke. "You want the name?"

"No. I'd like to keep what little sleep I get at night. Unless you want to take that too."

"Oh now, would you listen to this? You make it sound as if you're the victim!" He barks a laugh and swivels in his chair to face the bar. "Is that what all of you think? That I'm the bad guy, come to destroy your lives?" He turns again, addressing Cadaver and the kid this time. "That you're all just innocents, forced to do the bidding of some wicked higher power?" He shakes his head in amazement. "Don't fool yourselves folks. Until I came along you were hanging in Purgatory, waiting for a decision to be made either way. You should be thanking me that you're not all roasting in the fires of Hell."

"So that's not what this is then?"

He leans close, eyes dark, twin threads of blue smoke trailing from his wide nostrils. "Not even close, Deputy Dawg."

We stare at each other over the table. I try to will the kid to take his shot. I don't even care who he hits. But the kid isn't moving, just watching, just like everyone else. The rain keeps raining and the thunder keeps thundering, but inside Eddie's there isn't a sound, until I speak.

"This will end, you know." It's a threat that has no weight behind it. I want this to be over; I want things to be the way they were before my wife died, before the kid got it into his head that my skull would look better spread across the wall; before we all ended up here as slaves to our sins, but it's too late. There's no turning back now. Things have gone too far. Hill knows this, knows surer than shit that all of us are going to be here next Saturday night and the Saturday night after that, and the one after that until we've paid off whatever debt it is he's decided—or more accurately, whoever *controls* him has decided—we owe.

But tonight isn't going to be that night, and as blue light fills the cracks in the rundown bar, I reach across and slide the keys toward me.

"I know it will end," the Reverend answers, and pauses to take a deep drag on his cigarette. "Tonight it ends for you."

I close my fist around the keys and let them bite into my palm.

"You get a thief and his girlfriend," he continues. "The guy shot a pump jockey in the face, killed a woman and injured a little kid. The girlfriend's an addict and a whore. No one will miss them."

"Someone will. Someone always does."

The priest sits back again and smiles. "That's not for us to worry about."

"Not for you maybe."

"These missives from your goody-goody conscience are getting to be a real bore, Tom."

"This, from a priest."

His smile fades. "You'd best get moving, Sheriff. Your people need you."

I throw back what's left of the whiskey, then grab the bottle to keep me company. Hill won't object—he likes us good and drunk—and though Gracie might be pissed that she's out a few dollars, she won't say anything either. She understands the nature of dirty work.

I stand and jingle the keys in my palm. "When this is over," I tell him. "You're the only one going to Hell."

He doesn't answer. Instead he slides my glass in front of him and puts his own thumb over the print. It fits perfectly. He chuckles and turns his chair around so he's facing the bar. Flo avoids his gaze and slips her hand over Wintry's. Everyone goes back to doing a real bad job of pretending nothing's amiss.

At my back, Cobb grumbles on.

The few steps to the front door feel like a condemned man's walk to the electric chair, the lightning through the windows only adding to the effect.

As I reach the door and grab the brass handle, the lightning reveals the skeletal profile hunkered nearby, the shadows of the coin towers like knives jabbing at his chest. He's looking out the window, darkness pooling in the hollows of his eyes as, in what passes for a whisper, he says, "Someone's comin'." Then I hear it. Hurried footsteps, confused shuffling, and I move back just in time to avoid getting my face mashed in by a hunk of weathered oak as the door bursts open almost hard enough to knock it off its hinges. Rain, wind and shadows fill the doorway. Without knowing, or caring who it is that's standing on the threshold, I lunge forward, plant my hand in the middle of the figure's chest and shove them back out into the storm. "Get the hell out of here," I tell them, in as hard a voice as I can muster under the circumstances. Hill would love this, more recruits for his twisted game. But whoever it is I've just tried to dissuade, grunts, pivots on a heel, slams back against the door for balance and reaches out an arm toward where I'm standing, ready for anything.

Anything but the gun that's suddenly thrust in my face, the steel barrel dripping rainwater. "Get the fuck back inside," a man's voice says, and then a woman stumbles forth from the darkness and collapses on the floor. The rain that drips from her sodden form is pink. She's bleeding somewhere but right now all my attention is focused on the black eye of the gun that's three inches from my nose.

"Flo, Gracie…someone help the lady," I call out.

"Don't you touch her," the man says. I wish I could see his face, but so far he's only a voice and a pale sleeve with a Colt .45 at the end of it.

I'm getting real tired of having guns pointed at me.

3

"Move back," the gunman says. "Now, or I redecorate this shithole with your brains."

"God knows that would be an improvement," the Reverend chimes in, sounding not-at-all annoyed by this intrusion.

The woman is shuddering, and there's that goddamn instinctual need to help, to touch her, make sure she's okay, but that bullet blower keeps me in place.

"How come you don't have a piece?" says the man.

"I do, just not on me."

"Anyone else in there likely to act the hero?"

I consider Kyle. He's got a gun, and the guy's probably going to find that out sooner or later. But "No," I tell him, because later's better.

"You better not be lying to me."

"I'm not."

"Carla, you alive?"

On the floor, head bowed, dark wet hair almost touching the boards, the girl slowly shakes her head. She's bleeding something fierce.

"She needs help." It's an obvious statement, but considering the guy is still standing in the doorway pointing a gun at me, I figure he could use the reminder.

"Yeah, no shit. Don't suppose there's a doctor in there?"

"No, but we can at least patch her up, stop the bleeding. Give her something for the pain. You're not doing her any favors leaving her on the floor."

It doesn't take him long to realize I'm right. He waggles the gun in my face. "Back up. All the way to the bar, and keep your hands where I can see them."

I set the whiskey bottle down on the floor and do as I'm told, walking backwards, hands in the air, until I'm just about level with the Reverend's table. "You plan this?" I ask him, though somehow I know he didn't, not unless he was suddenly stricken with guilt and decided to save me gas money.

"It would seem," he replies, "that we'll have to suffer an unscheduled interlude."

"I find it hard to believe you don't make allowances for this kind of thing."

"Oh, but I do. Before this night is through, that man and his little trollop will be still be so many pounds of mashed up meat branded by the tires of your truck, Tom. Doesn't matter what they do to piss away the meantime."

"Shut your mouths," the man with the gun says. He steps into the light and at last I'm able to see the face of my intended victim. He's little more than a kid, it seems, not much older than Kyle, wearing a cream colored suit that was probably nice before the blood spoiled it, with a white shirt open at the collar. Shoulder-length blonde hair frames a face hardened by the many pit stops on the road to a Hell of his own design. He slams the door shut behind him and stands there, gun trained on me, then at everyone else in the room, before coming round to me again.

"This isn't the way to do it, son," Cadaver says, and the thief almost jumps out of his suit and the skin beneath. I wince, waiting for him to pump a few rounds into the shadow in the corner, but he manages to restrain himself. "Who the fuck is *that?*"

"Cadaver," I tell him. "He's just an old man. Leave him alone."

"The fuck's he doing hiding?"

"He's not. That's his table. Light just isn't so good. It's how he likes it."

"Yeah?" The kid doesn't sound convinced, and his fingers dance on the butt of the gun like he's deciding whether or not to illuminate Cadaver's corner with some muzzle flash. "Move out here with the others."

Cadaver doesn't make a sound, nor does he make a move.

The kid clicks back the hammer. It makes the same sound Cadaver does when he swallows.

"Look kid…" I take a step forward, and realize a split second after I've done it that it's a mistake. The gun finds me again. Now I have two of them pointed at me. If Kyle and this guy fire at the same time, I may very well hit the ground with two shadows. I raise my hands palm out. "Just hang on a second, will ya? No one needs to get hurt here." Which is a damned lie. Sooner or later, someone's going to get hurt, and satin-pillow-in-a-pine-box kind of hurt. Right now though, the question is not who, but how many, and that's not good enough.

The kid catches sight of Cobb. Frowns. "Why's he naked?"

"Because I choose to be," Cobb states boldly. "Ain't got no use for clothes."

The kid smiles, and for a moment I see the *real* kid, the one hiding deep down inside that suit, the kid who watched his manners when his aunt came to visit, said grace before meals, and shook in his shoes when he showed up at the door for his first date. An All-American kid run over on the road of life, relieved of his dreams, then fixed right up with some choice drugs, a gun and a whore and sent on his way. Only to end up here, with his would-be executioner trying to talk some sense into him.

"Some bunch of fuckin' loons we got us here, Carla."

The woman on the floor doesn't respond, but I almost don't notice because now I know her name, and it dances before my eyes in lurid neon, mocking me. I wasn't supposed to know. I don't want to know, but now that I do, their ghosts will have names too.

Wintry turns around in his seat, his huge head sheened with perspiration, and stands. The expression on his face is unreadable, but that big nose of his is flaring at the ends like a bull about to charge.

"Hey now." The kid is visibly intimidated. "Sit right back down big man, or I'm going to have to cut you down."

Wintry doesn't move, but his eyes move to the fallen girl.

"What are you doin'?" Flo asks, and grabs his sleeve. "Sit *down*."

But Wintry doesn't. He glances at me and nods one time, as if it's the cue to do something, as if he figures I'm clever enough to read those large brown eyes of his, or maybe he thinks he's already shared his strategy via some telepathic link. Whatever it is, I don't have time to figure it out because Wintry's already moving, brushing past me, his jacket making a zipping sound as it grazes my outstretched fingers. It smells of pinesap and smoke.

"Wait…"

My objection is overruled by Flo's panicked cry. "Wintry, don't!"

Wintry keeps walking.

The kid stiffens. "Hey, I said sit *down* man."

"Goddamn it," Gracie pipes up. "Do as he says."

The kid aims the gun at the big man's chest, licks his lips.

Wintry keeps walking, but he's not heading for the kid. He's headed for the girl, and surely the kid sees this. Surely he'll read the big black man's intentions, understand what I didn't, and—

There's a bang as if thunder has slipped under the door, a burst of light, and Wintry finally stops walking.

Flo screams, her hands flying to her face like a mask made of fingers. The girl on the floor whimpers and looks up. Her face is a mass of ragged bloody scratches. The rain has smudged her mascara into raccoon-like circles around her glassy eyes. Her lipstick runs clear across her cheek. She looks at us all in turn as if she's just realized we're here.

My ears are ringing.

I wait for Wintry to look down, to assess the damage like folks do in the movies before they finally acknowledge a mortal wound and drop to the floor. Wintry'll make a hell of a thud when he falls. My mind races, trying to think of something to do or say, but that shot might as well have passed through my brain.

"Wintry…" Flo sobs.

But when the smoke that coils like low fog between the big black man in the parka and the couple by the door finally dissipates, it's the kid who staggers back and drops to a sitting position, his back against the door. On his face is shock, and confusion; on his shirt is a blossoming crimson flower.

"My, my," says the Reverend.

I hear Flo's breath catch in her throat.

Smoke continues to drift out from beneath Kyle's table. The kid came here tonight to shoot someone, but the bullet that has my name in it now sits lodged in the belly of the man I was supposed to kill. I'll wait to ponder the irony of that. There's no time now.

Silence weighs heavy in the room. At last I find my tongue. "Wintry, go on." He does, stopping by the girl, though his eyes are on the wounded kid, and the gun that's still in his hand.

Cadaver, in an uncharacteristically animated move, emerges from the shadows looking grim, his black plastic raincoat swirling around him. His hip jars the table; another coin drops from its tower. Aside from Wintry and the girl, he's nearest the kid, and knows it, and so hurries to his side, hunkers down and gives the kid a sympathetic glance before relieving him of his weapon. The kid doesn't resist. Because the little microphone that Cadaver needs to press against the metal box in his throat to enable him to be heard is back on his table, he wheezes his words, and no one but him and the kid hear them. The kid stares at the old man as if he believes Death himself has come for him and replies, "Brody. James Brody."

And just like that, my nightmare is complete.

"Fuck," I mutter and squeeze my eyes with a thumb and forefinger.

There comes a crashing sound and everyone jumps, startled, no doubt wondering what calamity has befallen us now, maybe the storm, God's Hand, has come to smite us all one by one, like we damn well deserve. But it isn't anything so dramatic. It's Flo, who has swept her arm across the bar, sending a bunch of glasses and bottles crashing to the floor.

"What the hell?" Cobb stands up, looking down at himself and the shattered remains of his Bud, but I know what she's doing and silently commend her for it.

"Bring her here," she calls to Wintry, and he lifts the girl as if she weighs no more than an empty sack.

Kyle's still watching Brody, who's gasping in the corner like he's taken a slug in the lung. If he had, I figure he'd already be dead, but it's hard to predict any man's reaction to having his body insulted by a bullet.

Cadaver, still with Brody, looks over his shoulder at me and mouths the words, "Needs fixin'."

I know he does, but the Reverend's presence is like an extra shadow at my side, reminding me of the futility of our actions. Whether we patch those two unlucky kids up or not, they're still going to die before the night ends. But Cobb is with Flo now, looking like the world's unlikeliest orderly as they lay frayed towels out across the bar. Gracie is talking in soothing tones to the girl, who I can see now has a wide gash across her chest, another somewhere in the tangle of her hair that's sending rivulets of blood down the back of her neck. Flo takes her hand as Wintry lays the girl down on the bar and heads back for her boyfriend. With the exception of Kyle, who I guess is in shock himself, the Reverend, and me, everyone is helping, even though we're all privy to the same awful truth, truth we have no business knowing.

Those kids are doomed.

But right now, that doesn't seem important. After all, they're here when they shouldn't be, and the keys to my truck, the keys to their fate, are still in my pocket.

So I do the only thing left to do. I go to Kyle.

I stop a few feet from his table, blocking his view of the wounded kid by the door. "You all right?" Another dumb question, but the only one I've got.

"What do you care?"

"You did the right thing, you know. If you hadn't, it'd be Wintry bleeding to death on the floor. Any one of us might have done the same thing."

"But you didn't."

"We would have if we'd had the opportunity."

He looks up at me slowly and blinks, all of the hostility gone from his face, along with the color. "Is he dead?"

"No, but he's hurt bad."

"He going to die?"

I consider my answer, then decide on the truth. "Hell, everybody does, but maybe not tonight."

"I'm going to Hell."

"Why do you say that?"

"Because I murdered him."

"Not yet you didn't. And even if it's too late and he expires on account of that bullet in his belly, all you did was hasten what was coming his way tonight anyway."

"We're all going to Hell."

"Probably. Doesn't mean we have to be in any hurry though."

"That bullet wasn't meant for him."

"I know, but we can either stand here debating who should be dead and who shouldn't, or we can help these kids out."

"Why?" He frowns and the sweat pools in the creases. I'm overcome with a sudden and alarming urge to hug the boy, just crush the fear out of him. But to do that I'd have to be calm myself, and I'm a long way from that right now. Besides, while I suspect he's shot the last man he's ever going to, I've been surprised before, and I'm in no rush to test the theory. Not yet, anyway.

"Because they need it."

He laughs soundlessly, a wheeze that could have come from Cadaver's mouth. "I could put this gun in my mouth right now."

"Sure you could."

"Would you stop me?"

"I reckon I'd try."

"Why?" When he looks up at me, the emotion in his eyes is more powerful than any bullet, powerful enough to make me drop my gaze and immediately feel ashamed of it.

I clear my throat, the words like glass tearing their way up my throat, slicing open my tongue. "Because no matter what you think of me, you're still my son."

He scoffs. "My father's dead."

"No I'm not, I'm standing right here. You're looking at me, just as you've been looking at me every night since your mother died."

"Since you killed her."

"I didn't kill her."

"Yes you did. You killed both of you."

"If that's true then why do you come in here every Saturday night with a gun pointed at me? Can't kill a dead man, y'know."

I'm fighting a losing battle to keep my composure. I want to hug the little son of a bitch, squeeze the hate out of him, reclaim him while I still have the chance, force him to understand.

But I don't understand it myself.

"The bullet wasn't meant for you either," he tells me and finally brings the gun out from beneath the table. I recognize it of course, seeing as how it used to have a home in my holster. No police issue weaponry in Milestone, no sir. You just take whatever you think you'll need to get the job done. Back when there was a job to do, that is.

"It was for me," he says, and I feel my heart shatter into a thousand pieces.

Whatever I might have said, whatever magic words I might have summoned from the ether are blown away by the woman's scream. Both of us turn toward the bar, and see Carla convulsing, chopping that scream into stuttered wails as Flo, wincing, presses a damp cloth to the girl's chest.

"Jesus." I give the kid one final glance, hoping he sees the plea for another chance to talk this over, then I'm gone, storming across to the girl, my heart and soul in ruins as surely as if I was the one stretched out on the bar.

I haven't gotten far, when Brody, slung over Wintry's shoulder, calls out, "Go easy on her. She's pregnant."

And that takes what little wind is left in my sails right the fuck out of them.

I turn on my heel and Reverend Hill slams his glass down on the table and stands. "Enough."

I want to kill him. Rage boils within me, fueled further by regret over Kyle and his intentions, rage at my blindness, at my cowardice, for never questioning the speed with which my world grew dark, or the pain I dealt the people fumbling around within it. "You son of a bitch. You never mentioned a child."

"What difference does it make? People who cause fatal accidents very rarely get the luxury of counting their victims beforehand. Had everything proceeded here as it was damn well supposed to, you'd never have known any different, and that murderer's conscience of yours would have been spared an extra little slice of reality." He steps close, until our noses are almost touching. "Never forget, Sheriff, that I am the only thing standing between you and eternal damnation. *I'm* the closest thing you have to God, and as such I own you, so it would behoove you to stop questioning it and accept it as truth."

"This *is* eternal damnation," I counter, "And it seems to me that God would know what the fuck was going on, which you clearly don't."

Brody moans with pain as Wintry sets him down in his own chair next to Flo. Even in times of stress he knows better than to seat anyone in Cobb's place.

The Reverend looks over my shoulder at the kid, then smiles. "Then let's find out why things *haven't* gone according to plan, shall we?"

Cadaver regains his seat amid the shadows.

Gracie spills bourbon over the girl's exposed chest—the wound is deep—eliciting another agonized shriek from her, and I know I'm right. This is eternal damnation, or at the very least, some kind of waiting room where all we get to do is sit and stew and wait for our number to be called. I decide in that moment, without even the faintest idea how it's going to go down, that more than these kid's numbers are going to be called tonight.

The Reverend stands before the kid, who has a blood-soaked hand clamped over his belly. "Well now," he says, "Looks like you're in a bit of a pickle here."

"We need a doctor," Brody says, his pallid face slick with sweat. "Please."

The Reverend cocks his head. "And why should we do something like that for a man who introduced himself by shoving a gun in a lawman's face, then threatened to shoot the only fella in here who seemed inclined to help him?"

"Gracie, call Doctor Hendricks," I tell her, but the Reverend raises a hand he'd like you to believe was made to heal sinners.

"Do no such thing."

"Reverend," Cobb says. "This ain't how he's supposed to go anyhow, so what harm is there in fixin' him up?"

I look squarely at Cobb. "Can you help them?"

He nods frantically.

"Will you?"

Everybody present knows what it will cost Cobb if he does, but damned if he doesn't go on nodding that big old shaggy head of his. For a brief moment my envy extends from Wintry to this sad old man with his sagging body, who, if nothing else, has the kind of heart most of us would, and have, killed for.

But then the Reverend glances up at him and scowls. "You stay out of this, Cobb. When we need the black magic of heathens, you'll be the first to know. "

The dying kid fixes the nudist with an odd look. "Your name's Cobb?"

Cobb, equally perplexed, nods. "Yeah. Why?"

The Reverend sighs. "Shut your goddamn mouth. Now listen here, kid. All I want from you is a simple answer. This town's reserved for the dreamless, the lost and the hopeless. You may be a no-good piece of shit, but I bet you've got ambitions, right?"

"Sure. Seeing another sunrise was one of them."

"From somewhere other than Milestone."

"Yeah."

"Why is it, then, that instead of being in the driver seat of your nice new—*stolen*—midnight blue Corvette heading North, right the hell out of this burg, maybe with that filthy whore of yours giving you a blowjob while you listen to some of the devil's music on the stereo...why is it that you're sitting here dying?"

Brody's eyes widen until they seem to fill his face. "Shit, I'm dying?" He starts to chuckle. "Fuck me, Dean. Looks like we get to do that duet after all."

The Reverend slaps him, a quick dry open-handed slap that knocks the mirth right off the kid's face. He looks stunned, his breath coming in short hard rasps, then angry. "Preacher," he says, mustering as much iron into his words as he can. "You're lucky I'm down or I'd have to beg my Momma for forgiveness for busting your nose."

And on hearing that, God forgive me, I find myself warming to the bastard.

"Answer the question, sonny," Reverend Hill tells him. "Now, or I guarantee that shot to the gut will seem like a bee sting by the time I'm done with you. You see, here we follow a strict set of guidelines. Sinners atone for their sins by ridding the world of filth, just like them. There are outposts like this everywhere. Each one has its own methods too. Here at Eddie's, you get to drive. But seeing as how you're past doing anything of the kind, and therefore, all but useless to me, you'd better start answering my questions. So, for the last time, *why* are you here?"

Brody ignores the priest and glances at Cobb again. "She had the same name as you."

Cobb blanches. "Who did?"

Brody starts shaking, worse than before, and suddenly his eyes are on me with such intensity, even Hill looks over his shoulder. "Sheriff," the kid says. "Mind if I give you something?"

"Go right ahead, as long as it isn't a bullet."

"In my pocket...two twenty dollar bills and a five."

"Okay."

"Can you give them to that man there?"

"Cobb?"

"Yes."

I resist the urge to ask him why he didn't just get Cobb to take it himself.

"Not much life in you," Hill says, dropping to his haunches. "Better start talking. Just because you die doesn't mean I can't reach you."

Brody swallows, looks at Cobb, then away. "She came out of nowhere."

Cobb takes a step forward, but is stopped by the Reverend's glare and Wintry's hand on his shoulder. "What's he talkin' about?"

"Your wife, I expect," Hill says, with no emotion at all, then reaches forward and tilts the kid's head up until their eyes meet. "Am I right?"

"We didn't see her. She must have had her lights off. And if you don't get your fucking hand off me, Preacher, I swear I'll use every last ounce of my strength...to put you through the wall."

As I'm listening, I picture Eleanor Cobb, hunched over her steering wheel, trying to look as small and inconspicuous as possible, afraid of being seen by anyone, even in the storm, lights turned off on a quiet road because she doesn't imagine she'll encounter another car, and doesn't want to draw attention to herself if she does. But she hasn't counted on a thief and his woman traveling on that same quiet road, pedal to the metal, eager to be clear of a town that reeks of death.

I lower my head. "Jesus."

"Hang on, kid," Cobb says, and his tone is both desperate and disbelieving. "You must be mistaken. She doesn't come to get me. She never does."

"She did tonight," Hill says.

"No."

"I took her wallet. Figured…with the state she was in…she wouldn't need it. Saw her name…I'm sorry…you can have the money…I'm—"

I look up in time to see Cobb lunging for the kid, but Wintry's got him in a firm hold, and all Cobb can do is struggle until the strength leaves him and he turns, embraces the big black man and weeps uncontrollably.

"Get him a drink and sit him down," I tell Wintry, and he does. I'm surprised anyone is listening to me. Nights as wild as these badges count for nothing.

All the fight has left Cobb.

Reverend Hill stands up and scratches his chin. He sighs heavily. "Sheriff," he says. "Looks like you and I have a bit of a problem."

4

Considering the amount of blood on the chair and the floor beneath him, I don't reckon the kid has much time left. His face is the color of fresh snow and he's propped up against the bar like a guy who's had too much to drink and is trying to remember where the hell he's found himself. And, aside from the drink part, maybe that's exactly what he's doing.

The girl on the bar turns her head. Her tears are silent. Seems all the fight has left her too. She closes her eyes, jerking occasionally and gasping as Flo and Gracie tend to her. "She's goin' to die if we don't do somethin',"

Flo informs me, and it's hardly a revelation, but the one man willing to do something is way past doing it now. It's not like I can waltz up to Cobb and ask him to mend the people who killed his wife. That's the saddest part of all. I doubt he'd have been all that worried if his gift allowed him to raise the dead. But it doesn't. He can heal, that's it, and only wounds, not diseases. And right now, I'm willing to bet Cobb's second-guessing the limits of his power, wondering if it might work on his wife.

The priest turns to look at me. "You've got a job to do, Sheriff. Lucky for you, there'll soon be one less victim to worry about. Your boy gets that one. It's almost poetic, isn't it?"

"What is it you want me to do, exactly?"

"You gonna just let me die?" Brody croaks. "I knew there was a reason this town stank."

The Reverend shrugs. "No more than you were planning on doing all along. I want you to get in your truck and drive through town, fast as that piece of shit can carry you."

"Might want to watch the profanity there, Reverend. It being the mark of an ignorant man an all."

"Just do your job."

"For what? The kid's dying and—"

"Quit saying that, wouldya?" Brody interrupts.

"—his girl's bleeding out on the bar."

"True…" Hill shows his teeth. "But dying means they aren't dead *yet*. I reckon if you work fast and get them in your truck, you can still take care of business. Hell, I'll give you a break and just get you to take care of the girl."

"Can't you just let this one be?" Flo asks. "She's with child, for God's sake."

Without glancing her way, Hill says, "As are you, but you wouldn't expect anyone to forgive you *your* transgressions just because you spread your legs for a man."

Flo doesn't look shocked or stunned. She looks angry, and when she looks at Wintry, who is kneeling next to Cobb at the table where I first sat down, that anger turns to shame. Wintry, however, doesn't look quite so impassive anymore. Sins, the threat of Hell, death and murder don't make him blink, but finding out he's a Daddy sure does. His mouth is open, just a little, and I reckon even though he can't talk, he's saying something.

Thunder rolls like boulders across the roof.

Lightning shows me Cadaver in the corner, counting.

Me, I feel no more envy. Instead, I feel bolstered a little, aware that all those long-winded old passages you find in the bible about life and death and retribution may mean something after all. All we know, all we have known for as long as I can recall, is death. Now there's life. Even if we can't help poor Brody and Carla, even if we can't save her baby, Flo is pregnant, and the significance of that single fact is so great it makes my head hurt and my heart beat a little faster. Flo, a creature of death, is carrying life. Untainted life. Life Reverend Hill, for all his threats and blustering, cannot reach. Yet.

Flo is pregnant.

And whether or not she ends up filling that empty vessel with hate, or sadness, or sin, right now, for me, it represents just the tiniest bit of hope.

It's enough.

And it would seem I'm not alone in feeling that.

Without any of us, even the supposedly all-knowing Reverend, hearing his approach, Kyle is standing next to the priest, and the gun that has held so much meaning tonight, is gripped firmly in his hand again, the determination I've watched for three years back on his face, the muzzle nestled firmly against Hill's temple.

"I'm not driving tonight," I tell the priest, but Kyle has other ideas.

"Yes you are."

I look at him, wondering if this is how he finally intends to rid himself of his long-dead father. A man, who, despite all the nightmares and all the people he's killed on someone else's behalf, only ever felt guilty for the death he didn't cause. Cold as that sounds, I reckon there's a lot of truth to it.

"Me and you and the Reverend are going to take a ride tonight," Kyle says. "We're going to take that girl with us, and we're going to get her to Doctor Hendricks."

The priest chuckles. "Is that so?"

"Shit," Brody intones, struggling to sit up straighter. "What about me?"

He is ignored. We're not going to abandon him. That much I know. Not if there's a chance to save him. But Kyle's calling the shots now, so we're going to play it his way for the time being. The girl looks a lot worse off, so she goes first, is what I'm guessing is Kyle's reasoning here, though it would be just as easy to take them both. Maybe I'll suggest that once the gun's been lowered.

"Yeah, that is so," he says in response to Hill. The gun trembles in his grasp. I'm not yet at the point where I'm doubting my earlier opinion on whether my son will ever shoot a man again, but I'm not confident. What I am, however, is damn proud.

"Let me ask you something, Kyle. What exactly do you think shooting me will accomplish? Do you think I'll just drop like a rock? Like all these other weaklings? In case you haven't noticed, I'm the landlord here. Everyone answers to me, just as there are higher forces I answer to when the work has been done. When their *penance* has been done. And you, boy, have a lot of making up to do."

"And when is the penance done, huh? How many corpses amount to penance in your eyes? Ten, twenty, a hundred?"

"You'll know when it's done."

"Right," Kyle tells him. "When you've had your fill, maybe, you sick fuck."

The Reverend sighs. "Is it your intention to see how much suffering you can bring upon yourself? Pull that trigger then and we'll all see just how—"

Without warning, Kyle does as he is asked. The Reverend stands where he is for a moment, then topples. The echo of the gunshot rivals the rage of the storm and the sound of blood dripping could be the rain tapping on the window. What used to be Reverend Hill's head is now spread across the wall next to where Flo is standing, spattered in his blood. She doesn't seem at all put out, merely inconvenienced. Her eyes, white periods in a gore-smeared face, widen. "There's no way it can be that easy."

"Doesn't matter," I tell her. "He's down, and that's the end of it."

And yet no one moves. Instead we watch Hill's corpse warily, waiting for some sign of the power that has kept us bound for years. We half-expect the brains splashed across the wall to fly back into the man's ruined skull, the blood to return to the cavity Kyle's bullet burst open, the wound to heal. We wait for the Reverend to rise, murderous rage contorting his sallow face as he chooses which of us to destroy first. We wait. We watch.

But what happens is infinitely more surprising.

Nothing.

The all-powerful Reverend just lies there, minus most of his head, and deader than dog shit.

"I've never in all my years seen so much blood," Gracie says, and it sounds like a comment that should be followed by tears. But this is Gracie, and I'm willing to put money down that she's already stressing over the cleanup. "Guess he was just a man after all."

"I want to go home," the girl on the bar says, and that pulls us from our trance-like state of expectancy.

"We'll get you there, honey." Flo's hands tremble as she sleeves some of the priest's blood from her face.

"It's gonna be all right babe," Brody soothes, though he's in too much pain to sound sincere. "We'll be out of here soon, then it'll just be you, me and Dino."

Kyle is still holding the gun out, still pressing it against the ghost of Hill's temple, and I put a hand on his forearm, urge him to lower it before it goes off and adds someone else to the rapidly rising number of dead. For a moment he resists, then the tension ebbs away.

"It's okay son."

"Kyle," he mutters.

"What?"

"You don't get to call me 'son'."

"Okay."

Wintry is still tending to Cobb. The old man has downed half a bottle of whiskey. I'm sure wherever his mind is, it doesn't know what just happened, and maybe that's for the best. Wintry locks gazes with me and in that brief glance, we're like two old farts trading war stories. What's happened here tonight won't ever be forgotten, no more than will the things that led us here, the errors in judgment, the wrong turns, the simple little mistakes that all add up to an express elevator ride right into a nightmare no amount of waking up can cure. But this is a lull, and a welcome one, and I figure everyone (except maybe Brody and the girl) is going to savor it before the next unwelcome development. For however briefly, this is Eddie's bar, the only functioning water hole in a near-dead town, and right now, for the first time ever, these people truly are my friends.

Wintry goes back to silently consoling the inconsolable Cobb. Gracie heads into the ladies room and emerges with a mop and bucket that are filthier than the floor but don't, to my knowledge, have human remains on them. Flo tries to get the girl to stand up. It isn't going to happen.

"We need to take him too," I tell Kyle with a nod in Brody's direction.

"No."

"Why?"

"Yeah," Brody adds. "Why? If it's because you shot a perfectly nice guy like me, and don't know how to apologize…hell…that's all water under the bridge." He grins and there is blood on his teeth. "I don't hold grudges."

"He's a murderer," Kyle says.

I lean in close. "For fuck sake, Kyle. *Everyone* here is a murderer."

"Not like him we're not. He enjoyed it. Did it on purpose."

His logic makes my head swim, and the only thing I'm really sure of is that I don't agree with it. "Listen, you have to—"

"Leave him," Cobb says dreamily, as if our banter has woken him from a doze.

Everyone looks in his direction. He, however, does not look at us.

"Cobb…"

"Leave him. I'll take care of him."

I can't be blamed for taking that like it sounds. Sure, Cobb can heal folks, but considering we're talking about the man who just killed his wife, I don't imagine healing has anything to do with it.

"Take care of him how?"

"Fix him up, Sheriff. What else?" His eyes are swollen from crying, his face almost as pale as Brody's.

"Any number of things," I reply. "He can die on his own if that's what you're figuring to help him with."

"I said I'll fix him up. Weren't like he killed Ellie on purpose."

"You don't know that."

"No. I don't." He takes another slug of whiskey. "But why are we here?"

I don't know how to answer that. Seems no one does. But for the low whimpering of the girl, the room's awful quiet.

"We come here to try to make peace when there ain't none to be had. We come here to be forgiven. Way I figure it, Sheriff, is if I don't do what every ounce of me wants to do to this kid, and instead I fix him up, like I want to be fixed up myself, like I can never be fixed up, then maybe it'll count for somethin' in this great goddamn plan we're all so fuckin' tangled up in. What do you think?"

I consider that for a moment because it's worth considering. Then: "I think you may be onto something," I tell him.

"Yeah?"

"Yeah." I look at the girl. "What about her?"

"Nothing I can do for her. Maybe Hendricks can pull a miracle out of his hat, but not me." He glances down at Brody. "She's too far gone."

Brody sighs shakily, tries to stand and fails. Although Cobb has agreed to help the kid, I figure we've just seen his revenge. Telling the kid his girl is going to die is about the only weapon he has left to use, I guess. Hurt him as much as possible before he heals him.

"All right."

Cobb nods, and goes back to his drink. "Don't leave Ellie out there on the road, Tom. She deserves better."

"I'll see to it."

"You're leaving me here with *him*?" Brody asks, appalled.

"It's the one good option in a dump truck full of bad ones," I remind him. "Take it or leave it."

Gracie comes around the bar, flips that lock of hair out of her face and sets the mop and bucket down by the priest's body. "Think we should burn him?" she asks, as casually as she might inquire about the weather. "Bury the ashes and salt the earth?"

I understand her concern completely. No one wants to see that son of a bitch get back up. "If he was anything as dangerous as he led us to believe he was, he'd already have done something. And if he still plans to, then I don't reckon cooking him or seasoning the mud's going to do us a whole lot of good."

She sighs, and it's the most human I've ever seen her look. There's the urge again, to hold her, but this time I know it's because *I* need it, not her. So again, I restrain myself.

"Why didn't we do this three years ago?"

It's a good question, but I leave it unanswered.

I walk to the center of the room, Cobb and Wintry's table to my right, Cadaver still lost in the shadows by the door to my left.

"You okay, Cadaver?"

"Just countin' what's left," the electronic voice from the dark replies, followed by that familiar clink of pennies.

"Let's get this done," Kyle says behind me, and I'm glad to hear it. It means two things to me: First, he's still in control. The shock of shooting two men in the space of twenty minutes hasn't yet reduced him to the wreck it makes of others, and eventually will make of him when he least expects it, and second, it represents action, movement, right when my bones are threatening to turn to jelly and leave me a quivering, sobbing mess on the floor.

We move.

I'm stronger than Kyle, so I slip my hands beneath the girl's arms; he takes her feet.

"Hurry, for God's sake," Brody moans. "Don't let her die."

We carefully time the move, and with Flo ahead of us, we're out the door and loading Carla into the back seat of my truck before the second hand of the clock has made a full sweep.

We leave a trail of pinkish blood behind us.

5

The rain is pelting down like machine gun fire, the wind trying its best to wrench the truck doors right off their hinges as we bundle inside. Makes me wonder if this is the Reverend's 'boss' gathering his fury, preparing to blow us all to whatever the alternative hangout is for the kind of deities that would consider Hill a valued employee.

I'm still too scared to believe this is over. It's an ugly feeling I know well, and can only hope will abate as soon as we have Carla at the door of the good doctor, provided she lives that long. As I gun the engine into life, and look at Kyle, who's wiping the condensation clear and peering out at the rain, it occurs to me that if this is really the end of the night-mare, I have no idea what to do with myself. There won't be any glorious sunshine through my window in the morning, marking the equally glo-rious beginning of a new chapter of my life. I'm still a murderer; there's still the guilt, and there's my son, who thinks I'm dead and doesn't mind. All that will really change will be the venue into which I bring my suffer-ing. I don't imagine next Saturday I'll be at Eddie's. Instead I'll sit at home without those faces to act as mirrors for my own self-loathing.

I guide the truck out of the parking lot, careful to avoid the other cars, and turn out onto the road that will bring us to town, and to the doctor who I know won't take too kindly to being roused at this hour of the night, especially to tend to an injured whore with needle marks parading up her emaciated arm.

"Faster, she's not looking too good," Kyle says, looking over his shoulder as if he's been peeking in on my thoughts. "Think the baby'll make it?"

"Hope so." I resist the urge to remind him what Cobb said about her chances.

It's damn near impossible to see anything beyond the glass, the high beams like swollen ghosts staying three steps ahead of the grille. I'm going fast, aware that at any time I might inadvertently fulfill my obliga-tions to the dead Reverend and run somebody over, or mash the truck into some poor drunk driver's car as he struggles to make his way home.

"C'mon for Chrissakes, she's bleeding bad."

It isn't a long drive, but the storm buffeting the truck and Kyle's end-less needling make it seem like hours. Lightning turns the world to rainy daylight as I turn off the main road onto Abigail Lane, where the good doctor has his home.

Hendricks' place used to be a farmhouse, through the windows of which long gone farmers watched the world fall victim to the voracious appetite of progress. Mining companies bought out the land for the fam-ilies of their employees, and people got greedy. Then the money ran out, and so did the people. Hendricks, an M.D. from Alabama who claimed he was "just passing through," saw no reason to move on when he caught sight of the sickly state of those who'd stubbornly refused to leave Milestone in the great exodus of '79, and when he heard the asking price for a house nobody wanted.

As we pull into the drive that slopes upward to the block-shaped two-story house, there are no lights in the windows, which doesn't come as a surprise. I find myself wondering, if we had kept going instead of turning into Hendricks' drive, how long it would have taken us to come upon the twisted wreck of Eleanor Cobb's Taurus.

Despite the forbidding darkness of the house that looms over the car, Kyle's already hurrying to get the girl out. Not the smartest move considering the Doc might not even be here, so I leave him to his grunting and trot to the door.

Knock, knock. No sound from within.

"Leave her there," I call back to Kyle, who's as good as invisible behind the car's lights.

"What?"

"I said leave her *be*. If Hendricks doesn't answer, what good will dragging her out in the rain do?"

"What else *can* we do?"

"I don't know. We'll deal with that if and when— "

"Sheriff?"

The front door is open; the storm deafened me to the approach of the bespectacled man now standing there squinting out. "That you, Tom?"

He's a reed-thin man and heavily bearded. I've always suspected that, just like the deceased Reverend, vanity has driven the doctor to dying his hair to keep from looking his age. And though in this light he doesn't look much healthier than the girl in the back of my truck, I'm glad as hell to see him.

I summarize the situation as calmly as I can. It doesn't sound calm in the least by the time it reaches my lips, but Hendricks steps back, his face a knot of concern. From upstairs, his wife calls out a demand to know what's going on. The doctor turns on the hall light. It's the warmest looking light I've seen in quite some time, and the shadows it casts are gentle. "Bring her in. I'll see what I can do." He reaches the stairs and yells up, "Queenie, I'm going to need your help down here."

And in what seems like a heartbeat, the doctor is bent over the girl where she lies prone on the couch and swaddled in comfy looking blankets. The towels wrapped around her head make it look as if she's being prepped for a massage, nothing more. The blood running between her eyes spoils that illusion though. She's shivering, which is good. Means she's still breathing. "Lost a lot of blood," Hendricks says, pressing the cup of his stethoscope to her chest. "You said an auto wreck?"

"Yeah."

"Anyone else hurt?" He appraises Kyle and me. "How about you guys? You look pretty shook up."

"We're fine," Kyle says. "She going to be all right? She's pregnant, you know."

Hendricks frowns.

"She told us," I add quickly, covering Kyle's blunder. "Right before she passed out."

I can't tell whether or not he's buying it, but he says nothing, just presses that stethoscope to the girl's breast and breathes through his nose. His wife stands off in the corner, arms folded over her dressing gown. She looks pissed, and I can't blame her.

When at last the doctor looks up, his face is grave. "I'm sorry to say I don't think there's a whole lot I can do for her, boys. The baby's gone. That I can tell you right now for certain, and it's only a matter of time before she follows. I'd have to open her up to say for sure, but my guess is she's busted up pretty bad. Judging by that blood and the way she's breathing, seems she's got a punctured lung too. Pupils are dilated. Head's cracked open almost clean through to the bone. Frankly I'm amazed she's not dead already." At the looks on our faces, he continues, "But you fellas did real good. Wasn't much more you could have done for her. She'd have appreciated it, I'm sure."

Another life lost. For nothing. Though at least when I dream of this one I'll know it wasn't entirely my fault.

"Uh…Sheriff?"

I look back at Hendricks.

"You just going to leave her here?"

I'm about to argue with him, but it slowly dawns on me that he's right, that I'd have asked the same question. Hendricks, unlike me or

Kyle, still has a life, and I don't reckon we should leave a dead whore on his couch to remind him why we're different.

"Sorry, Doc. We'll take her back to Eddie's."

Hendricks looks confused. "Eddie's? Why there?"

"Because it's quieter than any graveyard. Most of the time. We can bury her out back right next to Eddie himself. I figure he deserves the company after all the shit we've done under his roof. Besides," I move close to the girl. "We've got some burying to do anyway."

"Who else died?" Queenie asks, her first words to us since we arrived.

"The Reverend."

"Oh."

I smile at the lack of emotion on her face. "Yeah. Ticker gave out on him while he was preaching to us about the evils of drink."

Hendricks shakes his head. "Man had way too much time on his hands."

"You got that right, Doc."

We stay for a while, exchanging the kind of uneasy banter unique to folks who're waiting for one among them to die. Kyle paces, torn between refusing to accept that the girl is gone, that we couldn't save her, and eager to be in a room larger than Hendricks' parlor so he doesn't have to be within touching distance of me.

At last there comes a single hitching sigh. The girl frowns, as if in her dreams she's stumbled upon something dangerous, then she shudders once, and that's the end of it.

No one says anything for a moment. We all just stand there, trying to read the story of the dead girl's life from the lines on her face, the punctuation marks on her arm, the commas at the corners of her mouth from too much time spent grimacing in pain. I reach down and brush a strand of hair away from her face.

"C'mon, Kyle."

For the second time that night, we load the girl into the truck. I imagine she feels lighter, that the soul, or whatever leaves us when we die, has weight, and hers is somewhere better now, somewhere no one can touch it, and use the stains on it against her.

Our drive back to Eddie's is a silent one. There's plenty that could be said, but no need to say it.

At least, not until we see the fire.

"Aw *Christ no…*" Kyle says and is out of the truck and running before I have time to draw a breath.

6

Eddie's is in flames, a funeral pyre burning against the dark, turbulent maelstrom of the night, and though the rain is still beating down and pockmarking the mud, it's not doing much to put out the blaze.

My first thought is that Gracie has finally had enough, that the Reverend's death is the catalyst she's been waiting for, the escape she's longed for all these years. I imagine her chasing everybody out, leaving the Reverend's body and Brody where they are, dousing the place from top to bottom with kerosene or spirits, then standing in the doorway, flaming rag in her hand. I see the light burning away the shadows on her grim face, making her seem young and innocent again. Then she tosses the rag, and the fire races across the floor and up the walls, a raging thing, but pure, and cleansing.

But as I watch the lithe silhouette of my son racing toward the inferno, I remember what I thought when I stood in there looking down at Hill's body, waiting for him to suddenly resurrect himself. Cold dread grips my heart. Is this the surprise we expected from him? Did he burst into flame moments after Kyle and me left the bar? I picture his almost headless corpse erupting into bright searing flame, claiming the lives of those standing nearest him first before they're even aware what's happening, then spreading out and cooking the rest as they try to escape.

And then I think of Cobb.

I pull the truck to a halt in the parking lot. Flames rise up, licking the sky; the rain falls down. Glass shatters in the heat and I have to shield my face. Not before my eyebrows are singed away.

Kyle is not alone, and his company is not a decapitated burning thing. I make my way over, all but blinded by the light from the fire. It isn't until I'm right there next to Kyle that I see it's Cadaver who's with him. His eyes are narrowed against the glare, but still there's an odd look on his hollow face, almost like reverence.

"Cadaver, what happened?"

Kyle looks like a ghost, his eyes filled with fire. "He says Cobb did it. Just after we left, he went crazy and torched the place."

Cadaver nods, but adds nothing. I notice his little microphone is absent, which explains his silence. Just like Brody must have thought when the old man hunkered down next to him, Cadaver looks like death. More so now than ever before, the orange-red light only adding deeper shadow beneath the sharp outcroppings of his cheekbones.

"Where is everyone?" I ask, afraid of the answer, because I've surveyed the area more than once on my way up here and I'm surveying it now again, and I don't see anybody here but us, and that feels to me like a brand new nightmare fresh from the devil's womb, waiting to be christened by the ignorant.

Kyle looks at me, and the flames shimmer in his eyes. "Gone," he tells me. "Cadaver says they're all gone. All but Brody."
"And where's he?"

Cadaver nods in the direction of the burning building, off into the shadows the fire is weaving to the side of it. I don't see Brody, but I trust that he's there.

"Jesus." I put my hands to my face to block out a reality that seems to be getting darker by the second.

There's a story here, I suppose. Cadaver must have seen it all from his place by the window, before he hotfooted it the hell out of the burning tavern. He might whisper to me of Wintry's bravery, how he tried to carry as many people as he could out of the place before one of the big timber beams came down and cracked his head open like an egg, dropping him and suffocating beneath his weight those he'd carried in his arms, his beloved Flo among them. He might tell me the details of Cobb's descent into madness, how one minute he was a sobbing wreck, the next a raving lunatic, whooping and hollering and raging, spinning like a top with spirits flying from the open bottles in his hands. Then a match, the smell of sulfur, and a small flame ready to birth an all-consuming fire. He might say that Gracie fought Cobb to the end, maybe cold-cocked him with one of those bottles, or gutted him with the sharp end of a broken mop handle before the smoke took them both, laid them down for the fire to burn them in their sleep.

Good for Gracie.

Cadaver might tell me these things, but I don't want to hear that choked whisper from his cracked lips. My imagination is louder anyway. "Is there a chance anyone else survived?" Kyle asks the old man, who shrugs and looks at me.

Like Wintry, there's more truth in his eyes than could ever roll off his tongue. But I'm stubborn, and what pitiful little sleep I have these days will be robbed from me tonight if I don't see for myself. There are no screams from Eddie's, no sound of anyone begging to be saved, but then we've all been damned for longer than we care to admit, and we've never cried for salvation.

I start moving toward the bar.

Kyle's hand falls firmly on my shoulder.

I start to turn, and the roof caves in. It sounds like a tree falling, a splintering crash that sends a plume of dirty smoke up before fresh fire rushes in to fill the hole, fed by the air that has tried to escape.

"Sonofabitch," someone cries out from the dark, and finally I see a shape rolling around in the shadows, batting at sparks that are trying to ignite his clothes. If the kid's able to roll, then could be his injuries are no more. We'll have to wait and see.

Crackling, spitting flames, but still no screams. On some level I know I should be thankful for that, and for the fact that this atrocity was not the Good Reverend's work, but I'm not. Not just now. Kyle is weeping, and as his hand slips from my shoulder, Cadaver's hand finds his before it occurs to me to comfort him.

"This shouldn't have happened," I say, without knowing whether or not I'm even saying it aloud, or who I think I'm saying it to if I am. "They didn't deserve this."

Another dumb, obvious statement in a night loaded with them.

"We should call someone." Kyle walks away and sits down, his back to the rickety wooden fence that separates the parking lot from the grassy slope down to the road. I start after him, rehearsing words of comfort that sound wooden, and useless, like pretty much everything I've ever said to that kid. He wants his mother back and he won't get it; he wants his father dead, and he can't get that either. If early life experience scars you for the rest of it, then Kyle's nightmare hasn't even started yet. He raises a hand as I draw near. It's as good as a signpost saying ROAD CLOSED, and all I can do is stand there feeling helpless, which is exactly what I do until I hear a sound I never thought I'd hear again.

The sound of pennies being counted.

"Cadaver?"

He's still facing the fire, but his head is bowed, all his attention on his upturned palm. I give the kid one brief, regretful look, then head back to the old man. Back there in the shadows, Brody's still cursing.

As I draw abreast of the old man, I see there's only two pennies in his palm. I guess the fire took a little something extra from him. But when at last he raises his head, not only does he seem calm, he's almost smiling. A thin thread of blue-gray smoke drifts from the small hole in the box in his throat. Opaque eyes settle on mine, and they look ancient.

The smile.

The pennies.

It dawns on me then, the not-so-quick-witted Sheriff of a town on life support, that there was something to Reverend Hill's threat after all. It was there right from the beginning. We were waiting for a great black winged demon to come bursting up from below, or the devil himself to come strolling in the door with a brimstone smile and eyes like glowing embers, all those peachy images the Good Book tells us we should be watching for, when we should have been looking at that ever-present patch of darkness in the corner. To the man counting his change.

Fear overwhelms me, and my legs, which have done a respectable job of holding me up through the madness, finally give out. I stumble. Cadaver's hand lashes out and clamps on my arm, somehow keeping me upright.

"You all right, Sheriff?" he whispers, head cocked slightly in an admirable impression of genuine concern.

From the fire comes a great hiss. It might be a serpent; it might just be the rain meeting flame. I'm not so certain of anything anymore. Only that Cadaver's the reason the air smells like burning flesh.

"'Just counting what's left,'" I say, recalling his words to me before we left the bar. "You were talking about us."

He nods, glances back at Kyle, then steps closer. There should not be enough strength in his old bones to keep me from falling, but there is.

His hand on my elbow might as well be a metal brace.

"There's no accountin' for human emotion," he says, his whisper tinged with sadness, aided by the expression of regret on his worn face. "Especially the love of a frustrated old woman for her shameless husband. Because of Eleanor Cobb, everythin' went sideways on us. You were right. This shouldn't've happened."

"But it did."

"Yes it did, and that's a shame." He closes his fist around the pennies. "If it means anythin'—and I don't expect it will, at least not for a while—this isn't what I wanted. They were my friends too."

I'm bitter, and scared, and more than ready for him to reach inside my tired body and wrench out my soul, whatever's left of it. "Am I supposed to believe that? Or is it just customary where you come from to burn your friends alive if things don't go according to plan?"

He purses his lips, then squints at me like a short-sighted man trying to read the fine print on a legal document. "The Reverend got what was comin' to him. They all did, unfortunate as it is. Wintry…" He shook his head, a wry smile on his wrinkled lips. "He can talk you know. He just chose not to after— "

"I don't want a litany of their sins," I interrupt. "It hardly makes a damn bit of difference now. All I want to know from you is what happens to Kyle."

He nods his understanding. Anyone looking might think we were discussing the latest decisions of the coaches of our favorite football teams. "Repentance is the name of this game, Tom. Don't matter whether I influence it or not, or whether you both live to be a hundred and ten or die tomorrow, the debt's got to be settled. It's the price you have to pay for makin' the wrong choice when both were available to you."

"You didn't answer the question."

He sighs. "I'm a reasonable man, Tom."

I can't help myself. I laugh long and loud at that little nugget of absurdity. The contradiction to Cadaver's claim is burning high and bright before us. Sure, he didn't strike the match, but if not for his influence, none of us would have been there to begin with.

He releases his grip on me. I don't fall, but there's not a whole lot of strength left in me. I stay standing only so I can look him in the eye when he tells me what's going to become of my son. And maybe when he does I'll have just the right amount of energy left to punch his fucking face in.

But he doesn't answer right away. Instead he grabs my left hand, forces it out of the fist that I've made to follow up on my unvoiced threat, and drops his two pennies into my palm.

I look up at him.

His eyes probe mine, and my guts squirm as if a surgeon has put his cold fingers in there. I'm afraid I'm going to be sick. "Consider it a loan," he says, and closes my fingers around the coins.

"Why?" I ask, as he starts to walk toward the burning building, the smoke whipping itself into specters that chase each other around the flames. Sparks dance like giddy stars.

At the threshold to the inferno that used to be Eddie's Bar, he stops, seemingly unaffected by anything but the light from the blaze. He squints back over his shoulder at me, and though his voice is still a whisper, I hear it as surely as if he's said it right into my ear.

"It's all I have."

7

Eddie's is still burning bright by the time we snap out of whatever cocktail of grief and shock and confusion has held us there like moths, and I give up waiting for Cadaver to come back out and explain just what it is that's making two cold spots in the palm of my right hand. Whatever he is, he's right where he belongs, but that doesn't make me feel much better. I thought for sure that Hill's death meant it was all over, that at last the shackles had been removed and we were free to move on, if we could ever figure out a way to do it without taking the guilt and ghosts with us.

But nothing's over. There won't be any new chapters here. And Eddie's might just as well be standing untouched by fire because after this, even though the numbers are lower, Milestone's purgatory is still going to house a few folks pretending to live their lives while they wait for someone to come collect a debt they're never going to be able to repay. Only difference is next time the debt collector won't be a cocky bible-thumping Reverend with dyed hair, but a skeletal man with an electronic doodad where his larynx should be.

Kyle's still watching the fire with tear-filled eyes, and I don't have a goddamn clue what I'm supposed to do next, but because I need to move, I have a quick word with Kyle, watch him head for my truck, then I make my way over to the shadows, where I can hear Brody hacking and coughing as he stumbles away from the burning building.

"You're alive." The announcement is my way of letting him know he's not the only one, in case he was wondering. His face, clear of the shadows and lit by the flames, is streaked with soot, his eyes narrowed as his lungs convulse and force another phlegmy cough from him. The nice suit is officially beyond saving.

"Yeah, no thanks to you."

"How's that?"

"You left me with that crazy man, didn't you? The healer? Executioner, more like."

I reach down, slip an arm underneath his elbow and yank him up. "You're looking a damn sight better than when I left you. He did *something* for you or you wouldn't be standing here." I inspect the front of his shirt. The bullet hole is still there, but I can't tell if there's one in the flesh beneath it to match.

"I owe that to the big black dude."

"Wintry?"

"Guy threw me right through the fucking window after your naked friend went nuclear."

"Nuclear, how?"

He takes a few unsteady steps, and leans against the wooden fence. "The guy put his hands on me. Cobb did. And yeah, he fixed me up just like he said he would, but then..." He shakes his head, a humorless smile on his grimy face. "Then he starts bawling and whatever invisible shit's pouring from his hands into me turns to fire. I tell you, I've been around—don't be fooled by my age, I've seen plenty—but I've never seen nothing like that before. Blue fire, man, streaming like piss from his fingers. I don't think even he expected it, but he just went right on bawling about his wife, about how he wasn't going to let her go, then he raises those hands so the streams are about an inch from the top of my head—

Christ, it was like looking up at an electric fence—and POW, he cooks the hot chick right where she's standing."

"Flo?"

"Yeah, the one looks a bit like Marilyn Monroe."

"Goddamn it."

"Yeah, no kidding. Hell of a waste. So she drops, and that sets the big guy off. He grabs a handful of my shirt, the world starts spinning and next thing I know I'm doing a swan dive through the goddamn window."

"What happened to the others?"

"Don't know for sure. Didn't see it; but it isn't that hard to figure out, is it? Guy grieving for his wife finds his hands have turned into flamethrowers. Three seconds later the whole place goes up in smoke. Looks like your friend had himself a barbecue."

Kyle finds us and with a grim look at Brody, hands me the set of handcuffs I keep in my glove box. Can't remember the last time I had call to use these. Brody straightens a little. "What are those for?"

"You're lucky to be alive, boy. You shouldn't be, and that's a fact. But you're a murderer, and that's a fact too, so you're going to cool your heels in my jail for a while until I decide what to do with you."

He stiffens, takes a step back, and I'm suddenly more aware than ever that I don't have a gun.

Kyle does though. "Stay where you are," he says, weapon trained on Brody.

"You've got to be fucking *kidding* me. After all the shit I just went through, you're going to stick me in a cell?"

"That's the plan."

"You don't have proof to say I did anything."

"I've got you threatening a police officer, and that's enough for now."

"Aw that's *bull*shit. Besides, my gun is in there," he says, jerking a thumb at the burning tavern. "Without that, you haven't got squat."

"Your girl didn't make it," Kyle says then. The guy's expression falters, but only for a moment, like a breeze across a calm pond. "Yeah, I figured that. Thanks for breaking it to me gently, though, you asshole." He rubs a hand over his face. "Naked old guy with flamethrower hands, fruitcake holymen…and a hick Sheriff and his trigger-happy boy trying to railroad me. I mean, for Chrissakes…where the hell *am* I anyway?"

"Milestone." I motion for him to start moving. *And Hell isn't a million miles off the mark either.*

❦

We put Brody, cuffed, in the truck. He doesn't resist, but I can tell by the tension in his muscles that he'd like to. "This is a crock of shit." His grumbling lasts only until Kyle and me start unloading the girl from the truck bed. "What are you doing?" he asks then, his voice muffled. "Where are you taking her?"

"She needs burying," I call back, and ignore whatever else he says. He probably thinks being her lover gives him some right to dictate what happens to her in death, and ordinarily I'd agree. Fact is, though, this isn't an ordinary situation. Fact is, she's dead because he was going too fast, hightailing it along dark twisty roads probably looking for somewhere to rob. Doesn't matter how he felt about her in life. For her, life's over, and he drove the hearse. So fuck him and his sense of entitlement. We're planting her.

❦

Kyle stands and draws the back of his hand across his eyes, carving clear furrows in the dust and soot. He glances at me for a moment, then shakes his head. I can't figure out if the gesture is more disdain for me or regret for the tragedy that's befallen our friends. Guess it doesn't matter now. I get back to work clearing the debris from my own head. After all, we're standing over a dead girl, about to put her in a hole far from home where no one will ever know she's planted and won't be able to visit her if they care to. But I'm guessing she was just as lost as the company she kept in her final hours, and probably won't raise a fuss about where I lay her bones, and no one else will either. No milk carton appearances for this one, just an unceremonious burial out back of a burning tavern.

I turn away from the flames and it's like walking from night to day. Raging light and heat behind me, cold rain and darkness ahead. A few feet away, Kyle's watching.

"You got a shovel?" he asks.

"No. Why don't you take that piece of yours and shoot some earth loose for me?"

"The hell's that supposed to mean?"

"You need me to explain it to you?"

His face contorts with rage. "Hey, I saved your fucking ass in there."

"That so."

"Yeah it goddamn well *is* so." He moves to stand close, in my face, his eyes black fire. "I saved *everyone* in there. I stopped that guy from killing Wintry, and God knows who else. I stopped the Reverend from sending us all out on our little death drives. Permanently. So what the hell's your problem?"

"You saved us?"

"Damn right I did. No one else had the guts to do it."

"That what you think?"

A step closer. "We're standing here aren't we?"

"*We* are, yeah."

He doesn't answer, just stares until I can't meet it anymore. I hunker down to the girl. She smells of sweat, or maybe that's me, but there's no question where the faint trace of perfume is coming from. The feeling I had earlier about the girl weighing less is gone now and my arms and legs quiver as I carry her up the slope. I figure it's because I'm exhausted. All the fight has left me, along with everything else.

"What are we going to do with him?" Kyle asks, looking back toward the truck.

"I don't know yet."

"I could take him back."

"If it's all the same, I'd feel a lot better taking him in."

"You don't trust me?"

I look up at him and shrug. "You just killed a man, Kyle. I bet you're even wondering if you've got the nerve to kill me, so no, I don't trust you. In fact, I'd rather set that guy free than let you take him in."

"You're a real asshole, you know that?"

"Yeah well…doesn't change the color of that bullseye on my back, now does it?"

"Fuck you." He stands there for another moment, a black ghost with the flames of hell behind him, then he turns and walks away. I watch him go, waiting for him to lunge toward my truck and the unsuspecting guy handcuffed in back of it, because as little as I've known about this son of mine, I know even less about the one with the cold look in his eyes and the big goddamn gun in his hand, so I'm watching, waiting to see what he'll do next.

But he doesn't go to my truck. He goes to his Chevy, and doesn't look back. The car's lights make gray funnels in the smoke as he reverses out of the lot and back down the hill.

I'm left to ponder the irony of protecting a murderer from my son when I was all too willing to leave the guy in Cobb's care. Could be I trusted Cobb when I had no right to. Could be not letting Kyle take the guy in was my way of protecting, not Brody, but my son, keeping him out of further trouble. Yeah, sure.

With a sigh, I circle the fire as close as it will let me get without burning the hair out of my ears. There's a plot of land back here where no one should rightly be put to rest. It's stony ground and hard, and its closeness to a tavern should disqualify it if the fact that its unconsecrated doesn't. And when the toilets quit working, as they often did in Eddie's, people pissed out here. That's the smell I'm getting now, despite the rain and the smoke, because the smell of piss is stubborn like that. It'll hang around, get stronger, no matter what you try and do to get rid of it.

Here's where the whore's going to get planted, in rocky unblessed earth that smells like the men's room.

The fire's close. If I stood up right now, turned and took a dozen strides I'd be right on the edge of it feeling what little hair I have left shrivel up. It dries my back as I lay the girl down and set about finding a rock with enough of a point to work as a tool. I'd use my hands but it would take me until this time tomorrow to get it deep enough that the coyotes and other scavengers would let her be. Takes me a minute, but I find what I'm looking for. It's a spade-shaped rock half-buried in the wormy earth, and though it takes some persuading, I eventually get it free and start hacking at the earth.

Nothing here to say it's a graveyard. No markers, no lumps in the ground where the dead have pulled the covers up over themselves, and no flowers. There's a reason for that. Anyone planted here isn't meant to be mourned, and so far they haven't been disappointed. Looks like a damn vegetable patch that's been let go to seed, but under all that stone and dirt and weeds, there are a number of folks I used to know and don't miss. Among them is 'ol Eddie, a rat-bastard of the highest order and, I'm guessing, another reason this patch of ground reeks of piss.

You're a real asshole, you know that?

Kyle's got a girl. She's not much, but she's company. Used to be she ran a pretty good store out of one of the old buildings on Winter Street, selling clothes and trinkets and such. But in Milestone, the days of prosperous business for all but bartenders, undertakers and whores has ended, and Iris Gale knows that well, which is why she's now self-employed in the latter trade. I figure she doesn't charge Kyle for her services, on account of how he's got no money, or at least none that I know about outside of the odd jobs he does for those willing to open their doors to him. Maybe that's why he was so concerned about Carla. Maybe Iris has changed his opinion on whores and the like.

Doesn't matter.

He's gone, and now it's just the dead girl and me with her boyfriend sulking in the passenger seat of my truck.

Or maybe not, because all of a sudden the back of my neck's cold and that's not right at all, not with the fire still fighting its blazing fight against the wind and rain. Someone's watching me. I'm sure of it, and I cast a quick glance at the whore before standing, both knees crackling loud enough to make me wince. "I'll get you there in a minute," I let her know by way of an apology. "Just hang on." That damn spied-on feeling grows stronger, until it makes my skin crawl. I have to wonder if it's the rain after all. Maybe it's just gotten colder. Maybe the fire's finally admitting defeat. Maybe Brody's throwing daggers at me from my truck. Maybe, maybe, maybe. It's all bullshit. My way of trying to pretend I've gone through all I'm going to for one night.

I start to turn around and I'm full sure I'll see Cadaver coming back out of the tavern, or studying me from the inferno. But it isn't Cadaver.

The fire's getting a little lower as it runs out of fuel to feed on, the heads of those flames whipping hungrily to the left, toward town, but with no way to get there, I reckon in an hour or two, they'll be nothing the rain can't handle. It's still hotter than hell though, except here near the back, where I'm standing. The cold is coming from the almost perfect circle that has appeared through the smoke and the flames, forcing them to bend around it. Goddamndest thing I've ever seen, but sure as I'm standing here with a dead girl at my feet there's a tunnel, tall enough to step into, drilled into the fire and stretching about ten feet into the tavern, like someone just stuck a great big glass tube right into the blaze.

At the end of that tunnel, brass foot rails reflecting the shunned fire, sits the bar itself. It should be a charred hunk of nothing right now, but there it is, untouched, and as always, unpolished. And behind it, busy fixing a couple of glasses of whiskey, and looking equally untouched and unpolished, is Gracie.

8

For a moment I just stand there, nudging my right foot against Carla's cold body to make sure I'm really here. The cold air wafting from that tunnel makes me shiver. The combination of temperatures is going to leave me with one raging bitch of a head cold on top of everything else, so I do what I guess I'm supposed to do, and make my way toward the bar.

It's like stepping into a freezer, or jumping into a lake of ice.

"Jesus Henry," I moan and rub my arms like a worried housewife. The cold makes me instantly aware of every spot on my body the fire didn't dry, and my breath turns to mist. I have to question why it needs to be *this* cold. If Gracie's dead, then she's dead. Keeping her on ice can only be someone's idea of a sick joke. Or maybe it's freezing because if it wasn't, I'd be one crispy critter right about now, given that I'm at least four feet past the threshold of fire. It laps at the invisible walls around me, spreading out across the surface like some kind of amber marine creature desperate to suck me out of my shell.

Strange, but I figure it's better not to analyze too deeply something that's keeping me from being roasted alive, so I focus on Gracie, who for all I know might at any moment give me a little finger-wave and vanish, along with her little invisible asbestos test tube. I speed up my approach, and the closer I get, the less cold it becomes.

Gracie looks up at me. She doesn't smile, but nods a greeting and tucks that rogue lock of hair behind her ear. If she's dead, it's been kind to her, but the drab unflattering outfit she supposedly burned to death in hasn't been improved any.

"Sheriff."

"Gracie."

I test the reality of the bar by brushing my fingers across its surface. They come away black with soot, but underneath, the bar is there.

"Sit," Gracie says. It's not a request.

There's only one stool, and I'm about to take it when it occurs to me to ask, "This wasn't Cobb's, was it?"

"Weren't anybody's."

I sit. Gracie slides one of the glasses in front of me. I look at it, wondering how I'm sitting here in a bar that's all but burned to the ground, about to enjoy a whiskey that doesn't exist with a woman who died in the fire. It's a couple of questions too many, so I figure maybe I can tackle them later. "For Blue Moon." I sink the drink. It burns, scalds my throat on the way down and sends fumes rolling back up that I vent through my teeth. It's real all right, and the conclusion forces me to accept that everything else is too, even as the fire dances around us.

Gracie slams her whiskey without effort, without expression, but that's Gracie for you. Woman could get shot in the ass and wouldn't blink.

"I'd be lying if I said I expected to see you here, Gracie."

"Why's that?"

"You died, didn't you?"

"I did, but you know as well as I do that the only reason I spent every wakin' hour behind this goddamn bar is because my daddy—may he burn in Hell—made sure I would. Last thing that sonofabitch said to me was "This is your place, Grace, and it always will be. Nowhere else right for you and you're not right for anywhere else. Turns out it was more'n just words."

"You don't seem too put out by it all."

"Wouldn't be much point in that, now would there?"

"Guess not."

She looks as tired as I feel, and that's somewhat discouraging. If you don't get find rest even in death, where can you find it?

"So that's why you came back?" I ask, holding out my glass. She tips the bottle, holding back a little, but I figure she's earned that right, being as how she got cooked and I didn't. "To look after a bar that's not here any more?" As I say it, I feel the solid wood beneath my elbows and shrug. "Or at least, shouldn't be."

Filling her own glass again, she says, "Lotta things none of you barflies knew about my daddy, Tom. He made promises and broke 'em just like every other fool on God's green earth. Nothin' special about that. But then there were the kinds of promises he made *sure* couldn't be broken. Learned ways to guarantee that there'd be a price if anyone broke their word. Some tried, of course, and ended up ass-up out where you were puttin' the whore. Others went about tryin' to find a way to have the promises dissolved, with magic and other nonsense. But my daddy, he had a little 'ol ace up his sleeve in that wife of his."

"Didn't know he married again after your Momma died."

"'Course you didn't. No one did, and that's how he liked it. His little secret. I was only eighteen at the time, and she—*Lian Su*—wasn't much older. Said he won the little bitch in a poker game on one of his trips to the Orient, but figured out after too long that he'd been the one who'd come away a loser, on account of how she wasn't…right. Saw things she shouldn't have been able to see, made things happen, could hex people and the like. Could make people forget themselves, cause accidents, summon quarrels from calm. All manner of voodoo shit."

"I'm not sure the Chinese have voodoo, Gracie."

"Well whatever it was, it wasn't natural, and it was dangerous. My daddy was afraid of her at first, tried to lock her away in the guest room upstairs, but given the kind of man he was, it was only a matter of time before he started figurin' ways to benefit from her 'gift'. Next thing, he's winnin' poker games all over the place and those few unfortunates brave enough to challenge him end up missin', or worse." She shrugs as if the recollection doesn't bother her, but it's plain to see it does.

"If he was winning poker games, what'd he do with the money? No offense but this place was never what you'd call fancy."

"He was a gambler, Tom. Anything he made got lost just as quick."

"Right."

"So a year later, Lian Su gets a letter tellin' her her Momma's sick, and she begs my daddy to let her go home. Not quite sure why she felt the need to get his permission. Never could figure out what his hold on her was, considering she could probably abracadabra him into a possum if she had a mind to. Whatever it was, he agreed, but on the condition that he be allowed to go with her, I suppose to make sure she wasn't scheming to leave him. I know he was secretly wonderin' if maybe her momma was rich and left Lian a fortune that he could then add to his own pocket. Lian had no choice but to grant his wish. So they went. Before they did though, she did somethin' to me at my father's request. Made sure I stayed right here tendin' to his shithole till he got back."

She steps back from the bar, her gaze hard, and slips the strap of her dress off one shoulder, letting it slip down almost to the nipple of her right breast. If she'd done this earlier, I might have been grateful for the glimpse, and eager to see more, but there are two reasons why there isn't anything even remotely sexual about this moment. First, there's the obvious fact that she's dead, and as much as I was attracted to her in life, that's a line even I won't cross. Secondly, there's some kind of symbol branded into the flesh of that breast, a large ugly pink thing that looks like a couple of wigwams behind a crooked fence trapped inside a square. Hovering above the whole mess is a couple of rough Japanese or Chinese symbols.

"What's it mean?"

She shakes her head, tugs the strap back onto her slim shoulder, and I'm somewhat disturbed to note how hard her nipples are beneath the material, and how harder still it is for me to ignore the fact. "I don't know, but it's how he kept me here," she says. "S'why I'm *still* here. Night before he took off, he tied me down, took off my shirt and had the bitch spout gibberish over me before she drew that symbol on my tit with the business end of a red hot Bowie knife."

"Jesus. You ever try to leave?"

"First time I tried stepping over the threshold of this place, it made me sterile and ejected the baby that was busy growin' in my belly at the time."

"You were—"

"No great loss. It was my daddy's child anyway, so he did me a favor."

"I'm sorry."

"I put it down to coincidence and tried again. That one gave me such a pain it dropped me to the floor and left me there for two days, paralyzed and bleedin' from every hole in my body. So I gave up, figurin' if I tried a third time, it might be the last."

"Might've been a mercy too."

"This look like mercy to you?"

"Guess not."

"So my daddy comes back. Lian Su isn't with him, and he's loonier than a goddamn fox-gnawed hen."

"What happened?"

"Beats me, but it don't take a genius to figure out what might have happened to a Western man in an Eastern house of witches, does it?"

I shudder at the thought, or maybe it's the cold, but despite how unnatural my circumstances might have become, the whiskey is once again doing its job and blunting the edges.

"He locks himself in his room for a week, and I leave him there, happy to have him starve to death, till I remember he's the only hope I have of ever steppin' foot outside this place. So I go up there and I find him curled up on the bed like a child, naked and whimperin', and I grab him by the throat." She extends her hand and throttles the air between us. "And I tell him I'm glad he's gonna die, that it should have happened years ago. And I tell him I'll help put him out of his misery if he just tells me how to get out from under the bitch's hex. And you know what he does?"

I wait for her to continue.

"He laughs. That cocksucker laughs in this hysterical girly laugh and tells me this is my place, nowhere else right for me, and then gets right back to laughin'."

"So he could have done something about it if he'd wanted to?"

"Don't know. Maybe he knew how to lift the curse, maybe not, but I didn't give him a second chance to tell me."

I drain my glass, and damn that whiskey's hitting the spot now. I 'm even wondering if Gracie will object to letting me take another bottle off her hands for old time's sake. But her eyes are all glassy. She's back in that room with her daddy for the moment so I guess it's best to hear out the end of her account.

"You kill him?"

"You bet I did," she says, the fire in her eyes hotter than the one at my back. "Fucker had it comin'. Should've done it years ago, first time he came into my room reekin' of bourbon with his pants around his ankles. Should have stashed a knife and cut off his prick, but I never dreamed he'd do it. Could've done it any night after that but I guess I was too afraid, too stuck on the Bible and what it tells you about vengeance and righteousness and all that bullshit. He unlearned me of those lessons, I can tell you. My only regret now is that I left him off easy.

Smotherin' him with a pillow was a hell of a lot better than he deserved. I should have tied him down and…" She waves away the thought. "S'all the same now."

"And here you are. Still."

"Here I am."

"The hell happened in here tonight, Gracie?" I want more than anything for her to be able to give me a straight answer, tie up the whole goddamn mess in one quick sentence, because she died, and surely that gave her the opportunity to see who pulls the strings in this little nightmare.

But all she does is shrug. "Don't know."

"So what now?"

She looks around at the fire outside our little magic tunnel. "Guess I'm gonna have to start putting this place back together. Not gonna stand around in a pile of ashes for the rest of forever, and a girl's gotta make a livin'." This time she does smile, just a little.

"I'd be glad to help."

"Appreciate the offer, Tom, but it's not like I don't have the time."

"Not a matter of time, Gracie."

"I'll figure out what needs doin', and the way I see it, if I can blow cold bubbles that keep the fire from eatin' me up again, I can sure as shit make myself some walls and a roof."

"I guess that's true."

"Besides," she says, shoving aside her empty glass and taking a long swallow from the bottle. "You've got problems of your own."

I sigh. "Don't I know it."

"Not yet you don't."

Setting down my glass, I feel the return of the cold. You can dispute bad news from just about any source, but when it comes from the dead, who I figure are more likely to know the score than anyone living, then you best listen. So I do.

Gracie's dark eyes hold me in place. "Tonight," she says. "This tavern, this whole town, has been rotten for a long time, Tom, and so are most of the people in it. Some more than others."

None of this is news to me, but she's building up to something, and I find myself getting edgier with every word. She's trying to be gentle with me, and that's not in her nature, so it doesn't work, and that's the worst thing of all, because if she's trying to soften a blow that's coming, it's going to be a bad one.

"Tell me."

She puts the bottle in front of me, nods for me to take it. I do, and with it comes the feeling that it's a parting gift, that she suspects one of us isn't going to be here when the sun comes up. That lock of hair falls over her eye. I wait for her to tuck it back. She doesn't.

"It's your boy," she says. "You have yourself a Judas."

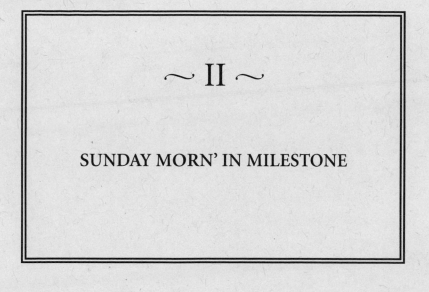

~ II ~

SUNDAY MORN' IN MILESTONE

9

Wintry's in agony, and it's not the kind of pain he's accustomed to carrying with him. This isn't the same as walking around with guilt pinned to your chest like Sheriff Tom's badge, or keeping it in your eyes like Gracie, or in your heart like Flo, or like Cobb trying to shed it with his clothes as if sins are snake skins. It's not the same as waking up every morning to find the faces of a few murdered men glaring at you in the mirror. This is a different kind of pain altogether. Oh yes. This is like being dragged for ten miles naked across a gravel highway until you tumble into a mound of salt and fire ants after being skinned alive and havin' boilin' water poured over you.

He sits atop a rock on the bank of the river, eyes closed, rocking like a child and whispering for forgiveness that isn't likely to come any time soon. Most of his body's burned, and burned bad, but despite the insistent demand inside him for self-pity, he figures maybe he deserves the scalding pain. Figures he should probably be dead so that those waiting for his end would finally get what they've been praying for. He knows for a fact that there's a widow down in Atlanta who'd be overjoyed and more than a little relieved to hear the fire took him, or that he died right here crying like a baby on the bank of a foul-smelling river. Of course, Wintry doesn't smell anything but the aroma of fresh-cooked flesh.

The problem is, that poor widow down in Georgia hasn't gotten her wish, at least, not yet. Seems her prayers, just like Wintry's, aren't going to be answered for a while. But sitting here with the rain falling down around him and the black waters of the gurgling river rising up, he wishes to God they had been, that he'd joined Flo wherever she got off to when the fire was done with her and the child.

The child.

Instinct makes him want to rub his wounds, to soothe them, but he can't. Even the slightest touch makes the raw oozing flesh on his body sing, so he keeps his hands pressed to the sodden grass, wishing the cold would help, but he's beyond believing it will. He's already washed himself in the river once, and for one brief moment, when the shock of the icy water hit him, there was relief, but then the fire returned with renewed force, eating him up from the inside out. So here he sits, and suffers, still sending up prayers to the Almighty to make the agony stop, if just for a little while.

And when, after some immeasurable length of time, with the rain coming down even heavier than before, hurting rather than helping every part of him it hits, he almost doesn't feel someone touching his shoulder. With eyes filled with rain because the flames have burned his tears away, he looks first at the hand, silently hoping it's the hand of a savior, or his executioner, both of which have come to mean the same thing in this night world of unprecedented suffering, then up into the face of the woman standing over him.

A smile splits his charred face.

"You alive?" says the woman. As brief as the first dip in that freezing river, Wintry feels love wash over him, easing his pain. He thinks of the child, he thinks of getting away, of second chances and God's grace. He doesn't consider the memory of that raging blue fire spreading from the hole in Flo's belly, burning her up as if she was made of straw, or the horrible choking sound she made when finally she dropped to the floor and lay still. He doesn't consider any of this and it doesn't matter a lick. She's here; she's alive, and he's not alone.

But then the raging red waves return and he gasps, not at the sight of his beloved Flo changing into a withered old man with a rusted box in his throat, but at the severity of the agony that consumes him.

The hand on his shoulder now is a gnarled one, and the grip is like a glove of fire, prompting Wintry to speak for the first time in years. "Who are you?" he croaks and the words are like glass scratching free of a scorched throat. He is not looking for a name, for it is one he knows. He's looking for the truth.

"Opportunity," Cadaver answers. "And punishment."

Wintry thinks of drowning, or bashing his own head in with one of those slimy black rocks at his feet. He should be dead, he knows that, and he knows too that it isn't going to take much to end it properly, especially now there's someone here to make sure he doesn't back out or come crawling back for the second time, even if it's not anyone he considers a friend. He reckons he's died with the only people he'd consider close once already tonight and shouldn't be too fussy about not being able to do it again. He figures suffering of this kind is made to have an end, and surely Cadaver won't stand in his way.

His head feels like it weighs a ton as he raises it to look at the old man, who smiles at him. "You might not think it, Wintry, but you've been through worse."

"You do this?" Wintry asks. "You bring me back?"

"No. You brought yourself back. Crawled out in a hurry once you saw there was nothin' could be done for your woman, or anyone else in there for that matter. Survival instinct got you out. Just like it got you out of prison. Just like it got you through life so far."

Wintry understands what he's being told, but he disagrees. He's never suffered like this before, and suffering is no stranger to him.

"You're a fighter," Cadaver says. "Always have been, my friend."

Wintry swallows a burning breath, and though his new kind of pain has inspired him to use his voice for the first time in fourteen years, it won't come.

There is the creak and pop of old bones and Cadaver is suddenly hunkered down next to him, his eyes pockets of shadow in a pillowcase face, the smile still twisting lips that look sewn from dirty thread. "I can help you," he whispers. "I can end this for you. Give you what you want. It's why I'm here."

Wintry shakes his head. Cadaver is the devil. He knows that now, and though what education he has comes from the street, the dingy alleys and shaded corners back in Atlanta, his fists the pen, hard faces his pages, he's smart enough to know the devil never offers anything without taking something in return.

"Let me be."

Cadaver sighs. It's the sound of a cold breeze on a summer's day. "You don't want me to do that."

"You…don't know what I want, and can't tell me neither. Go. Let me alone."

"I can end your sufferin'. All of it. I can free you from the ghosts. I can give you the chance to clear your soul. I can help you save yourself."

Wintry tries to smile but it's as if fishing hooks are holding the skin of his face together. His flesh sings with agony. He shudders, restrains a gasp. At length, he sags, adopting the repose of death, though that mercy stays maddeningly out of his reach. "What you want from me?" he asks, licking his lips with a sandpaper tongue. "What will you take?"

Cadaver shrugs. "Nothin'."

"You lyin'."

"That's one thing I never do. There's never any call for it."

"So you goan…set me free just cause you a nice…guy, huh?"

"No. You're goin' to free yourself. All I'm goin' to do is tell you how."

Before Wintry has a chance to say more, Cadaver stands and peers off toward the amber glow of the fire on the hill. Eddie's is still burning, the air still reeks of smoke and burned flesh, though how much of that is from himself, Wintry can't tell.

"You taught kids how to fight, Wintry. You trained them to defend themselves and inadvertently made them murderers. You beat a man to death with your bare hands, usin' what your no-good father made you learn from him. He compensated for his abuse of you by teachin' you how to use violence to get what you want. He hoped you'd use it on him someday if he pushed you hard enough. Hoped more than anythin' that you'd deal him a fatal blow and set *him* free of his misery. But you never did. You let him die by his own clock because it was the kind of fight you were guaranteed to win. Tonight, if you want an escape from your own skin, you're goin' to have to fight one last time, use those hams of yours and beat your demons into submission."

"Can't," is all Wintry can say.

Cadaver clucks his tongue. "You will if you want to be with your beloved when death does come for you."

"Can't fight."

"You can and will. It's the only way."

Wintry frowns, winces. The expression yanks on burnt nerves. "Who?"

Cadaver is by his side again, breathing foul breath in his face that ignites the ruined flesh. "Tonight, my friend, you're goin' to fight the fight you dreamed of for years through frustrated adolescent tears."

Wintry bares his teeth, feels anger cocooned in pain squirrel its way up his throat. "*Who?*"

Cadaver leans in close, his blind eye like a distant view of an icy sun. His whisper is almost reverential in tone. "Daddy."

~

I should sleep. I'm dog-tired, and stinking of grave dirt and old blood that's going to stay now that the rain's finally giving up the ghost. I don't look back at the tavern, though the heat's dropping. Eddie's'll finish it's burning soon enough. Whatever Gracie's putting back into that place isn't anything the fire's going to be able to touch. Not tonight, or more accurately—as a quick check of my watch tells me—this morning.

Not this fire, but maybe the next catastrophe that blows in when folks' sins start outweighing virtue.

Out there, past the willows and pines and beech and scrub, the sky's starting to lighten like someone's holding a flashlight down under the bedclothes. It won't take long to spread, but when it does and that horizon catches fire proper, it won't make Milestone any prettier. It'll only send long shadows racing toward the borders.

There's dirt caked beneath my fingernails and my knuckles are throbbing something fierce. Should've asked Gracie if she could conjure me up a shovel, but it's a little late. The whore's not buried deep, but she's planted all the same. If I put all my weight on the earth when I pack it down, it sinks until if I poked a finger into the grave I'd be able to feel her under there, so I go gentle, patting it with my hands until there's only a slight soggy hump in the earth to say anyone's here at all.

In a few hours there'll be stragglers on the streets as folks make their way to the church on Hymn Street. They don't want to go, not when they know God has fled the place, but they'll be there same as they always are, afraid Reverend Hill will come find them if they don't, as he's done in the past. They don't yet know he's dead, of course, so maybe if there's time and I'm still breathing I'll cruise on by the place and let them know. It'll be worth it just to see their relief that the old bastard is finally gone from their lives.

But what's gotta be done's gotta be done soon before there are too many people around to see it. Business of this kind always goes on when the town's quiet, so people can wake up in the morning and tell themselves nothing strange has happened while they've slept and the world's just as dark and shitty as it ever was without being helped along by sinners.

I finish patting down the grave, then retrieve the bottle of whiskey Gracie was good enough to send along with me without me asking for it, and I head for my truck.

I'm going to drive with the windows down so the cold keeps me awake, and alert, so I can try to pull some inspiration from my ass and figure out how I'm going to handle Kyle, who Gracie tells me is all set to sell me out.

"Can I get out?"

I know what Brody wants, and I guess I should give it to him. The man has a right to say goodbye to his woman. But I'm not going to. I doubt he gave the family and friends of the people he's killed such consideration.

Rich coming from me, I know.

"Just sit back and keep quiet."

"C'mon man…just a few minutes. I'm not going to run."

"Maybe later. Right now I've got some business to attend to."

I put the truck in gear and ignore his protests from the back seat. He's putting on quite a show, thrashing, spitting, cursing, but for all of that I've got the strangest feeling he really doesn't care all that much that his girl's dead. Not sure why that suspicion takes hold of me, but there it is. Maybe I'm way off base; maybe not. For now there's no way of knowing.

"I can't believe you, you hick son of a bitch. This isn't fair and you know it."

Yeah, I do, but your little crime spree took away any privileges you might think you deserve."

"She told me it was a mistake coming this way, you know. Should have listened to her."

"Yeah, you should have."

The truck rolls down the hill, the tires splashing through potholes in the dirt road that have filled with rain. Eddie's burns but the light is growing dim, the flames appear caged behind walls that grow more solid as their shadows band together. Brody keeps talking, but I've stopped listening. There's too much else on my mind. Kyle, for one, and where I might find him.

I decide to head for Winter Street, and Iris Gale's place of business.

Most folks think Doctor Hendricks came to Milestone to make his fortune, ignoring the fact that most of what he gets are corpses, or the living dancing at death's door, like the dead girl the Sheriff and his boy brought earlier. There's no money to be made here, but just because he insists on dressing real nice and being respectful toward anyone who crosses his path, he's labeled a gold digger. It's almost funny. There hasn't been anything worth having in this town for as long as he's lived here.

Good thing then that he came here to die.

As he sits watching the embers dying in the fireplace, a freshly brewed cup of tea warming his palms, he's aware, as always, of the long shadow above the mantel. It's his father's Winchester rifle. Now there was a man who decided young that he was going to be rich and didn't stop until he was, no matter how many people he had to step on to get there. There was your 48-carat gold-digger, a man who only ever smiled in the company of people he was going to ruin.

At home, Hendricks saw his father smile a lot.

A breeze against the window makes the curtains shift a little. There is no keeping it out. The house is old and draughty. Upstairs, Queenie's asleep, piled beneath enough covers to ensure she stays warm. She's not alone though. Never alone. She's got the cancer to keep her company, infecting her dreams with its promises of death, eating away at her brain while she snatches as much peace from her final days as she's permitted. For Hendricks, who despite his profession can do nothing but sedate her and feed her painkillers in near-lethal doses, it's become a lottery. First, he wonders if this morning will be the one he goes up to the room to find her dead. Then he wonders, if she does wake up, will she attack him, or scream hysterically because she's forgotten who he is? And lastly, he wonders if today's the day he takes that shotgun down and puts them both out of their misery once and for all.

He intends for it to happen, accepts that it must. The gun's loaded, ready to go. It's just a matter of when, and how many bullets he'll need. The thought does not disturb him. He has watched his beautiful wife lapse into psychotic rages and foul-mouthed fits for almost two years now. He has sat with her while she wept, and thanked the Almighty Jesus for her spells of lucidity and apparent health. For the past two weeks, there have been no episodes, no late night panic attacks or spells of spouting gibberish like a possessed thing. It's almost as if she's been his, and his alone. As if he hasn't had to share her with a parasite.

The lull won't last though. It never does, and he fears that this is merely the calm before the final devastating storm that takes her for good. If it does so before he takes that shotgun down, so be it, but he has no intention of surviving her.

There is a knock on the door. It surprises him, jerks the cup in his hand and sends tea sloshing over the side. He grumbles, checks his watch, then rises, sets the cup aside, and casts a final glance at the shadow over the mantel.

10

Though Milestone's creeping toward dawn, it always feels like deep night on Winter Street, and if you're looking for sunshine, you'd best look up on over the roofs and not through the windows.

Time was you came here for your groceries, or for a haircut, or for some new clothes to impress your latest date. If you wanted the fancy stuff, you'd have to carry your ass clear into Saddleback, which I've always thought is a long haul just to spend twice as much as you would in Milestone for more or less the same damn thing. Doesn't matter now though. These days, you come here to get laid or listen to the wisdom of Horace Dudds, one of only three town drunks who haven't yet realized the town's died around them. The others are Maggie, Horace's unofficial girlfriend, and Kirk Vess, though he tends to wander and isn't welcome on Horace and Maggie's turf. Apparently they have standards he doesn't meet. Politics of the homeless, I guess. If Maggie has a second name, she has never seen fit to reveal it, and no one ever asks. I guess we all figure when you've got nothing else to call your own, no one will begrudge you keeping your name to yourself.

I pull up outside a narrow gray building that looks like something from an angry child's drawing with its funny angles and not-quite-straight edges, boarded up windows and trash stuffed in the wide cracks between the short run of steps leading to main door. Through the gaps in the boards nailed over the store's plate glass window, a blinking florescent light shows a bunch of mannequins stripped of their clothes, and lewdly posed so they look like they've been frozen mid-orgy. A faded wooden plaque above the door bears the legend THE HOUSE OF IRIS.

On the opposite side of the road stands what used to be a clothing store for children before people stopped having them. Beneath the tattered red-and-white striped awning, sit two figures huddled against the weather.

"Evenin' Sheriff," Horace says, and offers me a toothy grin, at the same time drawing his bottle closer to his chest, like he's afraid I'm going to snatch it. Horace may be a drunk, but he's got a long memory, and can probably recall every bit of graffiti in my old drunk tank.

I nod my head, "Horace, Maggie," and slam the truck door behind me. The sound echoes along the street and returns as thunder. I join them under the awning.

"Bad night. You two should be indoors, by the fire."

Horace wears a purple peaked cap he won in a card game from an Irishman. A week later he played another game and lost everything he owned. Claims to this day it wouldn't have happened if he hadn't beaten that 'potato-eatin' Mick', who he says, "Went home with my luck snug in his ass pocket." Beneath the cap's peak, a huge nose keeps a pair of piercing gray eyes from meeting, though they seem determined, the pupils like black balloons anchored by dark red threads. His belt is a stretch of skipping rope with the wooden handles lopped off. People call him old, and he looks damn old, but the thing is, he's been in Milestone his whole life and it seems he's always looked exactly as he does now.

"Plenty of fire," Horace says sagely, "But it's too wet to walk a'far as Eddie's."

"What happened up there anyway?" Maggie asks. She's dressed in her signature floral print dress—sky-blue barely visible beneath an explosion of pink roses. Maggie's a formidable woman, heavy, and quick to anger. A tornado with a head of hazel curls. There's no doubt in my mind she could throw me from one end of the street to the other if I pissed her off. So I don't, even in the past when she's given me reason to. See the problem is that when Maggie's not sitting by Horace's side wherever he's chosen to settle, she's standing in the town square, blocking traffic and hollering her damn fool head off about the government and how they're going to round us up one by one and brainwash us to their way of thinking (whatever the hell *that* is). As if that wasn't bad enough, her pontificating and gesticulating is usually enough to allow certain parts of her to spill out of her loose-fitting dress, causing quite a stir among those who don't have the sense to drive around her. I've always thought that in another life she and Cobb would have made a happy couple.

"Cobb lost it," I tell her. "Burnt the place up."

"Oh," Maggie says with a shake of her head. "He had a lovely voice."

"Anyone inside?" Horace asks, after a puzzled look at Maggie. I know how he feels. No one I know ever heard Cobb sing, assuming that's what Maggie means.

"Yeah."

"Don't suppose the Reverend was one of 'em?"

"Matter of fact he was."

Horace nods his satisfaction. "Good. Bastard ruined this town. Place had a hope afore him."

Maggie shakes her head, effortlessly snatches the bottle, which I see is a flagon of cider, from Horace's protective clutches. "I wouldn't say he done ruined it. Minin' comp'ny and greed did that. Hill just helped is all. Set the stage for the men in suits and too-tight ties to come waltzin' in and make us regret ever settlin' down here." She ponders this for a moment, then takes a swig from the bottle that's so generous, Horace's eyes widen and he makes a grab for it. They scowl at one another for a few seconds like two dogs over a piece of meat, then Horace shakes his head and looks at me. "Your boy's okay though. Counts for somethin'."

"He's alive, if that's what you mean."

Horace smiles a little, and his bloodshot eyes gleam dully. "Yeah, that's what I mean."

"I'm assuming you've seen him around tonight, then?"

Horace shrugs. "Went in Miss Iris's place. Gone again now though."

Maggie grins. "He didn't stay long, did he Horace? Which is a shame, because usually them two put on some kind of a show for us less-fortunate types." She nods toward the double windows on the first floor of Iris's building—which, much like the main window on the ground floor, isn't boarded over enough to prevent the curious from seeing clear into the room, especially if the room is lit—and elbows Horace in the ribs. "I'm afraid one of these days it's going to put ideas into your head."

This is a conversation I have no interest in being a part of, so I bid them good night.

"Sheriff…?"

I stop, turn, look at Maggie. "Yeah?"

"You leavin' us?"

"What do you mean?"

"You look like a man flirtin' with the idea of runnin'."

"No," I reply. "Not yet anyway."

"Man's got a boy to look out for," Horace adds. "Man with responsibilities can't rightly run away from 'em or they'll dog him for the rest of his life. Ain't that right, Sheriff?"

"That's right." I get the feeling he's talking from experience.

"Well you tell that handsome boy of yours Maggie says hello, and that if he ever gets tired of that young gussied-up whore, he can come see *me*." She laughs uproariously and thumps a hand on Horace's back, nearly sending him sprawling into the street.

"I will."

"Hey, and Sheriff?" Horace again.

Exasperated, I frown at him. "What is it?"

"Town's awful lonesome this time of night, ain't it?"

"Yeah."

"You find yourself in need of company, or backup, you just let us know."

This sends Maggie into renewed hysterics, but Horace isn't laughing.

"Who's your passenger?" Maggie asks, loud enough for Brody to be alerted. His pale face presses against the window of my truck and he smiles.

"Never you mind, Maggie."

"Handsome," she remarks.

"Trouble," I call back.

I cross the street, ignoring Brody's toothy grin. There are no lights on anywhere on Winter Street, but that doesn't mean much. Iris's place is the only one occupied, and it's late.

My knuckles hurt like hell so I turn my fist to the side and thump the door like a pissed-off landlord coming for rent. It sounds like a gunshot, then the street gets awful quiet, as if I'm not the only one curious to see if I get an answer. Even Horace and Maggie have quit their banter.

Another bang on the door hard enough to send painful vibrations up my arm, and I hear soft slow footsteps descending the stairs on the other side.

A moment later, a sleepy voice filters out to me from behind the door. "Who is it?"

"Tom."

"Sheriff Tom?"

"None other."

"You here to arrest me, Sheriff?" I'm sure the playfulness in her voice is meant to be cute, and probably works for her customers, but it's late, I'm tired and I'm in no mood for it. "Open the fucking door, Iris."

"Not if you can't be civil."

"I don't have time for this. Where is he?"

"Who?"

I take a deep breath, time enough to consider kicking the door off its hinges and her off her feet in the same shot. "Kyle."

"He ain't been here."

"Cut the shit, Iris. I know he has, now either tell me where he went or I'll knock this door down and you'll spend the night behind bars."

She laughs, as sweet a sound as any woman's laugh, but it makes my teeth hurt. "Iris, so help me…"

"You seem awful uptight tonight, Sheriff. Tense. I'm almost afraid to open the door case you explode all over me."

"The only thing that's gonna…" I start to say, then decide to change tack. "Look, this is serious. Kyle's in trouble, so you need to quit the crap and either open the door or tell me where he is."

Her sigh is just loud enough to hear through the thick wood of the door. "Well now Sheriff, it's all a bit fuzzy. You can't come knockin' up a girl and expect her to have a good head right away, can you?"

I press my head against the door, and wish, not first time tonight, today, whatever the fuck it is, that I had my gun. But then there's the sharp snap of a lock, the door cracks open and I catch myself just in time to avoid pitching forward on top of the girl standing there with sleep in her eyes and a coy smile on her face.

"You're no fun," Iris says, her pout so dramatic I almost applaud. Her act might hold more water with me if I didn't remember her back in her store-owning days, when she'd blush at the slightest of compliments and get flustered as all hell when anyone got up the nerve to ask her out. She was a decent sort and I reckon somewhere beneath the too-thick makeup and scandalous facade, she might still be, if years of lying beneath fat sweaty old men, drunks, and addled young guns hasn't soured her on life completely.

She's short, about five feet tall, and most of that's legs, which are bare now beneath the hem of a man's logging shirt. Her red hair is cut short, not long enough to touch the small slopes of her shoulders, and the shirt's buttoned only at the middle, so when she moves her belly's exposed, and there's enough cleavage on show to let any man know what he's walked himself into. A soon as I'm clear of the door, she steps close, and despite my feelings about her and the urgency that's on me to find Kyle, there's a lot to appreciate right there in front of me.

Her hands find my shirt and she runs her fingers over my chest, her blue eyes gazing deeply into mine, a small smile on her soft lips. "I was hopin' you'd stop by, Sheriff."

"Yeah, why's that?"

"Well, why don't you come up for a coffee and I'll tell you all you need to know?"

She peers around me at the two hobos. I hear Maggie chuckling, then the door is shut and Iris is leading me by my hand up the dark stairs. Her skin is warm. Everything in me tells me to pull away, not to get suckered in by her games, though I'm full sure I won't, not with the way my mind's set, but this night/day hasn't followed any rules but it's own, and it's hard to keep track of it without the mind just shutting down. So even though I'm trying hard not to look at the pale curves of Iris's bare ass as she leads the way, I'm back to thinking of sleep, and it starts getting easier to imagine rest knowing there's a bed right up here complete with a woman to share her heat with me.

Sand fills my eyes, approving of my train of thought, and I yawn, then immediately clear my throat and tell myself to snap out of it. I'm in danger of putting a whore over my son's life, and though I'm guilty of a lot, I won't be guilty of that. I withdraw my hand, and she lets me, doesn't even look back.

"Long night, Sheriff?"

"The longest."

We're at the top of the stairs, and she walks ahead into a large room lit by more candles than I've ever seen in one place in my life, except maybe the church. They're spread out around the floor so densely I wonder if there's a trick to navigating it without setting your pants on fire. Not that I imagine too many folks are still wearing their pants by the time they reach this room. Iris doesn't look the patient type, and given that her customers are lonely desperate men, I doubt they need to be asked twice.

There are mannequins in every corner of the room, sexless, naked, and tilted back so they're all staring up at the ceiling with bored expressions on their plastic faces.

"Why don't you take off your boots?" Iris says and all that's missing from that suggestion is: *And slide 'em under my bed.*

"No thanks. I'm not staying long."

"Maybe not but you're trackin' mud all over my floor."

I look down and see that's she's right, but I've got no intention of taking off my boots. I'm sure I'm not the first visitor she's had who ignored the mat inside the front door in their eagerness to be right where I'm standing now.

"It isn't so bad that a quick sweeping won't take care of it."

"If you say so." She walks into the room, making her way around that obstacle course of candles with the sure step only someone who put them there could enjoy. The flames dance in her wake. The combined heat from those candles brings sweat to my brow and I search for a chair. There's only one, at the foot of the bed, facing it as if it's there for spectators. I sit. The room is large, and there's a door to the left of it, leading to a small kitchen area, and presumably a bathroom beyond. Iris stops here and leans against the doorframe. "How do you like it?"

"Black," I reply without missing a beat. "Two sugars. You trying to save money on the power bill?"

"No. Lights don't like me."

"How's that?"

"I turn 'em off."

"Why?"

"Not on purpose. They just switch off whenever I'm around 'em. If I'm walkin' the street, the lamps'll go out. Same in here. Turn on a light and it'll stay on just fine if I'm in the other room. Soon as I come in though…" She snaps her fingers. "Dark. Radios and TVs go crazy sometimes too."

"Oh."

"Been like that since the day I was born. Streetlight outside my house went off and the TV went snowy. Must be my magnetic personality."

"Interesting." My voice makes it clear I think no such thing. "Can't say I remember you having that problem when you ran the store."

"Well, it was usually daylight, wasn't it? And when it wasn't, I used hurricane lamps. You remember, you used to call 'em quaint, made you feel like you were at sea."

"No, I'm afraid I don't remember that at all."

"Maybe because they were better times. Some people hang on to those like prized jewels; others toss 'em as soon as misery comes a-callin'."

She disappears into the kitchen, where I hear the hissing sound of her filling the kettle, the scratch of a match and the whumping sound of a gas ring catching fire.

The bed is rumpled, and I have to wonder whether or not Kyle even spent time in it tonight. I was sure I'd find him here, but for whatever reason, his visit was a short one.

A few moments later, with impatience ticking a countdown in my head, Iris emerges from the kitchen. She's holding a single cup of coffee, which she brings to me. "I'm out of sugar," she says. "Hope it's okay."

"It's fine." I take a sip that scalds my upper lip and tongue, but I don't mind. It chases away some of the exhaustion that's clinging to me like a shroud.

Iris stands close enough for my breath to warm her belly, and crosses her arms. "So you're lookin' for Kyle?"

"Yeah."

"You're a little late."

"I figured."

She turns and makes her way through the labyrinth of candles to the bed, and watches me as she unbuttons the shirt and slips out of it. God she's a pretty thing, but I avert my eyes to the vapid stare of the mannequin in the opposite corner while she tosses the shirt on the bed and slips beneath the covers. "You're welcome to join me," she says. "Despite what you might think, that's not an offer I extend to just anyone."

"Then you may want to change your ad."

"Funny. You got nice ears, Sheriff. Anyone ever tell you that?"

"How long was Kyle here?"

She plumps her pillows and sits back, the sheet drawn up over her breasts, nipples hard points beneath the flimsy material. "Not long. He wanted some company but…" She shrugs, puts again. "Seems he wasn't up for it tonight."

"He say anything to you about what happened?"

"Sure. Told me Eddie's burned. No great loss if you ask me." She sighs, then her lips curl in amusement. "Bet you're wonderin' why you never saw me up there with the rest of you sinners, aintcha?"

In truth, I wasn't, but I am now, so I nod.

"Well I'm not real sure about that, Sheriff. Maybe it's because women in my line of work get special consideration. Maybe we're needed just like we've been needed all through history, so when it comes time to open that great big book of black sins, we get left out. Or maybe it's because Reverend Hill, despite his bible thumpin', was still a man at the back of it and needed his poke just like everyone else and couldn't rightly put me up on the cross for givin' folks, and *him*, what they asked for. Besides, it ain't like I force people's hands. And I ain't never killed a man. Least, not yet."

"What else did Kyle tell you?"

"That he wasn't sorry to see those folks killed. But he was lyin'."

"How do you know that?"

"Call it women's intuition. You sure you wouldn't like to join me in here where it's warm?" She pats the empty space beside her. "You look like you could use the release."

"No."

"No charge."

"I said no."

"All right," she sighs.

"So tell me."

"I don't think he gave a shit about the black man. In fact, I'm pretty sure he didn't, was probably glad to see the back of him if the way he talked was any indication."

"Wintry? Why?"

"Because he had the murderin' bitch."

"Why would that—?"

"Wake up Sheriff. I know you're tired, but you ain't stupid. Kyle had a thing for her. Didn't mind tellin' me neither, 'cuz y'know…I'm just good for one thing, right?"

She's still wearing that smile, but a hardness has entered her eyes, splintering the candle light and I feel a small knot of shame because that's exactly how I've always looked at her—Iris, former store-owner, current whore.

"Didn't give a shit about Cobb, or Gracie, and didn't care too much that he put a bullet in that young thief's belly. Only one he really cared about was Flo. Said he'd planned to run away with her, get away from Milestone and start a good life somewhere." She snorts a little laugh. "You raised yourself a gullible one, Sheriff."

The coffee tastes sour and I set it down between my feet. "What else?"

"Well, I've already told you he needed lovin' and I put on my best show for his poor soul. Didn't work though. He wasn't—"

"Yeah, you told me. He say anything else?"

She stares at me for a moment, and the expression on her face is unreadable. The light warms one side of her face, leaving the other in shadow. She sits forward, and the sheet slides down, exposing her breasts for a moment before she draws up her knees and crosses her arms around them. "He's gunnin' for you, you know."

"Yeah, I do."

"Know why?"

"Off hand I can think of any number of reasons."

"Know why he's plannin' on finishin' you tonight?"

"No."

"Because he made a deal and said he would."

"A deal? With who?"

"That old guy who looks like a corpse."

Cadaver. Not a great surprise, but it adds a layer of hurt to the pile that's already festering inside me. What does come as a surprise is finding out Kyle knew Cadaver was behind everything, even if the old man didn't start the fire. Now I'm wondering what they were really saying while they stood watching Eddie's burn. The idea of the two of them being in cahoots makes my blood run cold and those two pennies in my pocket are starting to feel like sandbags.

"You know what the deal was?" I ask Iris.

"Nope. Kyle wouldn't say, but I expect the end of you'll be his ticket out of town. Maybe he'll even get Flo back for his efforts. You never know."

We share a moment of silence, both of us burning up inside over Kyle's betrayal. I stand, careful not to send my cup of coffee flying, and put my hands on the cold bedrail. "He say where he was going?"

"He did."

I wait. She says nothing.

"Where?"

"Not sure I should tell you."

"Why's that?"

"You haven't settled up for the information you've already gotten outta me."

"What is it you want?" I ask, sure I already know.

"Come here."

"Iris. I have to get going. You know why."

"I do, so I'm not gonna be hurt that you ain't gonna stay with me. But that ain't it." She lays back, sheet to her waist, hands by her sides. "Just come here. It won't take long."

Against my better judgment, and struggling to keep my eyes from studying what's there to be studied, I sidestep my way through the candles until I'm standing next to her. "What?"

She reaches up, one hand finding the back of my neck, drawing me down even as her face is rising toward me, an odd look about her, her eyes like stars, and she kisses me. But my eyes are open, and in the honey-colored light from the candles, I see a deep angry-looking scar running from the top of her forehead back into her hair, like someone tried to split her skull open with an ax. I guess it shouldn't come as a surprise. Doing what she does is bound to put her in the company of some mean folks, but I don't like seeing it. I break the kiss, despite it making my body tingle with warmth that spreads across my chest and down to where I don't want it going, and I step back, look at her. Goddamn it's been way too long.

Iris hasn't bothered to draw the sheet up again, but that's all right. She's smiling, and the urge to say to hell with everything and just crawl in with her is powerful. But I can't, and she knows it. Knew it before she even opened the door to me, and I guess all this has been is a little betray-al of our own.

"We square?" I ask, after a few moments in which nothing needed to be said.

"I guess we are," she says dreamily. "Too bad you've got to go runnin' off though. I like talkin' to you. You ain't nothin' like your boy."

That's hardly a revelation.

"Maybe when this is over," she says. "If it ever is, and if you don't end right along with it."

"Where did he go?"

"The Reverend's house," she says.

"Why there?"

"Beats me."

This puzzles me. I can't figure out what he'd want up there, unless Hill had something he needs. Or something Cadaver instructed him to get. But what?

"I'm sorry."

She raises her eyebrows. "What for?"

"For…" I don't know how to apologize for thinking her nothing but a common whore. Don't know how to apologize for a scar I didn't give her, or for my son's casual and tactless confessions. Or for the fact that this whole town's gone to seed and I never once tried to stop it. And the only reason I'm saying a goddamn thing at all is because I'm not sure I'll get a chance to say it again.

"Sheriff?"

But there are no words, and if there are, I don't know them, so I do what any man does when what he feels he has to say gets lodged like a chicken bone in his throat.

I tip my hat and leave.

11

Hendricks opens the door to a scarecrow in a top hat.

"What?" he asks, unwilling to extend even the pretense of cour-tesy to a man he once caught urinating on his doorstep.

"Doc," Kirk Vess says, crossed eyes wide. "You're awake, good. That's good." As he searches for words that seem to be dangling just beyond his grasp, he snatches his hat from his head, revealing a greasy nest of hair that resembles a mound of limp noodles heaped atop a dirty upended bowl. Beneath the pallid brow and contradictory eyes, a single drop of clear snot, sweat, or water dangles from the tip of a fishhook nose, which in turn presides over an impossibly wide mouth, packed to capacity with thin black teeth. Hendricks has often wondered, judging by his scars and the man's erratic behavior, if Vess, at some point in his unremarkable life, donated his brain to science. It summons the comical image of a bunch of perplexed medical students clustered around a stainless steel pan wherein stews Vess's brain. *Good lord, it shouldn't be that shape should it?* one might inquire, while another asks, *Where's the rest of it?*

Of Vess, he knows very little, except that the man is homeless and given to outbursts of violence, and that come autumn, he will disappear, to reappear in the first week of winter. What he does during this absence is unknown, but there are few, if any, folks in Milestone who care enough to ask.

"Good, good," Vess says again, fingering with pale tapered fingers the brim of a hat as flaccid as the man himself. He wears a coat torn at the elbows and frayed at the hem, the lapels encrusted with a substance of some indeterminate origin. He reeks of urine, alcohol and vomit, from his scabrous scalp to his sole-less boots.

"What are you doing here?" Hendricks snaps. "If you've come to beg…"

Vess squints, leans in a little as if unsure of what's been said, then gasps and raises his hands, the hat flopping wildly as he protests. "No sir, no sir. Not money. What am I doing here? Big question. Keep asking it and no one has an answer. Course, they couldn't really." He shakes his head, dismissing a thought that perhaps didn't even make sense to him. "I didn't want to bother you for nothing, truth be told. But I had to ask someone who'd know where it might have come from or who might own it."

Annoyed, and loath to waste any more time on this odious creature, Hendricks takes a step back, intending to close to door. Vess's pleas stop him. "No, wait! Sorry, sir. Just a tick. A sweep of sixty, please. I'll show it to you." He starts to rummage around in his pockets, which look flat and empty. "I kept it safe as I could, but it looks dead a long time."

Intrigued despite himself, yet fully expecting the man will produce a dead rodent from one of those pockets, Hendricks only closes the door half way, just enough to let Vess know if this is some ridiculous scheme, it will be revealed to the morning breeze and a quiet street, but not a gullible doctor.

Frustrated, Vess begins to chastise himself in what sounds like an alien dialect. "Fffteck! Shlassen shlack!" Then with an apologetic look, he calms himself and reaches into the inside pocket of his coat. "Yes, yes. I knew it. I'm a fool," he says and slaps a grubby palm against his forehead hard enough to make Hendricks jump. "Yes, hidden and safe," Vess tells him and withdraws from the pocket a small brown bundle, which Hendricks mistakes for a stubby cigar. But as he prepares a suitably bemused tone with which to deliver his verdict, Vess, pale worm-like tongue poking from between his teeth, reverently unwraps the small parcel and holds it up, inches from the doctor's face.

"I found more, but I wasn't sure whether disturbing it was a good idea. I don't need no ghosts on my tail. Isn't that right? Not when I'm out of place."

Hendricks doesn't answer. Instead, ignoring the smell from the man, he adjusts his spectacles and steps closer.

"Told her I'd bring it back before she even know'd it was gone. Have to respect women you know. Even I know that and I've forgotten a lot."

Hendricks raises his eyes and appraises the man anew, not because he has developed any kind of respect or admiration for his guest, but because he is now as suspicious and wary of Vess as he would be toward any man who showed up at his door with the remains of a human finger in his pocket.

～⌒～

Iris is on my mind as I steer the truck out of Winter Street. Woman like that makes me think of the future, no matter what she does for a living or how screwed up she may be because of it. Makes me want to help her, to fix her somehow, and in the process maybe fix myself. And that doesn't make a lick of sense. I don't know a damn thing about her except that she's a whore, that she's been with any number of men, including my son, and I'm not sure that's something I wouldn't see in her every time she smiled at me.

I can't shake the feel of her lips on mine, though. It's enough to distract me, take me away from the cruelty I've brought down on myself, to a place where everything isn't sharp edges and pain, death and ruin. A place I'd like to stay, and might have, if Brody hadn't just jerked me out of my thoughts.

Check that out," he says, sounding amused. "There's someone out there."

I check the rearview to see where he's looking and then I spot it.

I'm a little ways past Hendricks' place when I slam down hard enough on the brakes to make the truck shudder into a fishtail. The smoke from scalded rubber sweeps past my window.

"Jesus," Brody groans, grunting as he shifts himself back onto the seat.

Bloodshot dawn glares at me from over the hills.

Between this road and the river, there's a field. Dan Cannon, the previous occupant of the house Doc Hendricks now calls home, used to grow corn there. Now it's barren and yields only a harvest of rocks. Tonight, someone has lit a fire in there a few feet from an oak tree with spindly branches that was the bane of Cannon's prematurely short existence, and from here, I can see a figure moving sluggishly around it, the flames revealing a craggy ruined face I'm too afraid to admit I know, disfigurement and all.

"Isn't that…?"

"Yeah," I mutter. Milestone doesn't have two giants. After what happened at Eddie's it shouldn't even have one. But that's Wintry up there, doing what looks to be some kind of a slow-motion drunken war dance around the fire.

 ⁓

"You know what to do," Cadaver says. He is hidden in the shadows beside the tree, shadows that refuse to be burned away by the light from the fire. Wintry tries to fill his lungs with enough air to power the words, but gives up at the realization that there is nothing he can say that the old man doesn't already know. He wants to die now, but it appears even in his darkest fantasies he's been wrong to think even an end to his suffering would come without a price. And tonight, here, that price has taken the shape of a dark pair of hands wriggling their way free of the oak tree's trunk, pushing forth from the rotten bark, thick fingers trembling.

It is dark despite the fire.

It is cold despite the heat.

And those hands, now clenching and unclenching at the end of scarred and meaty forearms, are hands Wintry knows.

Near the roots of the tree, a battered work shoe is wrested free. Dirt and bark tumble; the fissure widens. At the top of the tree, almost but not quite at eye level, pale white orbs, striated opals, fix Wintry with a raging glare. Beneath it a sharp nose, shooting breath to clear the passages of bark and rot. Inevitably then, a mouth, dirty teeth bared above a pointed chin bearded with moss.

"Loser," says the black devil as he jerks free of the tree to stand before his son. "No-good sonofabitchin' loser."

"You know what to do," Cadaver says again, but now that there are two men before the fire, it is unclear to Wintry who is being addressed. His father does not spare the old man a glance, but nods faintly.

"Pop," Wintry croaks.

"Lucius," his father says, and the mere mention of Wintry's given name is enough to unleash a cascade of unwanted memory:

That voice, resentful, and almost always raised in anger.

That mouth, sneering, twitching a little with each punch of those piston-like arms, smiling slightly at the cries, the injury, the fear.

Those hands, blackening his mother's eye, shattering her nose, loosening her teeth.

Those hands…tousling the boy's hair before bedtime, before the bad time.

Those hands, ripping off his clothes, breaking his bones.

Those hands. Around his neck, squeezing. And the words: *Toughen up you little shit. Fight me. I'll keep hittin' until you do.*

"How are you here?" Wintry asks, softly, not because he is threatened, which he is, but because his throat is raw and sore and the words feel like rocks being forced through a whistle.

"Don't matter." His father takes a step closer. He is a big man, bigger than his son but not as tall. The difference never mattered though.

His father's fists were always a great leveler, as Wintry suspects they will be now. "What matters is I'm here, and I'm more here than you, palooka."

He advances another step and Wintry, already quivering from the shock of his injuries, is close to rattling free of the shoes that have been melted to his feet. Into the firelight steps his father, a man who, until tonight, existed only in memory.

"I don't want this," Wintry says, then turns his head to look at Cadaver who appears to have woven himself into a mesh of dead branches. "Make it stop."

"Only you can do that, son," Cadaver replies.

Narrow face taut with rage, the man before the fire chuckles. "Hell, he ain't gonna do shit. He ain't never done a damn thing worth a damn thing. He nothin' but a worthless punk sent to steal all I had from me and make my wife ashamed of what she let into the house." His smile widens, teeth gleaming in the amber light. "Shit. He didn't find out till prison that we wasn't his folks."

Wintry sighs. "What do you want with me?"

"To put you down, boy. Just that. To put you down so's you remember what you done."

"I don't need to fight you to remember."

"Sure you do. You think you got ghosts now Lucius, but you're forgettin' all the good ones. All the real big mean ones, ain't that right 'ol man?"

Cadaver says nothing, just goes on watching.

"So right here, tonight, me and you's gonna dance. You gonna get the chance to swing a few, see if time's taught you somethin', see if you grew some balls up the river, and if you don't, then you gonna be hurtin' even worse by the time I get through with you. But I'll be your Pop for a spell and do you a favor, for 'ol times sake. I'll let you in on a secret."

Whatever the secret is, Wintry has no desire to hear it. The fire is licking at his skin though he's far enough on the other side of it to be out of reach of the flames, and the worst of the heat. Every nerve screams with pain, every muscle spasms, every organ revolts. He wants to lay down and die, most certainly does *not* want to be here in the heat facing down a man who died of prostate cancer while his son was in prison.

"For every blow I land on that cooked-up face of yours, you'll remember somethin' you forgot. You'll remember some of the bad things you done that you don't blame yourself for no more. You'll see the little bits of truth. You'll see yourself. Then maybe you'll understand why I was the way I was with you." His father leans over the fire enough to let the flames singe his short scraggly beard. "I saw what you was becomin' boy, and you was becomin' *me*."

For just a moment, Wintry sees an aspect of the devil floating in the flames. "You want me to fight you?"

"Yeah, that's it." His father is enthused. "Go a few rounds with your old man, see what happens. See what you remember. See if you've changed."

"I…can't fight. I'm hurt bad."

"Everybody hurtin', Lucius. That shit don't fly with me. Think I weren't hurt when my brother dropped you off on my doorstep with no money to keep you? Think I weren't hurt when my wife left me for a bucktoothed guitar playin' crackhead from San Antone? Think I weren't hurtin' when every bit of company I tried to keep got scared off as soon as they heard tell of a kid? Or when they fired me from a job I'd had for over thirty years? Fired for drinkin' and why, Lucius? Why was I drinkin? Because nothin' ever worked right for me, and you weren't nothing but another wrong thing in it. Everythin' I had I gave up to raise you right and you fought me all the way no matter what I did to toughen you up. So you stand tall now boy and be a man. Fight me for the last time. This here's long overdue."

Wintry raises his head, realizes that at some point during his father's seething monologue, he has fallen to his knees. The wet grass burns rather than soothes and it takes every ounce of strength he has left to stand again. When he does, the fire turns gray, then a darker red, and the hands, his father's awful hands are poking through it and separating, like a swimmer parting water.

Tongues of flame lash from the fire, one of them narrowly avoiding Wintry's face. Instinctively he ducks, groans and shields his eyes, wondering as he does so why his father spoke so passionately about fighting if he means to burn him alive. But the fire carries on past him until it touches the grass a few feet away and ignites. It is as if someone has touched a match to a gasoline trail poured in a perfect rectangle. The perfect shape for a boxing ring, the name of which has always puzzled him, because it isn't a ring at all.

"This won't…" Wintry starts to say, but gives up, the words too heavy in a mouth too weak.

"Straighten up," his father commands, and steps through the flames. Wisps of smoke curl from the shoulders and sleeves of his denim jacket, which he shrugs off to reveal a soiled and yellowed vest beneath. The gray tangle of his chest hair streams smoke, blackens and curls. He stands three feet from his son. "Let's go boy." Sinewy muscles grow taut as he assumes a fighting posture, shoulders hunched slightly forward, fists raised so that only his eyes are visible above the dark work-roughened knuckles. He bounces every so slightly on his toes, an old man trying to prove he's still as fast as he was in his glory days.

"I can't fight you."

"You can and will. Don't you disappoint me again boy. I've come a long way to see you."

Wintry shakes his head. "You're dead."

"Not tonight I ain't. Now put 'em up and <u>fight</u>, you little pussy."

Wintry looks at him, at this impossible caricature of his father, fashioned from oak and clay and ivy, and hate, and shakes his head again. "You want me to hit you. That all?"

"Be a fine start."

Cadaver is still just a shadow and quieter than the dark. Watching.

Abruptly, there is a sound like a baseball hitting a bag of cement and darkness explodes before Wintry's eyes. The world drops away, he falls—for a brief moment he is floundering weightless in outer space—and then the ground slams into his side, eliciting a silent cry of pain from him as burned flesh is crushed. Stars whirl across his field of vision; the wounds on his face ignite anew. The earthy smell of wet grass and the fiery agony in his skull keep him from tumbling headlong into merciful unconsciousness.

"Now," his father says. "That's one. You should've seen it comin'. Pay attention."

Wintry tastes fresh blood on his lips. He opens his eyes wide. Field and fire are gone; his father vanished. This is no longer Milestone, but a back alley somewhere in Georgia. Wintry is lying on his side in a puddle. It's cold, and soothing, and for a moment he relishes the relief, until he realizes there are people around him. He raises his head, into the rain of which he has only now become aware, and sees water sluicing down the groove in the barrel of a silver gun. Above it, made blurry by the rain, the gloom, the steam that billows from the vents in walls around the alley, and the proximity of the muzzle, which demands his attention, he sees a smile just as silver as the weapon. A man with a hat nods, cocks the hammer.

"Who the bitch now?" the man says and starts to pull the trigger.

Drawing from memory infinitely stronger than the pain, Wintry is on his feet, almost slipping on the slick concrete, then hunkered low and running, not away, but into the man with the gun, the man who he knows has been hanging around the gym, offering the kids little baggies, parachutes from which he promises an escape from the doomed plane of their lives, fairy dust to sprinkle on their troubles. Caught by surprise, the man does not do as he is expected to do. He does not quickly alter his aim. Instead he throws up his hands, the gun drawn back as if he intends to use it as a weapon, but by then it's already too late. Driven by fury Wintry plows into him…

…and there is fire, and cold, and pain. And his father, looming over him.

"Then what did you see?" he says.

And Wintry remembers.

Smoggy daylight.

The man is dead, neck crushed, skull broken, three silver teeth scattered around his head, one stuck to his lower lip. Wintry is straddling him, fists joined together and raised over his head, an anvil ready to deliver another fatal blow. The children, cowering next to dumpsters, holding each other, covering their eyes at the sight of one monster killing another, stop him. He looks at them, an unspoken apology on his lips, pleading in his eyes. Glances from one terrified face to another until his skin goes cold and the blood drains from his own. There is a man there, nodding sagely as if what he has just seen is confirmation of what he has always suspected. The stranger is not as sharply dressed as the man with the fedora, the man Wintry has just beaten to a bloody pulp. His smile is not silver, but it's just as blinding. He wears driving gloves, the leathery fingers on his right hand curled around the emaciated shoulder of one of the children, a small boy with tears carving clear lines in a grubby face. But while the boy may be deriving some solace from the stranger's hand, there is no compassion in the man's eyes. Only glee. And the knowledge that his efforts to contaminate these children will now go unhindered. The police won't care enough to feign concern. The children are poor and black, after all. And the one man who assigned himself their guardian is going to be put away for the murder of a pimp.

Wintry starts to stand and when he does it is the night that greets him.

"The wrong man," his father says. "But you been foolin' yourself, tryin' to make believe you been feelin' bad about killin' a man when all that's been botherin' you is not killin' the right one."

"What did you ever know about me?" Wintry asks, a new burning starting deep down inside him, a welcome flame that sears away some of the fear, numbs some of the pain. "What did you ever know about anythin'? Think now that..." His breath catches as new agony flares in his knees. He straightens, blinks once, twice. "Think now that you dead...think now that you know it all you can come along'n throw it in my face?"

His father is still bouncing on his feet, knuckles making creaking sounds, as if they're encased in leather gloves. Wintry sways, staggers and rights himself, draws up to his full height, and in two unsteady steps is in his father's face. "You know nothin' about me," Wintry says, and brings his right fist around in an arc, which his father watches with interest, approval, then avoids with a quick back-step. He follows the dodge with an uppercut that makes Wintry think his brain has been sent shooting from the top of his head.

Blood flies. He watches as it spurts upward and...

..."I can't make it stop," he moans and reaches down, his trembling fingers slick with the woman's blood. "Jesus please..."

White light in a bedroom.

The olive-skinned woman stares at him, but the life has fled her eyes. The accusation however, hasn't. She stares, peers deep into his soul and Wintry can hear her crying *Why didn't you see? Why didn't you know?* She is naked, lying in bed, her head propped up against the headboard, her wrists opened. She moves, jiggles, mimics life, but this is merely the effect of Wintry's desperate attention. He moans, wails, rages at the ceiling, at whatever cruel God is impassively watching this drama unfold. She is the love of his life and he knows now the reverse was never true. Had it been, she would still be alive. Had it been, she would not have betrayed him and herself, by waiting until she was alone to die.

Then, abruptly, her mouth drops open. His moaning subsides. Frantically, he scrubs tears from his eyes, narrows them, afraid to believe he has just seen what they are telling him he's seen.

And though no life returns to her face, she speaks, though here is where Wintry knows memory has slipped the rails. It hardly matters though, because what she says are the same words that have tailed him through life.

"You killed me."

With a roar that is animalistic yet filled with sorrow and rage, Wintry once more regains his feet and without knowing, without caring, whether his aim is sure, he swivels on his heel and jabs hard at the air. His father is prepared and smiling a suddenly silver smile. He dodges the punch, as Wintry knew he would. It is a feint, a ploy to induce the dead man to open up into a vulnerable position. His father has grown too certain, too comfortable, depending on his son's injuries and hesitation to make him predictable. In the old days he would have anticipated the feint. But these are not the old days.

An instant too late, he realizes his folly, tries to correct it. And in that instant Wintry unleashes a volley of punches: left jab, straight right, left hook, uppercut. His father reels, but refuses to go down, so Wintry does not stop. The anger in him rages to the surface, equals the fire in his wounds. Straight left, jab, jab, rabbit punch, right hook, uppercut…

"You fuckin'…" his father starts to say, his teeth connected by strings of black blood. Wintry steps back, watches his father try to regain his balance, and does not wait.

"Sonofabitchin' los—"

Uppercut.

It almost takes his father's head off.

"What…do…*you*…see?" Wintry says, his teeth grinding out a squeak as he punctuates every word with another punch, his arm pulling back, head jutting forward, knuckles crunching into yielding bone, skin slipping against tar-like blood. "What…do…you…*see*…you…son…of…a…*bitch*?"

"Wintry?"

99

The voice does not belong here, so he ignores it. There is no third man in the ring, no chief second howling advice at him, no cut man. There are no lights, no crowd, no world beyond the face that is caving in like a pumpkin but will not fall.

"Wintry, what the hell?"

"Fuckin' palooka, fuckin' tomato can," his father manages to spit between punches. He raises his hands, covers, tries to block the barrage of lethal blows, but Wintry is fast now, on fire, caught up in a memory he can never change and so uses to deliver him from the loathsome presence of a man long dead, a man who didn't need to physically return to haunt him. In the dark house inside Wintry's head, the man he called father is a permanent resident.

"Go down," he demands, the words slicing his throat. "Go *down*."

"Wintry!" A shout, right into his ear and he knows it must be addressed, knows it must be dealt with. He prepares his last blow, the last shot, a right hook he imagines as a scythe that will slice through anything it touches. His father straightens, grins bloodily, goading him.

Wintry swings.

His fist thuds into rotten oak.

12

"There's nothing I can do for you," the doctor tells him. "Take it to the Sheriff."

Vess sags and his suit starts to feel like a tortoise shell, waiting to conceal his addled mind from a world that rarely seems inclined to cut it a break. "I thought…She told me to—"

Hendricks scowls. "This isn't my business." He starts to close the door and Vess, in an uncharacteristically bold move, makes an obstruction of his foot, which the doctor looks at as if some unpleasant rodent has just insinuated its way into his domain. Fear ripples through Vess. This is not how he behaves. He has forgotten much, but knows that what he has just done is a violation of the doctor's sanctuary, his private quarters, and that if it suited him, the doctor could take any steps he deemed necessary to remove the foot, and its owner, and be well within his rights to do so.

So he speaks quickly. "She was shut up in a fridge, a white coffin. She wasn't supposed to be in there. She told me. Said I needed to find someone, let them know where she was and why she was there." He composes a sincere sorrowful look that nonetheless feels false under the glaring light from the doctor's spectacles. "She's a lady, Doctor, and no lady needs to be treated like that, left alone with no one to pray for her. And she doesn't want to be there any more. Can't blame her for that. She needs help."

Hendricks looks up from the offending appendage keeping the door open. "What is it you think I can do for her?"

To this, Vess has no answer. All he can think of is that surely a man as distinguished and gifted as Doctor Hendricks can do more for her than he can, but before he has a chance to organize those words into a proper sentence, he feels a jarring pain in his foot and quickly withdraws it. When he looks up, the Doctor's face is crimson.

"I have things to attend to," he snaps. "Now take your goddamn finger and bring it to someone who can actually *do* something about it, assuming you didn't swipe it from a boneyard somewhere."

"No, sir. Oh no this wasn't—"

The door is slammed shut hard enough to make his coat flutter. The gunshot-like echo is quickly drowned in the dense river of mist that has seeped up from the quiet earth. Vess stares at the door for a few moments, runs the tips of his fingers over the woodgrain, willing the doctor to come out again, then after a few moments, sighs and turns away.

"He wouldn't listen."

He has never claimed to be clever, or wise, and certainly not someone to turn to when a plan of action is required. He has drifted through these recent years with no responsibilities save one: to find the box and get home, but though he has vowed never to give up, his hope fades with every passing day.

"Find him," the finger advises, and he smiles down at where it lays unmoving, nestled in his palm.

"Are you cold?"

"*Find* him. He must know."

"It will probably be warm later today, but it isn't now. I don't want you to be chilly. Here," he says and gently lays the small brown bundle inside his hat and pops it on his head. The bones are cold against his scalp. "I was distracted. I let my mind get away from me again. I should have thought of you being cold. I'm sorry."

The finger doesn't reply.

Vess puts a long-nailed finger to his chin and scratches at the stubble.

The Sheriff is a member of an exclusive club that gathers at the tavern on the hill. But of course the tavern burned down last night. Still, this early in the morning, perhaps that's where the Sheriff will be, maybe picking through the remains of the place or making sure the fire is well and truly out. Barring that, he might be home, or at the jail, but one of the three sounds probable. If nothing else, it will keep Vess moving, keep him filled with that sense of purpose, keep him feeling useful.

For now, he is Kirk Vess, emissary.

Kirk Vess, soldier. And while there are no mortars detonating around him, no razor wire tugging at his clothes, no mud sucking at his feet, no bullets whizzing by, carving out the grooves in his face that he still bears today, no mustard gas tugging at his lungs, his charge seems no less important, no less thrilling.

He walks, and the small cold bundle pressing against his crown is a lock on the gate of his misgivings, holding back the tide of disappointment that has struggled to overcome him since the discovery that the metal box mired in the mud by the bank of the Milestone River was in fact just a fridge—albeit one with a body inside—and not the box he has been searching for since finding himself out of place, and out of time in this town.

Just a fridge, and not the box that can spirit him home.

~

"Hey, easy," I tell him.

Wintry rounds on me. His face is a picture of hellish madness, his breathing horribly irregular as if his lungs have been replaced with sacks of dust. His eyes are wide and black, dominated by his pupils. They fix on me and the hair stands up all over my body. I suddenly feel threatened by the last man I ever thought would make me feel that way. He withdraws his fist from the guts of the oak tree and takes a step toward me. I take a corresponding step back.

"Where he at?" Wintry asks.

I'm shocked to hear him speak, but don't dwell on it. No one ever said he couldn't talk, just that he'd lost his words. Guess I should have given those cryptic messages of his a little more thought. "Who?"

His teeth are bared; his lips, swollen from the burns, are split. Blood laces his gums. "The old man. He made me a bargain. Where he at?"

It's almost too much. Wintry's not dead. Burned to within an inch of it, sure, but still up and around, and not only is he alive, he's talking. For now I'm choosing not to think too hard about what kind of bargain he made with Cadaver, assuming that's what happened and the big guy hasn't just been driven crazier than a one-legged possum by his injuries. Right now the sight of those dilated eyes and the tattered state of his fists from ramming them into the oak tree, suggests it's not at all unlikely that he's gone off the deep end, in which case, maybe I have every right to feel threatened. Plus, there's the small fire he set here, which for a man covered in burns, doesn't seem like the sanest of ideas.

"I don't know," I answer. "I haven't seen him since Eddie's went up. We need to get you to a doctor."

Wintry takes another step toward me. His arms are trembling, fists clenched so hard that blood trickles from the cuts and drips to the grass. "I put him down."

"Wintry, take it easy, all right. It's me, Sheriff Tom."

That gives him pause. He stops moving but the expression of wild rage on that ruined face doesn't change.

"It's Tom," I tell him, hands raised, as if they have a chance of warding off anything he might throw at me. "It's me."

The expression falters, and although I can't be certain, it looks as if those eclipses in his eyes are passing. The rigidity that has held him upright, has kept his muscles taut, gradually subsides and then all trace of anger evaporates, replaced with suffering of the kind you'd expect to see on a man so badly wounded. He sags, leans, his shoulder hitting the tree hard enough to make it creak and sway back a little. Something in the branches above us lets out a startled cry. Wings beat smoky air.

"Sheriff?" he says, and blinks.

"You all right, Wintry?" I know he isn't, but it's all I can think to say.

"Hurts bad."

"We need to get you to Hendricks."

"No," he says, with a sad shake of his head. "You need to put me in the ground."

"Don't be a fool. You're still breathing."

"I don't want to be. Shouldn't be."

"Bullshit. We're getting you to the Doc."

This time it's him who raises the hand.

"Okay. We can wait a sec." Truth is, I don't have the kind of time I'm about to spend with him, but though I may have forgotten a lot about the way people should be treated, there's no way in hell I'm leaving this man to his suffering, not when there's a chance something can be done about it.

I walk up close and put a palm on the tree. It feels cold, oily. "Thought for sure you went up with the tavern."

"Got out. Ran and got myself into the river," he tells me. "Maybe should've stayed under."

"Don't say that."

His eyes find me. "Couldn't save 'em."

"I know, but that wasn't your fault, and you did everything you could. Wasn't you who started the fire. And you saved Brody."

He starts to lower his head, at the same time bringing up his ravaged hands to cradle his skull, but they stop short of meeting, as Wintry no doubt remembers the pain it will cause him to do so. "Couldn't save 'em, Sheriff. I always been tryin' to save folks and it never works out right. Reckon…one mistake too many got me here, no matter how good the intention. Path to Hell, an' all that."

"Well…" A sigh. "I can't put your mind at ease about that, Wintry, much as I'd like to. Fact is, we're here, no matter what the reason, but I got a feeling in my gut that we still have a chance to make it out of this. Could be I'm wrong about that too, and we're just killing time before a great big hand comes down and squashes us all. But I'm not going to just sit around and wait for that to happen, and you can't either."

"I was a fighter," he says.

"You still are."

"Naw, Tom. I'm done. Put my Daddy down and that's all there is to that."

I start to ask him what that means, but think better of it.

Pained eyes find me again. "Your boy all right?"

"I'm not sure. He isn't dead, if that's what you mean. It's where I was heading now when we saw you."

"We?"

"Brody's in the truck. Been meaning to stick him in the tank, but it hasn't exactly been calm tonight, y'know?"

"Where you goin'?"

"Hill's house. Or at least I was. Gotta get you to Hendricks, or the hospital in Saddleback now."

"Forget it."

"I'm not leaving you here."

"Then take me to the Rev'rends. Maybe I can help."

I don't see how he could be of help to anyone right now, but I meant what I said: I'm not leaving him. So I guess if he won't go to the hospital, or see Doc Hendricks, then he's coming with.

"All right, but when we're done up there, you're going to see the Doc if I have to haul you in there myself."

The idea of me trying to physically force the wounded giant before me to do anything is a comical one, and neither of us can let it pass without grinning at it.

"Okay, Sheriff."

I go to him, put my arm around his waist and let him lean on me. It's almost more than I can handle, and the smell of singed hair and burned flesh is enough to make me choke, but I manage to keep him steady as I guide him back to my truck.

From the back seat, where not so long ago his girlfriend lay dying, Brody's head is titled back, mouth open. Son of a bitch is catching himself a doze. I can hear him snoring from here.

We reach the truck. Wintry reaches out with an unsteady hand, braces it against the hood as I let him go and quickly open the passenger side door. "C'mon, get yourself in here." It isn't easy. He's almost too damn big to fit, but that isn't the worst of it. I can see how much he's suffering with even the slightest of movements.

As for me, I'm fit for nothing but sleep. I'm running on empty and the idea of bypassing Hill's house and just driving straight on to Saddleback and the hospital there is almost too tempting to resist. After all, what the fuck am I doing here anyway? Three murderers in a car. Sounds like the start of a joke. Heading for a dead priest's house to try to convince my own son—who hates my guts—not to betray me? What difference will it make if he does? We're both finished either way.

But I can't ignore it. Can't just leave. The clock might tell me it's a new day, but Saturday night won't end until all that's come about because of it has been dealt with. Wintry's alive, and still fighting. I've got a prisoner in the back. And I've still got two old pennies in my pocket from a loan I'm going to have to pay back whether I want to or not.

In the time it takes me to get back in the truck, the sun has dragged its head up over the hills, sending streams of fire through the trees. The road's become a latticework of red-orange light. I sit there for a moment, wishing I had the kind of brain that could appreciate such a scene, but it still feels the same as it has for as long as I can remember: Like a flashlight beam washing over corpses. It doesn't help that one of my passengers stinks of barbecued flesh.

"The hell are we doing here, Wintry?" I ask.

"Watchin' the sun."

It's not what I meant, but I figure it's as good an answer as any, so I let my hand slip away from the keys to my thigh, and I sit back, just watching that pumpkin colored light burning off the dark, chasing it underground, reflecting itself off windows that looked like dead eyes not twenty minutes ago.

Brody snorts in his sleep. It's almost mirthful, and as I reach down, fingers touching the cold metal of the keys dangling from the ignition, I catch a flurry of movement in the rearview and my seat is nudged from behind.

In the mirror, Brody is suddenly a hell of a lot closer.

Wintry's looking at me, agonized expression deepening.

I'm somewhat surprised to realize Brody's no longer wearing the handcuffs, and that one of those newly liberated hands is holding something cold and sharp to my throat.

13

Hendricks tips the cup and spills what's left of the cold tea onto the rug. Ordinarily he's the kind of man who'd abhor such sloppiness. He's always tried to keep a clean house, as hard as that's been considering how long it has harbored sickness, and how many years the town has striven to shove its filth under his door. But none of that matters any longer, and there is a great sense of liberation in watching the muddy brown liquid darkening the rug. It signals the beginning and the end.

He sets the cup on the mantel, and with quaking hands, reaches up until his fingers find the cold wood stock of the Winchester rifle. The fire, though all but dead, still warms his feet as he lifts the gun free of its brackets. It's an old weapon, meant to spend its final days as an ornament, but today it will get a chance to live again, to blast the killing shot from a cartridge, and breathe the smell of gunpowder into the stale air of this old house.

Hendricks lowers his arms, breeches the stock, his eyes moving to the couch, and the maroon stains on the towel crumpled there where the whore died. He feels a pang of regret that he couldn't prevent her suffering, but then he thinks of Queenie, how she woke up and spun into an immediate panic-driven rage when he crept into the room an hour later, trying not to disturb her. She looked at him as if he'd come to rape her.

Tears well in his eyes.

He couldn't save the whore.

He hefts the rifle.

But he can save his wife.

With a shuddering sigh, he makes his way upstairs. The steps are thickly carpeted and so his ascent is a silent one. The wood is old but doesn't creak, perhaps out of respect for his grim mission.

The gun is loaded. It has always been loaded, sitting there above the fire, waiting, as if it's known he would need it someday.

Silly. Silly thoughts. He shakes his head and a tear trickles down his cheek. He has thought of other ways, other options, but all of them have meant Queenie will be taken away from him, to die as she would die here, in agony. And if they let her stay, what choice would he have but to enter her bedroom each and every morning, his heart shattering, hope fading, each and every time she looked at him in terror.

Top step.

The landing.

He does not worry about visitors. It has been an unusually busy night, but no one will bother him now. Most people will be at church, he assumes, waiting for a priest who isn't coming. But no one will come here, not in time to prevent what must happen here.

He opens the bedroom door.

Queenie is sitting up, eyes narrowed against the brilliant glow of morning sun through the windows. She raises a hand to shield her tired eyes so she can see him.

"Bill?"

It does her voice so well.

Her eyes find the gun. The color drains from her face.

His heart breaks and he levels the rifle at her quickly, before she can fool him into believing everything is all right, that this brief period of lucidity is the rule and not the exception. Before the parasite can use his love for her against him.

"Bill…" Her voice wavers. She stiffens, gaze dropping to the Winchester's double barrel stare. "What are you doing?"

He eases back the hammer. "I won't let it do this to you," he says.

"Please…" she sobs, scooting back until she's pressed against the ornate mahogany headboard. "Please…don't."

She raises her hand and it looks like a blood-drained spider, splayed for dissection.

"I love you," he tells her. "So much."

She wraps her arms around her head, her knees drawn up below her chin, as if she fears the roof might fall in.

"So much," Hendricks says and brings the rifle up to his shoulder, one eye closed to ensure his aim is accurate.

"Oh God," Queenie whimpers, and begins to pray, then drops her arm. Looks pleadingly at him. "Don't. We can get help. You're not—"

Hendricks pulls the trigger.

The blast deafens him as the barrel coughs fire. Through the plume of smoke he sees his wife rise up as if she's going to leap from the bed.

But just as quickly she falls and the face that looked at him with such alien terror is gone in a burst of crimson and gray. Blood and bone rains down around her. She settles on the bed, kneeling, propped up against the headboard, her arms twitching, and suddenly he is deathly afraid that the ruin above her neck will turn toward him.

He is surprised to find that what has erupted from the addled shell of her skull is not black.

He weeps, bites his lower lip hard enough to draw blood and closes his eyes. It hurts, the pain of what he's done. It's so much worse than what he imagined it would be, worse almost than having to look at his wife dying every day in this room, turned against him by the invader that made its home in her head, an invader that's now splattered across the wall and can harm her no more.

"There you go," says a voice that barely filters through the ringing in Hendrick's ears, and his eyes fly open.

In front of him, between where he stands and the bed where his wife's body still twitches, is an old man.

Hendricks recognizes him, but that recognition makes his presence here, now, no less baffling. No less unwelcome.

"What…?" he starts to say, but falls silent as Cadaver's gnarled hand, the hand not holding that stubby little metal microphone to his throat, reaches out and forces him to lower the rifle so it's pointing at the floor.

Confusion becomes fear and desperation as Hendricks realizes the old man might attempt to stop him from finishing what needs to be done. He is not a murderer, no matter how this might look to anyone who doesn't understand what he's lived with. This isn't a crime. He does not deserve to go to prison. Can't go to prison. He intends to die, to join Queenie on the other side. There are no parasites in the afterlife. All that's left to do is to reload the rifle and set it up so he can end his own miserable existence.

Cadaver looks at him. "Damn shame that," he says.

Hendricks swallows, backs up a step, collides with the jamb, sidesteps and moves out into the hall. "She was sick. It was eating her brain. I had to do it."

"You're a bit confused, friend," Cadaver says, and follows him step for step. "Weren't nothin' wrong with *her*."

"She was dying. She wasn't right."

"The cancer's in *your* head, Doc," Cadaver tells him. "Care to come downstairs so I can show you all the envelopes you've been hidin' from her? All the test results and hospital correspondence that testifies to what's gone crooked in *your* brain?"

"Get out of here," Hendricks says, heat flushing across his cheeks. This is preposterous. He has never had much business with this man, and certainly hasn't treated him. Why now he should break into his house and make such cruel and preposterous claims while his poor wife lies dead a few feet away is beyond him. He knows what those letters he keeps locked in the bureau say. He knows who the patient is and what the diagnosis was. Therefore, he knows Cadaver is lying. Thankfully, he has the means to do something about that right here in his hands. "Get out of my house and leave us alone."

"I will. In a moment," Cadaver says, his voice an inhuman whisper. "Despite what you might be thinkin' right now, I didn't come here just to enlighten you."

"You have five seconds to leave." To emphasize the threat, he raises the rifle.

"You haven't reloaded."

He's right of course, but Hendricks stands his ground, does not lower the weapon. If it comes to it, there's nothing to stop him from swinging the Winchester and crushing the old man's skull. "What do you want?"

"You're a murderer now, Doc. And as such you've opened yourself up to certain obligations."

"What are you talking about?"

Cadaver glances over his shoulder, takes in the mess on the bed, clucks his tongue, then looks back to the doctor. "Call it an act of contrition."

"I want you out of here right *now*."

Cadaver reaches into the pocket of his coat and produces a set of keys. Hendricks recognizes them as the keys to his house and his Buick.

"What are you doing with those?"

"Nothin'," Cadaver says and smiles. "You're goin' to drive."

"I'm not going anywhere."

The old man's shoulders drop a little and his expression changes to one of regret. "I don't enjoy this in the least, you know—"

"Then leave."

"—But if I don't do it, then the consequences for us all would be cat-astrophic."

"Get out of my fucking *house*." Spittle flies from Hendricks' lips. Terror worms its way through him. He has rehearsed this scenario a thousand times and not one of them had a mad old man standing in his way.

Cadaver raises the keys between them. "Here's how it goes. You drive, you kill a man, and you get to go back to what you were plannin' to do before I rudely interrupted this very intimate execution."

"Kill a man? No."

"What difference will it make? You've killed once already today, and if you really do have the stones to kill yourself, no one'll be able to make you answer for it."

Hendricks shakes his head. "Not in this life, maybe. But afterwards…"

Cadaver reaches out a hand, pats him on the shoulder, ignoring the fact that the muzzle of the rifle is a half-inch from his chin. The doctor feels the cold hard cylinder of the old man's microphone digging into his flesh. Then Cadaver withdraws his hand, presses the mike to his throat again. "I don't offer many assurances, Doc, but one I can give you is that where you're headed, you won't have to answer for a damned thing."

"You can't know that. No one could know that." He swallows. "Who are you?" The rifle is slipping from his sweaty grip.

Cadaver's still holding the keys in his other hand. Now he gives them a little jingle, nods as if everything has been settled. "Time to…"

❧

"Hit the road, Jack." Brody's got the knife to my throat, but he's look-ing at Wintry, who isn't moving. "C'mon, beat it. And I don't think I need to tell you what I'll do to your friend here if you try something, right?"

Wintry still doesn't move. I'm overcome by a peculiar sense of deja vu, then recall the standoff back at Eddie's, how Brody kept barking com-mands at Wintry, which Wintry disregarded in his attempts to help the girl. I'm hoping to hell he doesn't try that trick again. Chances are it'll only get me killed first before the kid turns the knife to him, and though he looked fired up and capable of anything back in that field, Wintry doesn't look like he could bat away a fly right now.

"Just…take it easy." I raise my hands so Brody can see I'm not about to try anything. "You don't need to do this."

"Well, I appreciate the advice, Sheriff. Really. But if it's all the same to you, I think I'm probably the most qualified of the three of us to decide what I need, don't you think?" He looks back to Wintry. "The fire cook your fucking eardrums too? I said get the hell *out*."

"He's hurt bad, kid. We need to get him some help."

"My heart bleeds."

"He's also the reason you're not dead."

"Which is the only reason I'm letting him out here. Now for the last time, big guy, move!"

Only Wintry's eyes obey. He looks at me. Apology and regret swim like rockfish through the pools of his pain, and with excruciating slowness, he reaches for the door release.

"It's all right," I mutter. "It's going to be fine."

"That's right," Brody adds. "Everything's going to be peachy if we all do as I say."

"Hey," I call after Wintry as he eases himself out of the truck, his legs wobbling as he looks back at me. I lick my lips. "Name that tune."

He nods, gives me a flicker of a smile. "Good luck with that."

"The hell does that mean?" Brody asks, annoyed, and the blade digs a little deeper into the flesh at my throat.

"An old joke. Can you ease off a bit with the knife, kid? I'm not going anywhere, trust me."

"Trust you? Trust the guy that psycho priest said was supposed to kill me? The guy who left me with The Man with the Flaming Hands and buried my girl in a shallow grave behind a dive bar? Yeah, shit, Sheriff, we're the next best thing to pals, you and me. Let's not even start in on the whole you being a cop thing."

"Just listen."

"Go right ahead."

"I have no interest in turning you in."

He scoffs. "That so? Jeez, the handcuffs might not have been the best way to show that."

"I *did*, sure. But not anymore. All I care about now is getting to my son in time to help him. He's in trouble."

"That doesn't surprise me. Guy likes to ventilate skulls that much is bound to get his ass handed to him sooner or later. Hell, I know what that's like. I'll be lucky to live to see the Mexican border, and I'm all right with that. But what I can tell you right now is that I'm sure as shit *not* going to be run down in a backwater hole like this. So I'm taking your truck, Sheriff, and whether or not I leave you as a corpse in the dust all depends on what you do in the next five minutes."

"You can go. I won't stop you. I give you my word on that."

"Good."

"But you're not taking the truck."

"Say again?"

"I need it. It's the only way I can get to Kyle."

"Yeah well, that's touching as all hell but you're not going to be in much shape to do anything for the little prick if your head's no longer attached."

Our eyes meet in the mirror. Both of us are sweating, for different reasons. He's getting ready to kill me; I'm getting ready to die.

"Take the truck," I suggest then. "Just take me with you as far as Hill's house. After that you can get gone and you'll never hear from me again."

"No dice."

"Why the hell not?"

"Because I don't like you." The blade pins my Adam's apple in place, biting the flesh there, drawing blood I can feel trickling down into my shirt.

"We did everything we could for your girl." I'm hoping shifting the focus of the conversation might buy me some time. That's not something I was trained to do; it's just plain old common sense.

"It wasn't enough."

"Hey, you brought her here. If you hadn't—"

"Don't feed me that bullshit. We were here tonight because we were supposed to be here. I don't much like the idea of not being in control of what I do, but that's pretty much tough titty right now, right? Whatever juju you and your friends were doing up in that bar, *it* was what decided where we'd be, who would die and…" He shakes his head. "I'm getting out of here now."

Trying to grab hold of a coherent thought right now is like to trying to find a licorice whip in a bucket of snakes, so I quit trying and let myself relax. He's not getting the truck; that much I'm sure of. Everything else is up in the air, so I decide I'm going to end this, right after I ask him something that's been on my mind since last night. "Did you kill Eleanor Cobb on purpose?"

"I didn't kill her at all."

"How's that?"

"*She* came at *us*. Almost as if she was sitting there around that corner, engine idling, waiting for the first sign of headlights coming in the opposite direction so she could plow into them. Into us. Crazy old bitch."

No, I think and close my eyes. *Not crazy.* Lost. Stuck with a husband who grew older every time he took someone else's pain away, a man afraid to love her too much because he was going to die soon, whether because of his gift, or because of his sins and Hill's regulating, it didn't matter. She was going to lose him soon, and both of them knew it. Hell, everyone knew it. So she went first, and he followed.

"I have a favor to ask."

The kid frowns. "What?"

"I want to turn on the radio."

"For what? You're getting out."

"That's the thing. I'm not getting out. I can't, so I'd appreciate you letting me have the radio on. That way I don't have to hear you breathing when you do what you have to do."

Brody scowls at me. "Are you out of your fucking tree completely, or what?"

"No, but it looks like we've reached an impasse here, and you're the one with the knife. All I want now is some music."

"Just like that, huh?"

"Just like that."

He holds the knife away from my throat, just enough for me to see that it's a big son of a bitch, thick-handled, with a curved blade on one side, a serrated one on the other. The kind of knife my father used for skinning bucks.

He's breathing quickly, sweating more. "You and Carla and the goddamn music. I don't have this kind of time to waste."

"So don't."

I reach for the stereo, leaning into the blade. Flip the switch, and sit back.

A moment passes. Wintry is a helpless shadow beyond the window.

I start to tremble all over. My guts squeeze bile into my mouth. Brody's going to assume it's because of him, because of what we both know he's about to do. But it isn't that at all. I'm not afraid of him.

It's the goddamned stereo.

I'm afraid of the radio and what's going to happen because I've turned it on, something I promised myself I'd never do again. Not in this truck. Not after the last time.

Brody curses, brings the knife back to my throat, positions the serrated side beneath my Adam's apple but doesn't start cutting. Cold metal teeth nip the skin. I figure maybe out of respect he's waiting for the music to start. So we watch the stereo.

The green CD light blinks on. The disk begins to spin with a faint whirring sound.

Then at last, after what seems like years of silence, the music starts. Patsy Cline. "Crazy".

And with a sigh that might be regret, anger, or relief, Brody begins to cut my throat.

~

"We're closed."

Confused and struggling to accept that somehow his mind has been playing tricks on him, Vess lingers in the doorway of a tavern memory tells him burned to the ground last night but his eyes swear is still here, untouched by fire on the outside, only slightly blackened on the inside. Near the far end of the room, by the bar, a svelte woman clad in gray tempers a carpet of soot and ash with short sharp smacks from a ragged looking broom. The air smells faintly of smoke.

"Of course you're closed, but she's looking for him," Vess explains, but moves no further into the long narrow room. A single hurricane lamp has been set up on the counter, creating a murky twilight through which the woman moves like a delicate ghost. Thin shadows twitch spasmodically around the rows of bottles behind the bar. "The Sheriff I mean, of course. That might not have been clear. I don't always say what

I mean the way I mean to say it. Means I usually have to elaborate. I don't—*Hassak!*" Annoyed with himself, he wrenches the hat from his head and tugs at it, forgetting its contents until the bones hit the floor like pebbles and skitter away from him. "Oh." He drops to his haunches, stretches his upper body as far as he can over the threshold to avoid stepping foot into the room and therefore risking the woman's ire. A single phalange remains maddeningly out of reach.

"*Not here,*" whispers the finger.

What are you doin'?" the woman asks, and he jerks back. She has approached without his hearing her. He looks from the kernel of bone at her feet to her face and smiles involuntarily. She is without a doubt one of the most beautiful creatures he has ever seen, with her auburn hair and light green eyes. Often, on the endlessly lonely nights beneath the stars, he has dreamed—not of this woman—but of women like her. Maybe in his imaginings they were less severe looking, not so hard of eye or tight of mouth, but the basic model is the same. He finds his already muddled thoughts scrambling, his mind exploring fantasies he will never live to see made real, even if the same stars he sleeps under were to align and the woman decided to court a pauper.

"I asked what you were doin'?"

"Sorry," he splutters, attempting a half-bow despite his posture already being an approximation of one. It's an awkward feat that almost sends him sprawling, so he quickly steadies himself and rises, the last fragment of finger forgotten.

"I'm Kirk Vess."

"I know who you are," the woman responds icily. "I barred you from here, remember?"

He doesn't, but nods.

"What do you want?"

"A woman's finger brought me here," he says, nodding pointedly at the phalange two inches from her shoe. "To find the Sheriff."

"A finger?"

"Yes Ma'am."

"Whose is it?"

"I don't know. Just…a woman. A pretty lady, I'm guessing. She…she was in a fridge."

116

The barmaid's gaze is penetrating. Vess feels himself growing warm from the inside out, the color rising to his cheeks.

"A fridge?"

"Yes, like a white coffin or…They put her in it as if it was a boat."

Gracie frowns. "What?"

Vess squints, fearing his thoughts are squirming free of him and desperately tries to catch them. He runs the tips of his index fingers over his eyebrows and takes a breath. "Stuck in the mud," he says slowly. "That's where she was. I thought it was the box but it was only a fridge. Poor lady." He clucks his tongue. "She wants me to find the Sheriff. I tried Doctor—"

"Understood," Gracie says, her expression softening just a little. "You found a body."

Vess nods eagerly. "Her finger brought me here."

"Not here," whispers the finger. "*Not* here."

"I *know* he isn't," Vess whispers back, eager to silence the dead woman. Immediately he feels guilty for thinking her an intrusion into this unexpected scene, and grimaces. "May I…collect them?"

Gracie nods. "The bones? Go ahead."

He does, stroking each segment by way of an apology before depositing them into his pocket.

"The Sheriff ain't here," Gracie informs him, and heads back to the bar. "But chances are he will be before long."

Vess smiles. "I'll come back. I'll bring the finger."

"You could wait."

"Yes."

"Want a drink while you do?"

Vess immediately begins to question what he thinks she said, for he has never been welcome here, or any other bar for that matter, with the exception of the kinds of places where no one with any sense would go, places where people still get killed over cheating at cards and old men in expensive suits sit in shadowy corners discussing the undoing of their enemies. Vess has never been welcome anywhere, which is why he exists to be elsewhere. With that in mind, he decides jumping at what he is not convinced was an invitation is not the wisest recourse, so he doesn't, simply stays where he is and grins uncertainly.

"Well?"

"Think I heard wrong. Sorry. My hearing of things is like my speech. Trying to explain is—"

"Come join me for a drink while you wait."

The smile almost splits his face, and certainly adds deep wrinkles where there were none before. He almost floats across the floor to the bar, so elated does he feel by this offering of kindness from so magnificent a lady. A drink in a place he should not be, in the company of a woman he should not know, stews his mind further, until it sends tremors of confused pleasure though his limbs.

"Sit." She indicates a stool, and he takes it quickly.

Gracie produces two shot glasses from beneath the bar, and tucks a lock of hair behind her ear.

"Thought the place burned," Vess says. "There was a lot of light up here. Must have been imagining things. I do that sometimes, especially when my mind gets tired."

"You weren't imaginin' things." She fills the glasses to the top, slides one before him. "It burned all right."

"Oh. Wasn't too bad then." He sips the drink, savoring it and the moment. Accustomed as he is to cheap wine, the bourbon tastes like tears from Heaven. His mouth buzzes, tongue pleasantly scalded by the liquor. He coughs. "Bit of black and burnt, but still all right."

"I was bored," Gracie says, crossing her elbows and leaning on them, her face close to his, chin hovering above their drinks. "So I started to rebuild it. I'd rather be stuck in a room, no matter how miserable it might be, than a hole full of charred wood."

He raises his glass in agreement and takes another sip.

"Not that I intend to be here for much longer." She raises her own glass, starts to drink. Vess watches her, follows the single drop of bourbon that escapes her lips, winding its way down over her chin and throat until it disappears into the opening of her blouse. A new kind of heat flourishes within him and he grins.

"I'm movin' on," she announces, with obvious excitement. "After all these years in this goddamn town, I'm gettin' out, leavin' all these wretched people with their wretched lives behind."

Vess's grin falters. He wonders if she includes him in her estimation of the townsfolk, but then reminds himself that he is an outsider, a mere visitor, and a woman as pretty and smart as the barmaid would surely know this.

"Can I see the bones?" she asks then, slamming her glass down on the counter hard enough to make Vess jump.

"Oh yes. She might even talk to you," Vess enthuses, and scoops the bones from his pocket, scattering them on the bar like a voodoo woman about to tell a fortune.

Gracie studies the bones for what seems to Vess to be a considerable amount of time, her expression unreadable until she smiles and looks up at him. The feel of her studying him is not an unpleasant one, and he is abruptly cast into those green eyes as helplessly as a man bound to an anchor tossed into the sea.

His drink no longer seems important.

He is a traveler, and in her eyes, he is seeing a place he has his whole life been forbidden from visiting. He will not, cannot blink.

"That's hers all right," Gracie says, and though she moves back a step, she does not look away, and for that Vess is grateful. "Not that I can really tell from the bones." She chuckles and the sound is magical, like pipe music to wounded ears. "I know because I put her there." His smile grows. He is not really paying attention to the words, only the lush red lips that form them and the piercing eyes that hold him in place.

"*Not here, no not here!*" the finger seems to wail from the surface of the bar, which is now oddly slick beneath his fingers. He ignores the cry, watches his world jar, once, twice, and believes it is his heart, which feels like it may explode.

Somehow, it starts to rain inside the bar. The shadows thicken and reach for him, attempting to steal away this delightful interlude. He resists, struggling to hold on.

"Can't always ssssay it right," he admits. "Werrdener…"

The barmaid's scent intoxicates him. He does not want this to end, and is saddened a great deal to realize, as crimson tears flow copiously down his face, his skull deflating under the weight of the long metal pipe Gracie is bringing down upon his head like a woodsman cleaving a rotten stump, that it already has.

14

S tatic shrieks from the radio.
   Hands follow.
   "What the fuck?" The knife is gone from my throat, tearing off a strip
of my flesh as Brody propels himself away from the pale tendrils of mist
that are snaking their way free of the CD slot in the car stereo. "What the
fuck, man?"

I'm no less scared. While Brody's going to get hung up on the whole
unnatural or supernatural angle here (maybe it reminds him of something from a horror flick he caught at the Drive-In with his high school
sweetheart), this is a repeat of a moment I have been trying to avoid since
the night Jessica died.

Brody claws at the door. "Unlock it for God's sake!"

It isn't locked. At least it wasn't, but maybe she locked it.

The hands spread out, push further into the car, the tips brushing
against my chin, making me flinch, bringing me dangerously close to
soiling myself. It's cold in here now. I can see my breath. I can see Brody's
breath too, pluming over my shoulder.

"Open this goddamn door!"

The mist separates, the CD slot gapes obscenely, lit from within by
white smoky light. The black plastic cradle keeping it in place begins to
crack. And all the while Patsy Cline keeps singing "Crazy" at the top of
her lungs, loud enough to make my eardrums vibrate with pain. I feel a
hand on my shoulder and bat at it in terror, but it's Brody, trying to pull
me through the seat. "What is it? What did you do?"

"It's our song," I tell him.

He starts kicking at the door.

She won't let it open.

Her face emerges sideways, slipping impossibly from the too-narrow
gap, her features distorting, forming and reforming, coming apart like
windblown cigarette smoke only to be whole again before the eye can
track the movement. There is nothing but a rope of smoke connected to
her head as it rises like a tethered balloon from the CD slot. Her face settles. The face I loved. A face I am terrified to see looming over me now.

Brody screams at the sight of it, renews his assault on the door.

"Oh shut your trap," Jessica commands and the door Brody is so desperately trying to break open is suddenly blown from its hinges with a tortured shriek of metal, clear into the trees on the other side of the road where it smacks against the trunk of a pine, falls, and is still. Brody doesn't wait to see whether she intends him to be the next object thrown at high velocity from the car. He hurries out into the road, and straight into the bruised, burned and bloody knuckles of Wintry's fist.

The kid drops and hits the ground hard.

"Can I turn this down?" I ask, desperately trying to avoid looking at that blue mask hovering three inches from my face.

"Why are you shakin'?"

"It was a close call with the kid, that's all. I guess I'm not as tough as I used to be."

"Right." Even though the expression is made up mostly of dust, smoke, and air, and, for all I know, my own memories of her, the doubt sweeping across it is all too clear. I let out a long low sigh. The kid's down for a while, thank God, and Wintry's holding on hard as he can. But in my frightened mind I can still hear a clock ticking, still feel those cold pennies in my pocket. I don't have time to hang around talking to my wife's ethereal head, no matter how sentimental that song makes me feel.

"Looks like quite a mess you've made for yourself," my wife says.

"Looks like it, yeah."

"It didn't have to be this way you know."

I smile, but it's a cold one. "Yeah, I do, but please spare me the list of reasons why. I don't have time to hear 'em."

The smoke coils in my vision. I'm tempted to close my eyes but that only leads to the dreadful thought of what she might do to open them, so I stare at the dashboard, at the undulating tendril that's keeping her tied to the mangled stereo. Somehow, it's still playing that song.

"You're still actin' the fool, Tom. Still pretendin' life will eventually work out just fine if you keep walkin' through it with blinkers on. What you can't see can't affect you, right?"

I say nothing. Have nothing to say.

"You shouldn't be in the least bit surprised that it's come to this."

"I'm not. Just didn't figure it would happen so soon is all."

"What wouldn't happen so soon? Do you even know what this is?"

I shrug, still can't look at her.

"It's not Hell," she says softly. "It's not damnation other than the one you condemn yourself to. The Hell inside yourself. Shun love and ignore hate, hurt people and dismiss those who truly need you…that's the best way to find yourself stopped at an intersection in Milestone lookin' up at a traffic light that hasn't worked in ten years, without any idea how you got there. When *did* you get here, Tom? Do you even remember?"

I nod slowly. Sure I remember, but I don't want to. Thankfully, it's a question that requires no answer, because she already knows it. What I can remember without fear is the woman who worked in the library in its last year of service, the woman who at first sight encompassed every adolescent fantasy I'd ever had of the quiet bookish brunette, hair tied back, spectacles perched on her nose to downplay the sultry beauty you knew in your heart was there. But Jessica was so much more than that. Within ten minutes of getting up the courage to talk to her, I realized she was way out of my league, not only with her looks, but with her frightening intellect and resolve. She was witty, clever, and iron-willed. The mating ritual was of little interest to her. No let's do dinner, then play phone tag until I trust you enough to fall into your bed. She was stuck in a small town that died a little every day. Her job was in danger. She needed a man to love her and provide for her, but railed at the slightest suggestion that it meant she would stay at home and play the good wife. No. She intended to study, paint and make enough money so she could get out of Milestone, maybe go back to school, and someday teach. A damsel in distress she certainly was not. A homemaker only under duress. Aprons would be worn not to bake cakes or apple pies, but to prevent the spatter from her paint from ruining her clothes. She was a bohemian, and if a prospective mate couldn't understand that, or considered it something that would pass once she discovered the joys of Betty Crocker and Martha Stewart, then they would be sorely disappointed.

She frightened me, she enthralled me, and I knew the day I left her company for the first time and stepped out into noon sunshine that looked a little brighter, a little cleaner than ever before, that I had to have her.

She frightened me then; she frightens me now, for the same reason: She was always right.

"I'm sorry."

The smoke clucks its tongue. "Too late for that, and I'm not the one you should be apologizin' to, unless your goin' to play the same game with me that you're playin' with Kyle."

"I'm not—"

"Save it." Her face whorls, and reforms right in front of my face, close enough for us to kiss. It's hard to see her as my wife, so I avert my eyes once more. There's no denying where the voice comes from though.

God, I still love her.

"Why didn't you tell him?"

I shrug and it's pitiful. "There was never a good time."

"Bullshit. It would have required too much of you. It would have meant you'd have had to sit your ass down and talk to him like a man. You'd have had to face up to somethin' for the first time in your life, but like everythin' else, you turned your back on it. Just like you turned your back on me."

"I didn't—"

"What else do you need to lose before you see what you've done to yourself and the ones you love? How many more people need to die before the sun breaks through the clouds around that thick head of yours?"

"I have to go."

"No."

"I have to help him."

"Why?"

"Because he's…because I have to."

"It's too late."

I slam a fist on the steering wheel. "It isn't, and don't you say that." Panic courses through me. Like I've said, she's always right, and right now, more than ever, I don't want her to be.

Again her face falls an inch or two, trying to stay level with mine. "Why do you care? Why now is it so important that you race to his rescue?"

"I don't have to explain it." *Because I can't, and I don't want to have to think about it.* "He's my son."

"He doesn't think of himself as your son. I don't think of him as your son, and on any other day you wouldn't either. Do you think this will save you?"

I give a bitter chuckle at that. "Save me? From what? Myself? This town? That old bastard with his coins? There's no salvation here and you know that as well as I do."

"Then why fight it?"

"I don't know. For Chrissakes I don't *know*, all right? Why does there have to be a reason? Would you prefer I just sit here listening to you while whatever happens to our son happens?"

"Why not? It's what you've been doin' your whole life."

"I don't need to listen to this."

"Then why did you turn on the stereo?"

I scowl and reach for the keys. "To get rid of the kid."

"You're lyin'."

"You think so? Take a look around. The kid's out there on the road, not here with a goddamn Rambo knife to my throat. *That's* why I turned you on…"

I feel her smile and the urge to share it is almost overwhelming, but I kill the compulsion by reminding myself that for whatever reason, she's trying to keep me here.

"I'm going, and I'm switching this thing off."

"Why?"

"Because I don't have time to talk anymore, that's why."

A sad sigh. "Nothin' ever changes in your world, does it Tom? The whole town could wake up buried under a hundred feet of ice and you'd still plod along with that badge pinned to your chest, swearin' to protect while watchin' them all freeze. And an hour later, it'd be forgotten, locked away for good in that holdin' pen in your skull."

I start the ignition. The truck rumbles to life. Wintry's shadow eclipses the light through the passenger side window, where he stands, and waits, aware that the business in here is not something he wants, or has any right, to be a part of.

Finally, I look at her face, into her eyes. Death has made her one of her own sketches, a pale imprint on blue paper. Only the eyes look alive, miniature galaxies swirling in pockets of deep space.

"I don't know any other way," I confess, and quickly look away.

"There's always another way, Tom, but you've never been interested or tuned in enough to seek it out. Your way suits you fine, and that's why you're here now, waitin', maybe secretly hopin' it is too late when you reach Kyle so you won't have to shoulder the burden of what follows. You're your own puppet, Tom, even if today, someone else is pullin' your strings."

"The hells' that supposed to mean? No one's pullin' my strings but me."

"There are two pennies in your pocket that say different. Sometimes, givin' selfish people what they want is enough to bring a town to its knees, as it will bring you to your knees."

"Wintry, come on," I yell out at him, disgusted by the quaver in my voice. I lunge forward, through the smoke, through *her*, and gasp. She feels like winter mist on my skin. I kill the stereo.

"You should have told him you didn't kill me," she says sadly.

"I know. There's a lot I should have done."

"That you didn't know how isn't good enough. Apathy is sometimes worse than murder." She starts to fade, dissipating like the Cheshire Cat, only it isn't her smile that remains clear while she dissolves, but her eyes. "You should have told him the truth."

"Wintry…"

He half-raises a hand in acknowledgment, and opens the door, then slowly, painfully, eases himself into the seat. "We goan leave the kid?"

"Yeah."

Wisps of smoke curl from the broken stereo. I sense him looking at it, then at me, and I put the car into gear to get us moving. I roll down my window. The fresh air cures the nausea.

"They ain't always right, you know," Wintry says.

"I know. But she was."

We head for Hill's house, Brody a dark dwindling shape in the rearview.

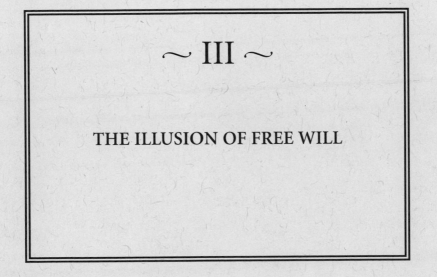

~ III ~

THE ILLUSION OF FREE WILL

15

Reverend Hill's house sits by itself on a grassy slope, segregated from the rest of the community by a short stretch of woodland on one side, and the river on the other. Hill's predecessor, the benevolent and much lamented Reverend Lewis, was never comfortable being so far from his flock, and was busy finalizing plans for the purchase of a smaller, more modest place in the town center when for reasons known only to him, he decided to string himself up. When Hill came to Milestone, he sneered at the idea of what he called an "odious hovel", and quickly made his home out here, in the tall narrow house he deemed just big enough to contain a man of his importance. "You'll know where I am if you need me," he advised his parishioners, "But know too that I have little time to waste on trivial matters that you yourselves have the power to cure."

The only time he would take an interest in the people was when one of them came to him with a blemished soul, but even those misguided few quickly realized that whatever god it was that Hill claimed to worship, it wasn't one they recognized, or wanted to have their lives governed by. But fear kept them—kept us—within his power.

From the get-go he was an asshole, and everyone knew it. A fire-and-brimstone man they didn't need, or want, but they were stuck with him, and as Cobb once said, "In troubled times, you can't be choosy about which preacher's voice you end up listenin' to."

Gracie's right. We should have killed him three years ago, as soon as it became clear what we'd been saddled with, but despite everything we'd seen and heard, and despite instinct telling us what the wise thing to do was, we did nothing. For three years we kept going back to that tavern, kept drinking ourselves numb and waiting for the keys to be jingled, waiting for Hill to tell us which sinners we were going to erase from the world as repentance for our own transgressions.

And every Saturday night, one of us would. Take the keys, get in the car, drive, and kill. Pretend the screams and the horrible thud against our hoods were deer, then come back, drink some more and wonder when that spiritual cleansing would kick in.

Never did of course, and never will.

He never wanted to save us from Hell. He brought Hell *to* us. But even he can't be blamed, not entirely, for what's happening in Milestone, tempting as it is to pin this nightmare on him.

No.

This town is dying because we're killing it.

~

"You want to wait here?" I ask Wintry, and watch his eyes slide slowly past me, to the house with its stained and buckled siding, leaf-choked gutters, unpainted frames.

He licks his lips, grunts with pain, and closes his eyes. "You might need my help."

"What is it you think you're going to be able to help me with in your condition?"

His shrug is slight. "Never know."

"Wintry, look. I appreciate the backup, but I'm not sure I have the time to wait for you. My boy's in trouble. I got to get to him, so do me a favor, all right? Wait here. If the ground cracks open and imps come flying out, or if the house takes off and starts spinning, then you come help me. I'm sure I'll be glad of it. All right?"

He smiles weakly, but I know he's not happy.

"See you soon," I tell him, and shut the door.

A long gravel path twists its way around a large granite boulder that bears the names of all the clergymen who have presided over matters of the spirit in Milestone, going back as far as 1820, when the town's soul was the charge of a Protestant minister by the name of Edgar Saxton. Seventeen men succeeded him. Sixteen of their names are etched there forever in the face of that boulder. Only Hill's name is missing, and I reckon it'll stay missing, unless his replacement decides he deserves the acknowledgment, if a replacement ever comes.

Though I'm running on fumes now and my head is threatening to split in the middle, I jog my way up the path, my pulse racing the closer I get to the house, and the red Chevy parked outside the main door. In a way I'm relieved to see it. It means Kyle's still here. But another part of me seems to have been betting on the fact that he wouldn't be, that either I'd make it here too late, or find that Kyle went home. Or back to Iris.

On the dashboard, there's a worn deck of playing cards wrapped in a rubber band. Next to them is a pack of Camel Lights, one cigarette poking from the foil. Maybe they belong to Iris, or someone Kyle gave a ride to. Maybe they're Kyle's. That I don't know is just another one of those things I'll have to sit down and chastise myself about later. No time for it now, even though I've just wasted five minutes staring at the damn Chevy.

As I skirt around the car and make my way to the door, the gravel crunches under my boots loud enough to give me away. No harm in that. I'm not here to surprise anyone.

As it turns out, the front door's shut, but not locked. It's got one of those fancy brass handles with the little button on the top you have to press down to open the latch. With a cursory check of the curtained windows for faces that aren't there, I depress the button and the door swings open without a sound.

I'm greeted by the smell of furniture polish, which isn't what I expected. Not even sure why. Maybe it's because the exterior has fallen into disrepair, or because the man who lived here up until some hours ago made everyone he encountered feel dirty so I naturally assumed his home would smell like filth. It doesn't though, nor does it look filthy. Just the opposite. I step into a hallway with dark varnished floorboards and a wide colorful rug which depicts the Virgin Mary in a typically beatific pose, her hands clasped in prayer, doves circling her head, her eyes rolled up so far to look at the Heavens she looks like she might be having a seizure. There's a bare coat rack to my left, the wood the same dark shade as the floor, and a few feet further in, a little ways past the rug, there's a small table with two drawers, the surface of which is completely free of dust and reflects the light from the quaint chandelier suspended from a small brass dome in the high ceiling.

I wonder if Hill had a maid.

The hall is short and opens at the end, where to the left, an arched doorway leads to the heart of the house. To my right, a set of stairs—as dust-free as every other surface I've seen so far—rises up and around behind me, running past the oval stained glass window above the door, and on to the second floor, the landing of which is overhead, and manned only by shadows.

It occurs to me that the sharp smell of polish and the immaculate cleanliness of the place don't make the place seem homely, but preserved. The kind of smell you get in a museum, or anywhere else you go to look and admire, but not touch.

At this point, I should call out for Kyle, just in case he hasn't heard me coming and does something rash because I've startled him, but there's a noise now, coming from somewhere beyond the arch; a shuffling sound, barely noticeable over the thumping of my own heart in my ears. Papers, I'm guessing. That's what it sounds like. The same sound the newspaper used to make when my father rustled it at the supper table. His way of telling us to shut up. For a few years I thought he was human only from the waist down, his upper half made of paper and black print.

I make my way into the darkness of the arch and on, into another short hallway, this one just as pristine as the last. There are windows to my right, and though the glass is regular, not stained, and clean, the morning sun seems to be straining to get through. On the opposite wall there are three doors, the middle one open. I cross to that side and poke my head in. It's a bathroom: sink, toilet, bath, no shower, and it's deserted.

The sound comes again, as if it's meant to draw my attention, to direct me, and it's coming from the room I've passed to get to the bathroom, the first door in the row from the arch.

My pulse quickens. Blunt pain taps at my right temple like an icepick. I go to the door, open it, half-expecting to feel a bullet rip through me before I get the chance to see who's holding the weapon.

But no bullet comes, and there's no weapon.

I'm in what I guess is the living room, and there's a man sitting on a brown leather couch across from two matching armchairs. I guessed right, he's reading a newspaper, but I don't have to wait for him to lower it to know it isn't my son.

"Took your time, Tom," Cadaver says in a hoarse whisper, as he closes the newspaper, folds it in half and sets it on the arm of the couch. He looks at me, expression grim, and motions for me to sit in the armchair opposite him. For a moment I don't comply, just watch as he retrieves his little microphone and jams it to his throat.

"Where's my son?"

"Sit," he commands. "This is how it's supposed to go. So do what I say." A sympathetic look crosses his ancient face. "*Please*."

Oddly enough, there is no mockery in his tone. The plea is a sincere one, so I take the seat, feel myself sink into it. Might be comfortable if I wasn't wired to the moon right now. "Where is he?"

Cadaver sits forward, one hand on his knee, the other holding the mike to his throat. "Upstairs," he tells me.

I start to move.

"Wait."

"What?" I'm already on my feet, impatient to be gone from this room.

"You ain't ready to see him."

"The hell I'm not."

He gestures at the seat again. "Please. I ain't fixin' to keep you from seein' him, but now's not the right time. You need to listen first."

"I'm not sure I want to hear what you have to say."

"Maybe so, but it will help you."

"And why would you want to help me?"

"I ain't your enemy."

"I seem to recall Hill said the same thing."

"Hill was an idiot."

"Can't argue with that."

"Please…sit."

I don't move. Can't. The door's not that far away and I'm standing.

"Kyle ain't goin' nowhere, Tom. He's restin'."

Resting? Here? Of all the ways I imagined finding Kyle when I got here, taking a load off sure isn't one of them. I can't tell if Cadaver's being straight with me. He managed to fool me for three years into thinking he was a harmless old man, and there's not much hope I'll be able to figure it out just by looking at him, so I do as he asks.

"Why is he here?"

"We made a bargain."

"I know: a one-way ticket out of here, right?"

Can't fault the kid for that. I don't think I've met anyone in this town who didn't dream of leaving it far behind them. But if that was what he got for his efforts, then why is he still here?

"That's right."

"In exchange for what?"

"I think you already know."

I do, but I want him to say it, to bring the gavel down on what I've been told, and what I feel deep down in my gut.

"Tell me."

"In exchange for you."

There's a glass-fronted bookcase behind the couch. In it I can see my reflection, but the gaunt overweight creature staring back at me with hollow eyes isn't someone I recognize. I bring my gaze back to Cadaver. "My life for his escape?"

"I offered to bring back the woman he loved. I offered to bring back Flo and grant him safe passage from this town."

"That's quite an offer. I'm flattered you thought it would take so much for him to sell me out. He'd probably have done it for a six-pack." I can't keep the ugly tone from my voice.

"You don't know your son very well, Sheriff."

"Neither do you, apparently." I draw my fingers down my face. "So if he made the deal, how come I'm still breathing?"

"It interests me that you assume he did."

"What?"

"Situations reversed, would you have accepted the terms?"

"This isn't about me."

"You couldn't be more wrong about that."

"I want to see him."

"I understand, but let me have a few more moments of your time."

I also want a drink, but even though there's a fancy decanter in view on one of the bookshelves, I'm not going for it. I don't want to be drunk for whatever's coming, and I don't want anything Hill might have touched. So I wait, and listen, and picture Kyle in a room somewhere above my head, sleeping, unaware that his father's downstairs, chatting with the devil.

Or whatever he is.

"Is this what you do for fun?" I ask.

He looks surprised, maybe even a little insulted. "Fun?" He scoffs. "Hell...I wish that were the case, Tom."

"Then why?"

He scoots forward a little, an intense look on his face, one eye like a white marble, the other in shadow. "I don't enjoy what I do anymore than you enjoy livin' in your own skin when your spirit's already shriveled up and died inside it. I do this because I *have* to, not because I want to." He sits back, drums his fingers on the arm of the couch. "You want to know what I am. I can't tell you that, and not because I ain't allowed to, but because no one's ever explained it to *me*. What I can tell you is what I used to be. It may surprise you."

I shrug as if I couldn't care less, but I'm interested. "A preacher?"

He grins and his cheeks vanish. "A salesman."

"Let me guess—bibles."

"You need to abandon the religious angle, Tom. I was a door-to-door carpet products salesman. Damned good one too. In my spare time I liked to paint. Still life's mostly."

I frown at him. He laughs and it sounds like a gust of winter wind through the eaves. "I know. Hard to picture, ain't it?"

"No shit. And when was this?"

His smile fades. "Can't remember."

I'm appalled to find myself feeling sorry for him. I have to remind myself why I'm here, and whose fault it is. But that's not so clear, no more than it's ever been. I can't be sure Cadaver wasn't toying with me by planting the seed of doubt in my brain. He hasn't said Kyle took the bargain he was offered. He hasn't said he *didn't* either. The fact that I'm alive is about the only thing keeping me from being convinced the latter holds true.

"Had a wife, and two children too," he continues, as wistfully as his artificial voice will allow. "Can't recall their names, or their faces. I know I cared about them a great deal though."

"So how did you get demoted to this position?" I'm hoping to get a rise out of him, simply so I won't have to feel sympathy for the old bastard anymore.

It's his turn to shrug. "Can't rightfully recall that either, but I'm sure it began with the scandal. See, I mentioned I was good at my job. Turns out I was maybe a little too good. I could talk the talk like no one else in the company. Had a ninety-six percent success rate you see, which means almost everyone who opened the door to me bought whatever I was sellin'. Which is good, unless it's discovered that what you're sellin' emits toxic fumes, which when inhaled, causes seizures, and eventually a very painful death." He shakes his head. "Sold an awful lot before the company recalled it, Tom. That's an awful lot of dead folk."

"And that's why you're—"

"No idea. You could say the death of all those people wasn't my fault, but we might have to argue about that. I've had plenty of time to think it through, and I suppose there could be any number of reasons why I ended up doin' what I do now. Could be because I shot my father to keep him from beatin' my Momma to death with a shovel, or because I shot a few bluejays with my BB gun when I was a kid.. At the end of the day, don't really matter why. I still am what I am and always was: a salesman sellin' death to whoever opens their door to me."

"And that's what we've done? Opened our doors to you because we fucked up our lives?"

"Because you fucked up the lives of others. Why do you think you're involved here? We both know you didn't murder your wife, but you keep tellin' yourself you did. Why?"

"I figured you'd already know."

"Humor me."

"Why should I?"

I search for words, but like the answer he's seeking, I can't wrench it free of the dark that's coiling inside me like oil in a spinning barrel.

"Who's the victim of your sins, Tom? Kyle?"

"Maybe."

"No." The word is flat, dead, delivered like a hand slammed down on a table. "It's you. You're the victim. You've let yourself drift on a tide of bad judgment, let this town suck the marrow from your bones and the ambition from your heart because it was easier'n puttin' up a fight. You're a quitter, Tom."

I'm a little stunned at the vehemence in his artificial voice. Whatever the motive behind his little rant, I'm inclined to believe he's just accused me of an unforgivable crime, not on some malignant whim, but because he desperately wants me to know. Because I *have* to know.

I've heard some people say that when they were faced with extreme danger their lives flashed before their eyes. That's who Cadaver is, or at least a part of what he is. He's a reminder of all you've done, and should have done. He's an accountant who keeps track of how much you've squandered and how much you owe. He's a debt collector of the most ruthless kind because he deals in the currency of souls.

"You're a failure."

I'm getting angry, and that's about par for the course. I can't walk away from this like I've walked away from everything else, and with no distance to put between me and the man judging me, and no gun to shove between his eyes to force him to reevaluate, I have no choice but to defend myself with words.

"Is this supposed to make me see the light? Change my ways? Am I supposed to leave here with an arm around my boy, both of us skipping to the tune of *The Andy Griffith Show*, all because I was fortunate enough to heed the wisdom of a mass-murdering parasite? Fuck you old man. You brought Hell to this town just as much as Hill did. You infected it, infected us, and then have the gall to sit there like God himself judging everyone you've set out to destroy. Why not just wave a magic wand and blow the fucking place off the earth and be done with it. Why drag it out like this unless you like the suffering, unless it's how your limp dick gets to twitching?"

Cadaver seems unaffected by my outburst, but right now I want to wring his scrawny neck, or at the very least rip that goddamn box out of it so he'll stop talking.

"I've done nothin' in this town the people didn't ask for, Tom. I'm as cursed as everyone else, maybe even more than they are. I don't get to make choices. I just get to grant power to people who make them too freely, and without thinkin' them through. And I don't get to change them." He frowns. "So no, I don't expect you to see the light. That star burned out a long time ago. But whether or not you choose to understand what I'm tryin' to tell you, you'll learn to appreciate the message when the choice is taken away."

"Riddles." I stand, muscles trembling, hands clenched into fists I want so badly to use but know I won't. I can't. "You're speaking in goddamn riddles. What do you want from me? From Kyle? How do we end this? Do we have to die, to burn? Is that it? Tell me!"

Cadaver rises, a skeleton beneath plastic skin. The smell of his cologne will from this moment on remind me of death. "How these things turn out depends on the choices that are made. Sometimes it happens that everythin' turns out fine. But not often. It ain't in our nature to consider others when we're sufferin' ourselves. And unfortunately for Milestone, everyone gets to bargain if they want it, even the monster hidin' among you."

I'm standing as close to him as I am willing to get. His one good eye holds me as sure as if it were a loaded gun. "Tom, you were a good man once. You lost your way. Tonight you're goin' to lose everythin' else, and for that I'm truly sorry."

He's trying to scare me. It's working.

"What about the coins, the loan? What about—" Frantic, I dig in my pocket until I have those two cold discs grasped in my hand, then I hold them out for his inspection. "—these?"

"What about them?"

"You said they were a loan."

"I did."

"What if I give mine to you? What if…" Unsure what I'm doing, but praying it achieves the desired result, I shove one of the pennies under his nose. He backs away, looking slightly annoyed. "What if I let you have mine, *me*, right now, whether or not Kyle took the bargain? What then?"

"You misunderstood, Tom."

That's not what I want to hear.

"Just listen—"

He puts a hand on my wrist, forcing me to lower the coin from his face. "It was a loan for you. The coins ain't some kind of barter for your soul and Kyle's. They don't represent souls at all."

"Then what the hell are they?"

"Time. I let you borrow time."

I feel something being yanked away from me, the knot in the tug o' war rope vanishing into the darkness in the corners of a room that smells of death/cologne and furniture polish. The man looking at me from the glass over Cadaver's shoulder is a monster. His eyes are gone. My eyes are gone, but I'm not blind enough to miss seeing the picture this old man has drawn for me.

"He couldn't sell you out. I knew he wouldn't, no matter what I offered him. He's one of the few good ones, Tom, so I broke the rules for him. I gave you the pennies. Both were his. I gave you time to save him."

Sweat trickles down my neck even as a chill dances across my back. "How much time?"

From the room directly overhead, something crashes to the floor. The light sways slightly. Grains of plaster float down between us like sand from a cracked hourglass.

I feel a vibration in my bones, terror twisting my gut.

Helpless, I look at Cadaver.

"That much," he whispers.

16

I run, taking the steps two by two though the sweeping angle of them seems designed to slow me down. As my feet make sounds like gunshots on the steps, I feel a part of me rip away, a part of me that wants to go in the other direction, back downstairs to Cadaver, to kill him, so there'll be nothing left to face when I return. In the split-second instances when my mind cuts away from the sight of my own filthy boots pounding polished wood on this fucking endless staircase, I can almost feel his body come apart beneath my hands, blood and bone, or maybe just dust and oil spattering the walls, wet and satisfying beneath my shaking hands. I'm ripping that box from his throat, taking no care with it, just yanking it free and delighting in the sight of the gaping void it leaves behind as his head lolls atop withered shoulders. I'm hurting him. I'm showing him agony. I'm showing him how I feel, how I felt long before I first stepped foot in that goddamn tavern.

I'm tearing him apart. Returning the favor.

But then the steps run out and the landing isn't nearly long enough for me to get my thoughts in order, to force myself to be calm. Three strides and I'm at the door I'm guessing is the one from which that thumping sound came. I don't wait a second longer.

I throw open the door.

It's a bedroom.

Bed, neatly made.

Sink in the corner, dripping.

Sunlight making shadows that lay flat upon the floor.

Window overlooking the yard.

There's no one here.

Cursing, I head for the next door, the echo of that sliding thumping sound bouncing around my brain. I know what that sound was, but I'm going to dismiss the certainty and tell myself I'm letting terror mislead me. But deep down inside where reality is a small dark plot of land under an indifferent sky, I know the truth. I feel it. Right now, there is no tiny dirt road I can sidle down to avoid that big sprawling highway that runs only one way—straight into the mushy black heart of truth, the true nightmare of this situation. I can't get away. Never could. But I could have gotten Kyle out of this and didn't.

Still, *Be there; be alive. I won't let you down. Not again,* I repeat in a mantra inside my head, a head that feels as if it's become a porcelain vase dropped from a height.

My hand finds the door knob.

Please. Just a little more time. One more chance. One more penny.

I open the door.

The hinges shriek.

There's light coming in the window.

My mouth's dry.

There's light coming in the window.

I can't see for the tears.

There's light coming in the window.

And there's a long thin shadow swinging in front of it, touching my own feet, which I let drop me to the floor. They've held me enough, held me longer than that creaking rope is going to hold my boy.

I can't look at him. Won't.

Then I do.

Help him down, goddamn it. He's still alive.

I'm back on my feet in an instant, hugging my boy's legs, my arms tight, lifting, lifting. Trying to unbreak his neck; trying to unchoke him. He rises, but doesn't make a sound. Christ…he doesn't make a sound.

No words, no breath. No life.

He's dead and gone.

Slowly, so slowly, and gently, I let him go until the rope is tight once again and his body twists in a breeze that isn't here.

Another man, another *father*, might persist, try to free him, try to save him, wailing and moaning all the while, crying out to God, promising retribution for this heinous injustice.

But I'm not another father.

And God isn't listening.

I find myself looking at my son's shoes, note that they are cleaner than mine, though we've walked the same paths tonight. Guess that probably means something. All I take from it is the fact that they're cleaner, and that the laces are untied, same way they always were when he got done with a day's work. He never could tie laces right, but he sure did a hell of a job with that noose.

His belt buckle is silver, a rearing horse locked inside an oval, and it glints in the sunlight, until the body swings around to the shadows again, then that silver mare turns black.

The floor hurts my knees as I let it draw me down again. Bare wood. I want to claw it to splinters, but I'll wait. I have to wait to see if I choke to death like my boy because the feeling in my chest makes me believe that's what's going to happen. Someone has their hands around my throat, but there's nobody here but us.

Just me.

Just me, and my boy, who's wearing a brown noose pulled so tight it's sawed almost clear through the skin.

Just me and my boy, who's sticking his tongue out at me like he did when I teased him about the girl he used to walk home when they were in second grade. How many years ago was that? What was her name? Nancy something. Ellis, maybe. Damn it. Pretty girl too, but she moved on. She didn't want to, and I guess Kyle didn't want her to either. But wish in one hand…

"Shit in the other," I say aloud, wondering if my voice is enough to make Kyle swing some more, because aside from that creaking rope, the room is deathly quiet, deathly still, which I suppose is only appropriate.

On the floor, there's a chair, lying on its back, one its runners broken. I wonder if Kyle changed his mind as he stood atop that chair until the chair decided for him. *Sorry, son. Too late now. Your old man hasn't spent your time wisely.*

I won't look at his face, though it begs me to.

I won't.

I've taken the blame for my wife's death though I wasn't even in the car. I got out, she drove away, and two hours later we pulled my Lexus out of the Milestone River. I never told Kyle that. Never told him that we found Alfie Tomlin, the banker, in the passenger seat either. No, I kept that stuff to myself because once she was gone, I was all he had left. I was what he needed. A target. Someone to blame, to hate, and I let him.

I let him.

You're the victim, Cadaver said. Not Kyle.

He lied, of course. For all his sympathy and confessions, he lied to me. I'm not the victim. I'm not the one swinging from the rafters or burned to death.

I'm alive, and though I'm about to make myself a promise that I'll rectify that before the sun goes down, I'm going to forget about Hell and devils and men with no voices and miraculous resurrections and ghostly spouses, and the cosmic or celestial balance that has made us all its slaves. I'm going to put out of my mind all thoughts of betrayal and lies and sin and hate and love.

Fuck all that.

Right now I'm going to restore the only balance that matters a goddamn right at this very second in my life.

And I'm going to enjoy every minute of it.

~

I expect to find him gone, fled like the yellow son of a bitch I know him to be, and when I storm into the parlor, he's nowhere in sight. Rage is making me shake harder than a man in an electric chair, but when I turn, there he is, the front door open, poised, waiting, as if for me to accompany him. Like we're about to take a nice pleasant walk of the grounds. The daylight doesn't reach far into the hall. Maybe he's holding it back. Maybe it doesn't know how to penetrate the sickness, death and misery he wears for a coat.

"You killed him."

He clucks his tongue, and I've just decided that's the first thing I'm going to rip from him.

"You know that ain't true." It's hard to hear him over the sound of my own blood roaring through me. "Maybe not in your head where the fury's flowin' from, but deep down you—"

Fists clenched tight and held by my sides, I start toward him. "I'm through listening to you telling me how I am, what I am, and what I'm supposed to do. And you're all done messing with folk's lives. You're going in the ground today, Cadaver, right next to Eddie and the whore and the only choice I'm giving you is whether or not you want to be dead or alive when I do it."

I need him to be unsettled, to look shaken. I need him to be afraid, but he isn't. Nothing about him has changed much, except maybe for his shoulders, which have drawn in a little as if he's waiting for the first blow. But there's no fear in him. Nothing. He just looks sad, like none of this is a surprise, as if he saw the whole damn thing in some fucking crystal ball.

"You know somethin'?" he asks, when I reach him. "I would very much like if you could do that. But you can't, and you ain't the first to offer. Not by a long shot. And every time I hear it, I feel somethin' I'm not allowed to feel, somethin' I've all but forgotten how to feel. The very thing you and everyone else in this town squanders with every breath you take: Hope. So by all means, Tom, do your worst. Make your last stand in a town that has nothin' left in it for you to protect even if you continue to pretend it does. Put me in the ground for a spell to teach me a lesson you still, despite all you've lived through, haven't learned yourself."

Words. That's all they are. More words.

I close the space between us with one lunge, and insane animal sounds fill the hall, like there's a pack of crazed starving jackals pouring down the stairs. Takes me a moment, but as soon as my hands find Cadaver's coat, and then his neck, I realize that sound is coming from me. Spit flies from my lips into the old man's face, flecks of foam stippling his sallow cheeks, and still, *still* he doesn't look threatened, and that refusal to be afraid, to at least pretend I have a hope of ending all of this by ending him, is going to drain the fight from me if I don't do what I need to do and fast.

"Bring him back," I snarl, grunting with the effort of trying to strangle a man whose throat is mostly metal. He shakes when I throttle him, but his eyes, one living, one dead, stare at me with aggravating calm, his hands by his sides.

"Bring him *back*."

"And what will you do for me?" he whispers.

"Just bring back my son."

He mouths the words, "I can't," and then the bastard smiles, adds a silent, "I won't" to it and my hands fly from his throat to his face, to those eyes. He jerks back, and somewhere inside me I'm celebrating the first reaction I've gotten from him, but I'm too focused, to driven to rejoice for long. His skin is cold—but not cold enough to indicate he's already dead and therefore can't be killed—and my hands brace his face, thumbs finding his eyes.

"If you won't fix it," I growl at him. "You won't ever again see what you've done to people." And as if I'm pressing them into fruit to test for ripeness, I let my thumbs sink into his wrinkled sockets, into the too dry but soft orbs of his eyes.

He doesn't make a sound, but he's beginning to sag. The feeling of victory increases, filling me with cold fire, igniting some part of me that's been buried for far too long, the part of me that knew once upon a time how to make others pay for their sins.

And goddamn it, I'm not stopping until *someone* has paid.

Cadaver's legs buckle beneath him. He's kneeling, arms still by his sides, face still cradled in my hands, a queer hissing noise coming from the box in his throat. That little microphone clatters to the floor.

"Fight me," I command him, because I want him to. I want him to fight for his life like everyone in Milestone has had to do because they were too blind to see it when it deserted them.

He gasps as his eyes give way beneath my thumbs. I increase my grip, letting them sink farther, drilling toward his brain, or whatever ugliness fills his rotten skull. Even without his eyes, he could be dangerous.

Sweat trickles down between my shoulder blades.

Cadaver mouths something as watery blood streams down his face, but I can only feel his lips move against the heel of my palm now. Dry and dusty, like the wings of a moth. I lean close. "*Fix it.*" It can't be this easy. But it seems it is. Three years being governed by an old man and a lunatic priest and they were both made of flesh and blood at the back of it all. What utter fools we've been.

Cadaver, who hasn't struggled from the beginning of this, gasps one more time and I feel his weight pulling away from me, his body headed for a resting place in the corner by the door.

Milky fluid squirts and reflexively, my grip loosens. There's a gruesome squelch as my thumbs slide free of the man's eye sockets. He falls back, legs folded beneath him, his skull thudding against the hall wall.

He's still smiling.

I wipe my hands on my pants, and stand over him. The fresh air drifting through the open door cools the sweat on my brow but I'm shaking so hard I'm afraid it will shake me to pieces. My guts seem about to escape through my throat. They're headed off by desperation. "How do I make this stop? How do I get him back?"

He gives the smallest little shake of his head.

"Goddamn it, *tell* me or I'll carry you out of here in a basket."

He does, but I have to bend low to hear the words. "It wouldn't interest you," he says.

"What wouldn't?"

The fist he brings up is trembling, and for a moment he looks like an old man about to waggle it at some pesky kids who've left a flaming bag full of dog turds on his stoop. But then a twig-like finger springs free and bends toward him, indicating he wants me to come closer.

I hesitate, and in that hallway where the light is hesitating too, time passes unmeasured by the fall of the old bastard's coins. I hunker down, knees crackling, my gut straining against my belt.

"Tell me what to do."

With that maddening smile still mangling his lips, he brings his head close and whispers in my ear. "You have to give me what *I* want."

~

Wintry's been near-death since the fire, but in Milestone, even if you don't have an old man's pennies in your pocket, you can draw the time out just enough to get your business done. I've been doing it for too many years to count, and Wintry's doing it now.

With his last reserves of strength, he leans against the doorjamb, awaiting my word. He says nothing, offers no condolences, asks no questions, just stands there, eyes narrowed against the gnawing pain, watching as I return from the kitchen, a bread knife clutched in one hand. When I ask for his help in cutting Kyle down, he dutifully steps over the threshold where Cadaver is playing possum, and accompanies me upstairs.

My boy is as I found him, though he's stopped swinging, his shadow like a painted thing on the polished floor. The wounds mask the emotion on Wintry's face as he supports Kyle's legs while I drag the bed away from the wall and far enough into the middle of the room to allow me to mount it and reach the noose. There is little give in the mattress, though I can feel the hard springs pressing through. The rope has been looped three times around one of the rafters. It won't be hard to cut and the blade is sure.

"Lift him," I instruct. Wintry does. The sound of his breathing is like a steam train leaving the station.

Kyle is turned away from me, and I'm thankful for that. All I can see is the back of his head, the dark unruly hair. I can't remember the last time I touched it, but I won't touch it now. Later, maybe, when Wintry's gone.

I begin to saw at the rope, tears or sweat running down my face, I can't tell which.

The first loop snaps with a labored groan.

Then the second. When the third gives way the boy is free, and falling, but this time it is not a noose that catches him, but Wintry, whose eyes now seem to contain an emotion I have never seen in them before. It's the same look he once drew from me whenever Flo lavished attention on him.

Envy.

And it's directed at the boy cradled in his arms.

17

Wintry carries the boy downstairs. He goes slowly because of the pain, and because he doesn't want to drop the boy. Doesn't want the Sheriff to have to try to hide his mourning any more than he's already doing.

So he takes the steps easy. Kyle isn't heavy. It's like carrying a baby, and right now Wintry wishes he knew magic, or had the power of healing, because he'd bring that kid back for the Sheriff lickety-split. But he doesn't know magic, and he doesn't have Cobb's power to heal. If he did, he'd surely use it on himself, and make the awful burning go away.

Though the stairs seems to go on forever, it has an end, and when Wintry reaches it, it feels like he's just come down off the mountain he calls home—used to call home—into the valley.

He stands there for a moment, ignoring the raging fire in his arms and the terrible pain from the muscles beneath, and he pictures Flo, who might walk in that door any second, smiling, delighting in his surprise. Just like the night he asked if he could walk her home and she agreed, except it was his home he walked her to. Just like she surprised him by refusing a drink, or anything but the short walk to the cot in the corner. Just like she surprised him by weeping all the way through their love-making, then asking him to marry her afterward. And sure, Wintry was no fool, he'd heard the stories, heard that she'd killed her husband, but at that moment it didn't matter. He'd said yes, and in the morning, when he watched her leave, watched her until she had descended the mountain and was little more than a speck, he decided that if she did kill her man, he must have deserved it. And maybe he would too, but he could think of worse ways to die than at the hands of the woman he loved.

Burning, for example.

Grimacing, he turns to look at the Sheriff, whose face is almost the same shade as his son's, and nods. For a moment it doesn't seem as if the man understands what Wintry's trying to tell him, so he adds, "Take him."

The Sheriff reaches out with the kind of look a man not used to holding babies might have when presented with one. But he takes his son in his arms, anguish rippling across his face, and brings the boy close to his chest.

"Let's go," he says, as firmly as a voice broken by tears will allow him.

But Wintry doesn't move. Instead he glances down into the corner by the door, where the man he wants to see, the man he came here to see is still sitting.

"Just a sec," he says to Tom, and leans over the man with no eyes.

"He's gone," the Sheriff says quietly, and there's a certainty to his voice that only the man who killed him can have.

"He welshed then," Wintry murmurs. "Didn't do what he promised he'd do."

"If I were you I wouldn't be surprised. The devil doesn't keep his promises."

Wintry straightens, a hard black knot of bitterness caught in his throat. With a sigh, he leads the way out into the sunshine, still taking it slow out of respect for Sheriff Tom's grief. *It ain't fair. Ain't fair at all.* He's real sorry for Tom, that's for sure, but he's sorry for himself too and impatient to be done with it all.

It feels like hours before they reach the end of the path, and here they stop.

"Thanks," the Sheriff says. "For…" He shakes his head, brings the boy's head close to his chest with one grubby, bloodstained hand. His eyes are filled with the kind of agony Wintry knows all too well.

Sheriff Tom blinks, as if to dismiss further conversation, or acknowledgment of his gratitude, and moves around the front of the truck, to where the sun through the overhanging leaves makes dancing patterns on the road, and he motions for Wintry to open the side door. Kyle's head begins to turn, as if he wants to see what Wintry's up to, or where he's going to be stowed, and the Sheriff gently puts a hand on the boy's chin, directs his gaze back to the gold star on his father's uniform. The light breeze ruffles the boy's hair, making him seem alive. But anyone who might come along this road need only look at Sheriff Tom's face to know the truth about the situation.

And then the sound of an engine getting closer tells Wintry that someone *is* coming along. He hopes, for the Sheriff's sake, that whoever it is doesn't stop to offer help, or ask questions. But then, this is Milestone, and people rarely do. Can't rightly be afraid of death if you've never had to look at it, which is why most folks in this town don't look anywhere but inside themselves.

"Wintry…"

It's Wintry's turn to apologize for being distracted by the car. "Car comin'," he says, and sets about opening the door for Tom. "We best hurry ourselves outta the road."

He feels a cold lance in his side at the thought that maybe the kid—Brody—managed to get his hands on a car and is racing to put them out of their misery once and for all. Wintry wouldn't mind, but he figures that's more than the Sheriff deserves.

"Best hurry," he says again.

The sound of the car grows louder. Should be just past the bend now, and it's coming real fast. Wintry's hand is on the door, on the handle, and has it cracked, just a little, when the engine roars, making him turn to look once more.

It's a red Buick. He recognizes it as Doctor Hendricks car, and as it gets closer, still going way too fast, sunlight flashing across the windshield, Wintry sees that he was right. There, hunched behind the wheel, is the doctor himself.

"It's the Doc," he tells Tom. "But I don't think—"

Even from back here, Wintry realizes two things: Hendricks either doesn't see them, or doesn't care. Whatever the case, he's not stopping. And in a matter of seconds, the men standing in the way are going to be road kill.

He has time for one thought only: *This is where it ends*, and it is not a frightening thought. He has never feared death, and that's just as well because here it comes now, bearing down on him, the Buick's silver grille like grinning teeth about to yawn open and swallow them all wide, the headlights wide like the terrified eyes of the pale man behind the wheel.

The sound of the engine fills the world.

The Sheriff cries out a warning. There is a hand on Wintry's arm. He ignores the pain it causes, grabs hold of the Sheriff's wrist, turns and thrusts the man, still cradling his boy, clear across the road, where the lawman staggers and falls flat on his ass on the verge of the slight embankment leading down into the woods. Kyle tumbles away from him, lands sprawled on his back in the grass, shoes pointing straight up at the sky.

"Wintry!"

There is nothing but red in his vision.

See you soon baby.

Wintry bends low, as if he's going in for a football tackle, head lowered, eyes forward, shoulders angled forward. He does not wait to die.

With his last breath rushing from his mouth in a strangled cry, he rushes to meet it.

~

"Didn't used to be this hard," Cadaver says, easing himself onto a stool. "Didn't used to be like this at all. Guess I'm either losin' my touch or people are gettin' smarter."

"The hell happened to you?" Gracie asks, her hands flat on the counter, eyes cold.

"The boy is dead."

"Shame."

Cadaver raises his head, and smiles at her, though the absence of eyes and the raw bloody holes where they should be negate any semblance of humor from it. "You almost sound like you mean it."

"Who says I don't?"

"I don't know, but if you're lookin' for character witnesses, you're runnin' kind of low. 'Specially with you killin' 'em an all."

"Vess would have told them."

"Could be they already know."

Gracie leans in, teeth clenched, red-veined eyes wide. "The only way they'd know is if *you* told them."

"Yeah." He nods slowly, picks a speck of soot from the counter and inspects it, which, considering he's blind, or at least should be, would seem amusing to Gracie under different circumstances. But she's far from amused. In fact, she'd love nothing more than to rip the old guy's head clean off his shoulders and preserve it in a pickle jar as a warning to future customers not to fuck with her. But of course, there won't *be* any future customers. She's getting gone and Cadaver's her ticket, so for now at least, she has no choice but to let him keep that rotten head of his, and to bide her time.

Gracie's hands become claws on the polished mahogany. "You dirty son of a bitch. *Why?*"

"Because you ain't the only one who wants out, and I've been plyin' my wares an awful lot longer than you have. Comes a time when it has to end, you see, when you start goin' to bed at night and instead of seein' nothin' you start seein' the faces of people you used to care about—"

"I don't believe I'm hearing this."

Cadaver ignores the interruption. "—Then you realize, one mornin' while you're busy materializin' in people's livin' rooms right when they're desperate enough to say yes to Hell itself if it means they get more time, that there might be salvation for you after all, an escape route you never believed existed. And then you start to *want* it, start plannin', until at last the time comes when you have no more faith in what you do, only in what you can do to be done with it all."

"You've got to be kiddin' me."

"For me that time is now."

Gracie brings her face close to the old man's, stares hard into his dead eye sockets. "Not before you get me out it isn't."

"I'm not a welsher. You'll get what I promised if your side of the bargain is met. All of 'em, you said, correct?"

She nods, struggling to restrain herself from raking his sallow face with her nails.

"Well then," Cadaver says, rising from the chair with a tip of an imaginary hat. "Let's hope the Sheriff doesn't live to see another sunset." He turns and walks toward the door. "Or you'll be watching a million of them from behind these windows."

～

I'm winded, and not altogether sure what I'm seeing is actually happening. Could be I'm dreaming it all. Since finding Kyle strung up in Hill's house, everything seems just the slightest bit off kilter. When I move my eyes, the world takes its time following.

But the sound, the earth-shattering explosion as steel meets flesh meets steel is enough to let me know there can be no mistaking this as reality. I saw Hendricks as the car approached, hunched over the wheel, shoulders raised as if he was manning a jackhammer. He was talking to himself, the sun making the tears in his eyes sparkle, face contorted in agony, the roots of which I'll never know. Maybe it was simply the knowledge that he was about to kill someone.

And that look stayed on his face until Wintry let out a roar, fists held at his sides, and rushed forward like a bull, head and shoulders ramming into the car as if he hoped to stop it. I swear he almost did. The car seemed to stagger a little. There was smoke from the wheels, a horrible sharp screech before the car slammed into the wounded giant, crushing him against the front of my truck, his upper body snapping back like a jack-in-the-box. Blood flew. Flesh was torn away. But that wasn't the end of it. The speed and the interruption Wintry presented to its passage didn't stop the car. It's front wheels reared up as if it was going to simply drive on over my truck. It didn't make it. Gravity intervened. Hendricks' car stalled and rolled back down on all four tires, the Buick bouncing on its chassis, but in doing so, crushed whatever was left of the big man beneath it.

The impact was so severe, I expected to see it had ejected the doctor from his car, but though the windshield was obliterated, he's still in the driver seat, though what's sitting there isn't recognizable as anything human.

Can I call this an accident or assume it's the result of another of Cadaver's little bargains? Guess it doesn't matter. The only thing that does is lying three feet away from me, spread-eagled, head cocked at an unnatural angle.

I have to leave here, but my truck isn't going to move. There's steam gushing out from beneath the crumpled hood and oil pissing from beneath it. It's done, as is Hendricks' Buick, so I guess I'm walking, unless someone comes along who doesn't feel compelled to use their car as a weapon. And in Milestone, at least over the past few hours, such people are rare.

I stand up, check on Kyle to make sure he's as comfortable as he needs to be, that he's not just lying there like a buck waiting to be skinned, then I look at the road, at the twisted metal, the blood, the chaos.

Wintry's gone, and though I know I should mourn him, I reckon he's exactly where he wanted to be. At least his suffering's over.

I step out onto the asphalt.

Though my truck's a wreck, the front end doesn't look all that bad.

There's a slim chance the stereo still works.

⟋⟍

Blue smoke, sad eyes. The smell of fresh blood and motor oil.

"Did you know?" I ask her.

"Yes."

"Why didn't you tell me?"

"I tried. You wouldn't listen."

Silence but for a faint dripping from somewhere behind me. Then, somewhere in the trees behind Kyle, a catbird does its impression of a hungry infant. I look toward the sound and see a flicker of dark gray, then nothing but green trapping the sunlight.

"What I'm going to do…will it be enough?"

"I can't tell you that."

"Can't or won't."

"Can't. And even if I could, I wouldn't."

"Why?"

"Knowin' what lies ahead can't change you, or make anythin' better no more than dwellin' on the past will. You've always done what your gut's told you to. You've never been a great listener to the voice of your heart, not because you're a bad man, but because you're not wired that way. It doesn't speak to you in words you understand, and that's just how it is."

I respond with a soft, bitter laugh. "So I can blame this *voice* for driving my son to kill himself? Jesus, that's a relief."

"Would Kyle have been happy if he'd sold you out, and got out of Milestone? Would you, in his shoes? Neither of us can see what would have become of him. He wanted out; he got it. He listened to the voice of *his* heart and it showed him the way."

"And what is my voice telling me to do now? Can you hear it?"

"No. But it doesn't matter if I tell you it's the wrong or right way, you won't listen. All that's left is to see this through."

"Hey," I say, clearing my throat and scratching at my scalp—my way of letting her know I can't discuss this anymore.

"I know."

I wave away her mind reading and scowl. "Well for Chrissakes just let me say it anyway."

"You don't know how."

"Then can I say I love you?"

The smoke curls into a smile. "Yes."

"Will you buy it if I do?"

"Maybe."

"I love you."

"What about Iris?"

"Don't start."

"Get goin' Tom. Do what needs to be done."

"Wait." I haven't turned off the radio, haven't told her to leave me alone, but when I search for her face, she's gone, curlicues of blue smoke drifting on the breeze from the open car door. I watch it fade until only the memory of her is left, and the sad fact that when I told her I loved her, she didn't respond in kind.

~

The sun's high in the sky and glaring like the eye of a dragon by the time someone comes. We haven't moved, Kyle and me. We're still just sitting, and catching up on old times, though of course I'm doing all the talking, and I figure I must have been staring right back at that big old sun because there are white orbs wherever I look, even when I shut my eyes.

This car is a familiar one. It's going too slow to present much of a threat, but in this town, who knows? There are no miracles in Milestone. Plenty of murderers, though.

The car stops a few feet away, and it's a woman that gets out.

"Tom?"

"Iris." I'm glad to see her, but I'm guessing she won't know that by the look on my face, so maybe I'd better tell her. "Guess your magical power of screwing up electricity doesn't extend to car batteries, huh?"

"Or telephones, or hairdryers. What happened?" She's blocking the light now, her shadow cool and welcome across my sunburned face. It gives her a red halo.

I fill her in on the details, laughing my way through some of it, blubbering my way through more, and listening to the rest as if it isn't coming from my mouth at all.

In the end it comes down to a litany of who's dead, an out-loud reading of tomorrow's obituaries. Iris is quiet through it all, and if she's upset as I reckon she should be seeing Kyle lying here lifeless at the side of the road, I can't hear it in her voice.

"C'mon," she says. "We gotta get you home."

"I'm not going home."

"Where then?"

"Your place. Just for a little while. I need to rest."

I expect her to ask questions, and there are certainly plenty of them, but we both know my son's body's got to be loaded into her car, so we say nothing more until the job is done and we're on our way back to town.

"What are you goin' to do?" she asks me, her voice laced with concern.

My eyes are closed; exhaustion's taking me away from all this to a cool dark place where there's only me, no one else, no angels with red hair or devils with no eyes. Just me. But I have energy enough to satisfy her curiosity as Cadaver satisfied mine, even though the dark wings of sleep have wrapped themselves around me and are already spiriting me away.

"Kill Gracie."

18

Brody closes his eyes. His jaw aches something terrible, and he suspects his nose is broken. His breath whistles through the coagulating blood. Still, all things considered he reckons he could be a lot worse off. He's still free, after all. There aren't any sirens sundering the air, no thundering cavalcade he could never outrun on foot. The maddening chorus of birdsong drills into his eardrums and he kicks at the high grass, roars at the source of the noise, but that only makes his head hurt more, so he shuts them out, massages his jaw, and keeps walking. He's heading out of town, tired, and sore, and on foot, but sooner or later a goddamn car has to pass this way and give him a ride.

He wipes his sleeve across his nose, winces and grunts with pain.

"Goddamn sonofabitch." The guy got him good, there's no denying that. In his haste to be away from the whatever-the-hell-it-was that came crawling out of the Sheriff's car radio, he hadn't thought of the big black guy, hadn't considered that there might still be enough strength left in him to get in his way. But there was, and he did, and the fist Brody ran into was like a brick wall.

Worse than being knocked out by a burned-up giant he hadn't had the sense to look out for though, is the fact that they tricked him. The Sheriff should be dead and Brody three states away by now, but the Sheriff knew what he was doing when he turned on that stereo, and all Wintry had to do was step up to the plate. Now they're gone, and though he knows where to find them, and vengeance demands he do that very thing, he's letting it go. There isn't time; he's wasted enough of that on these hicks.

He needs a car, and fast, and it's only when he stops looking over his shoulder at the quiet road a mile and a half later that he realizes he's been looking in the wrong place. To his right, through the trees surrounding a narrow overgrown path, is a small quaint little cabin. Smoke drifts from the chimney. There's some kind of a wooden figure standing on the rickety looking porch, and what might be a totem in the small overgrown yard.

Parked out front is a beat-up old Dodge.

Well I'll be damned.

Brody smiles and steps off the road onto the path.

～

The cabin is painted gray with crimson shutters. Dreamcatchers and wind chimes dangle from the eaves, tinkling away like tin-eared men trying to play a tune. A six-foot cigar store Indian either presides over the porch, complete with headdress, war paint, and battle scars. He's stationed right next to the small bungalow's warped and scarred front door, sharp-boned face upraised, ocean blue eyes staring reverently upward. There's a quiver of arrows on his back, a bow slung over one shoulder, and a curved wooden blade strapped to one muscular thigh.

Brody stoops to pick up a dusty rock, half-expecting to find a door key hidden underneath, but is disappointed. Nothing but a few earwigs and earthworms, and after a second, even those are gone. He sighs, but keeps the rock in his hand, nods at the chief respectfully as he mounts the creaky porch steps. *Now there's a guy who'd have taken no shit from cowboys*, he thinks as he raps a knuckle on the door. Immediately there comes a shuffling sound from inside the house. "Who's that?"

"Yeah, hi," Brody says, in as cheerful a tone as he can summon out of his aching head. "My car broke down a ways down the road there. I was wondering if maybe you had some jumper cables or something."

"I ain't got nothin' like that. Be on your way."

"Well, how about a phone so I can call someone?"

A dry chuckle. "You know where you *are*, boy?"

Brody groans silently. This is all he needs. Of course the option to just jump the car is still available to him, but if it turns out there's a real life Geronimo behind that door, he'd rather not end up with a couple of arrows in his back. Better to just make sure the guy's incapacitated one way or another.

"I need a ride is all. Doesn't seem to be much traffic out here this time of the day. Thought folks would be coming home from work at least."

"There's no work in Milestone, boy, least not the kind you'd understand."

"That so? Well, if you could help me out—"

"I know who you are."

Brody stops, sentence unfinished, and straightens. "That so?"

"Yep."

"Well I don't see how you'd know."

"I heard."

Brody puts his hands to the sides of his head, massages his temple. *Jesus on a cornstalk.* This is all he needs. Obviously the guy is watching him through a peephole or something, though Brody doesn't see one, and has recognized him. Could be his mug shot is showing on the guy's TV right at this moment, or on the front page of a newspaper spread across the kitchen table. But just as he's about to concede defeat, the guy mumbles something that gives Brody pause. "What did you say?"

Clearer: "I said the wind told me about you."

"The wind?" Brody rolls his eyes. Another loon. "And what did the wind say?"

"Said not to trust you. Said you murdered some folks, one of 'em a drifter who looked like Dean Martin, your girl's favorite singer. Said you tried to kill the Sheriff when he was just tryin' to get to his son. That sound about right?"

Brody grits his teeth. "Wow, that's quite a wind. Better than the main evening news."

"You best get out of here now. I have nothin' you need."

Brody glances over his shoulder. The Dodge is a rustbucket, but the tires aren't flat and he can see through the dirty window a set of keys in the ignition. With a smile he turns back to the door. "I need your car."

"Take it."

Brody stares at the door for a moment. Then: "Take it? Just like that?"

"Sure. I ain't got no use for it anymore."

"Why's that? You a cripple or something?"

"Nope. I just don't leave the house."

Brody smirks, already starting to feel better about things, even if his head still hurts like hell. "Town like this, can't say I blame you." Eager to be gone, he slaps a palm on the door. "Much obliged to you for the car. Can't say as it's ever likely you're going to see it again."

"Don't expect to."

"Right. You take care now."

Grinning, Brody turns, but halts so abruptly on the top step he almost falls. "The fuck?"

From behind him, the old man's panicked voice: "What is it? What do you see?"

Brody opens his mouth, but quickly closes it again, smiles uncertainly. "It's nothing," he says.

But it isn't.

No birds are singing, and the breeze has died.

There's no sound at all, even from the hundreds of deer that have somehow gathered in the old man's yard and are now standing motionless, heads lowered slightly, their dark eyes fixed on the house.

On Brody.

"It's nothing," he says again. "Just a bunch of dumb old deer."

"I'm afraid," the old man whispers. "They're a little more than that."

~

It's time to go. I've only slept a few hours, but it'll do. Iris's hand is cool against my bare chest, and though we're both naked and in her bed, we've done nothing except lie together. I didn't ask for anything more, and she didn't offer, and that sits just fine with me. It's not why I came here.

The breeze through the window has the candles snapping at shadows. In the kitchen a sink is dripping water with the sound of a clock ticking in an empty room.

I take a moment to breathe in the scent of her, of this woman I hardly know and likely never will, then I carefully remove her hand from my chest and set it down next to her. Despite my efforts to make as little noise as I can getting out of bed, I'm heavy enough to make the springs squeal and when I stand and look back at her, her eyes are open, and clear, as if she hasn't been sleeping at all.

"Leavin'?"

I nod.

"What's your hurry?"

"I have to get going. Have to 'tie up some loose ends' as they say in the cop shows." I'm trying to sound casual, like the darkness locked inside me isn't trying to eat its way out, but she's not fooled. She props her head up with the palm of her hand, her elbow digging into the mattress.

"What kinda loose ends?"

I avoid answering by pretending my clothes are proving tough to locate, even though they're laid out right here at my feet.

"Tom?"

It isn't until I have my underwear and pants on that I answer her. She's looking impatient, worried, ready to reach for something to threaten the information out of me.

"I'm turning over my badge tonight," I say.

"Why?"

"Because it's the way it's supposed to go."

"That sounds like a crock of shit."

I smile at her and sit back down on the bed. "Does, doesn't it?"

She scoots close, drapes her arms over my shoulders, rests her head against my back. "If you're plannin' some kind of heroic exit, that's one thing, but if you're figurin' to walk out of here without tellin' me why, you'll be doin' it without your balls."

"Nice."

This is a tough one, and I'm not sure how much I can say, how much I'm *allowed* to say, so I guess it's best to just keep it simple and hope she understands. "I'm done with this town, Iris, and it's more than done with me. I should've handed over the reins years ago to someone who might have done something more than stand around watching people die. Can't do it anymore."

"Then don't, but that don't mean you have to leave."

"I'm afraid it does."

Her grip tightens on my shoulders. "Then let me come with you."

"I would if I could."

"Why can't you?"

"Because you wouldn't much like where I'm going." I bring my hand up to hers, squeeze it tight.

"What if I don't let you leave? What if I keep you prisoner? I could do it you know."

"I don't doubt it."

She pulls her hand free, withdraws her arms and sits up. "What's going to happen?"

"Something good," I tell her. "And something bad."

She says nothing else, just watches as I get dressed. She doesn't cry, won't cry, but I can tell she wants to.

When I'm ready to go, I carefully pick my way through the candles until I'm at the door. There's no mad rush from Iris, no sobbing farewell. She just sits there, knees drawn up, hand on her chin, studying me.

With my fingers on the door handle, I give one last look at her. "You know just because you can't leave with me, doesn't mean you can't leave."

"I know."

"Big world out there. Could be a better place for you in it. Never know."

"Never know," she echoes, and scoots down under the sheets.

"Wish I'd had more time to get to know you."

"You had plenty of time, Tom. We've lived a stone's throw from each other for a long time."

"True. Guess I was busy."

"Guess you were. And blind."

I can't argue with that, so I don't, but when I start to open the door, she starts talking again.

"I've never loved anyone, Tom, and I'm not goin' to say I love you, because I don't. But I know people, and I know you better than you think."

"Yeah, seems everyone but me does."

"Your wife loved you though. No doubt about that."

"Hope so."

"I saw it in her eyes every time she looked at me. 'Course, we weren't friends or nothin' but you can tell a lot by the way someone looks at you. She was wonderin' if you'd ever spent time with me, or if you wanted to, if maybe when you were in bed you were thinkin' about me, and every time I saw that look, I shook my head, and she'd smile just a little bit. The kind of smile someone gives you when they've accepted a whore's wisdom but don't want them to know it."

Our eyes meet and something powerful passes between us, maybe it's some of that same power she has that knocks lights out. Maybe it's trying to quench my soul before I do more damage.

"You should go" I tell her. "Get the hell out of Milestone. Find some place where the people are still alive."

"I'm still alive, Tom. And with all the things I got stuck in here," she says, tapping a finger against her forehead, "it don't matter where I go. They'll follow. So I might as well stay right here. Same as it don't matter where you're headin'. You'll still be the same man tryin' to run away from his shadow in a place where the sun never stops shinin'."

"Iris…"

"Now you best get on if you're goin'."

"Take care."

"Take care yourself."

She turns away from me, and I guess that's my cue to leave, so I do. Three steps from the bottom of the stairs, I hear her sobbing.

❧

Cadaver dreams of two young boys, one blond, the other raven-haired, sitting in vibrant green grass, the sun warming their legs as they play with toy soldiers, which are scattered around them in the frenzied order unique to combat. The blond boy giggles as his plastic tank appears from nowhere and mows down his brother's army. The raven-haired child swats him, hurt and frustration on his face.

This particular war is defused in an instant by the soft calming voice of the woman sitting in a lawn chair a few feet away, a magazine spread open, obscuring her face. "No fighting," she says, "Or you can go right back in the house and help your father clean out the attic."

The boys are quiet, sulking, but once the raven-haired child locates a soldier the tank missed in its calamitous charge, a victorious smile crosses his face as he guns down his brother's ranks. They are caught unaware and fall accordingly. The blond boy shrieks, and calls in reinforcements. The battle is on.

The woman in the lawn chair sighs, but it is a 'boys will be boys' sigh, and not at all annoyed.

In this summer-lit yard, life is good.

Cadaver awakes, and he is smiling too.

He is sitting on a smooth flat limestone rock at the bottom of the hill, head bowed, and though his eyes are gone, the cool breeze invigorates him, reminds him of all he has lost and all he will soon gain.

Minutes pass. Night sounds carry on waves to his ears. He waits, ragged breaths whistling through the rent in his throat above the box that gives him his words.

It grows dark.

And then, ice crawls through his veins, chilling him from the inside out. As anticipated, there is pain, for he is aware that he cannot be released from his duties without being reminded of the suffering that has been his stock-in-trade. These are secondhand agonies, all of them hard earned, all of them real. He grunts. Something touches the back of his hand, then again. The breeze seems to be blowing through him now and he relishes the feel of it.

"Soon," he says and the smile cracks his face. Teeth drop into his lap, tumble and hit the floor with a sound like pebbles. The flesh begins to slide. The box in his throat starts to rust, disintegrate.

"Soon," he says, one last time, his hair shedding and tickling what remains of his face as it falls.

Flesh withers; organs shrivel. Bones begin to crumble.

Cadaver sighs.

In his mind, the woman in the lawn chair is peering at him above her magazine. He can tell by the wrinkles around her eyes that she is smiling—*Boys will be boys*—and when next the breeze blows, there is only an old raincoat full of dust for it to attend to.

19

"If you're plannin' on goin', now'd be the time, boy."

The animals have filled the yard now, necks straight, eyes glittering, but still they make no noise. It's as if they're waiting for something.

The sight of them standing there motionless, ears pricked up, is unsettling, but Brody knows better than to be threatened by so docile an animal, no matter how many of them there are. Hell, for all he knows the old man's got a vegetable patch out back and they're here to raid it. The only threat they could possibly present is if they stampeded and rushed him, but even then the car's much closer to him than they are.

"*Move* for Chrissakes," hisses the old man.

"Because of a bunch of deer? Man, take it easy." But as the words leave his mouth, the calm he has forced into them sounds utterly false.

"To *you*, maybe, but right now you're blockin' Red Cloud's shot."

"Shit." Instinctively Brody ducks, arms covering his head, and swivels on a heel to see where the hidden shooter is. He scans the house, then the yard, and it is here his gaze halts. The blood drains from his face. Somehow, the deer are closer now, almost level with the Dodge, and one of them has mounted the hood like some unfunny parody of a hunter's prize. It stares at him with black eyes, head cocked a little to the left, thick antlers like a bleached tree branch reaching for the stars.

Brody feels the air change, a sensation he is accustomed to only when he is presenting the threat. But to feel it now means there is a very real danger here, and that mystifies him, until he recounts the events of the past few hours and realizes that nothing should, or ever will, surprise him again.

This belief continues for a few moments more, until the deer on the hood of the car begins to speak. "*Come out Blue Moon.*" The voice is a croaking whisper much like Cadaver's, but stronger, and its lips don't move. Nevertheless, despite how insane it makes him suspect he might be after what he's gone through, Brody has never been more sure of anything in his life.

The *fucking deer* is talking.

Behind him, there's a sound like a stick swishing through air and then a thump and clatter as the deer on the Dodge tries to keep its balance, then crumples and rolls, hooves beating a tattoo against the metal. Blood smears the hood, and now the creature is making all-too-normal animal-in-pain sounds, which surprises Brody, who almost expected to hear it scream in a human voice. The deer hits the ground, still moving, and Brody can see there's a long stick protruding from the side of its neck. An arrow.

"Stay down, boy."

Brody does, but looks over his shoulder.

The formerly inanimate cigar store Indian pays him no mind as it thumbs another arrow into its bow and draws back the string.

Brody breathes disbelief, and pushes himself away until he collides painfully with the porch railing. "No way in *Hell.*"

The whispering has spread, pouring from the unopened mouths of the deer herd like a breeze through the canopies of leaves overhanging them. More sharp reports as hooves meet metal and Brody is forced to resign himself to the incredible reality of the situation: In the yard, there are talking deer. *Pissed off* talking deer, and all that's keeping them at bay, for the moment at least, is a wooden Indian whose every move is accompanied by a creak as flakes of dead wood fall like dandruff from his shoulders.

"*Jesus.*"

"Just stay d—"

"Yeah, I *heard* for Chrissakes. What the hell is happening here?"

The Indian lets his arrow fly. It hits home; another deer stumbles and falls.

"The short version: Long time ago my father and his friend made a mistake that got a lot of their tribe killed," Blue Moon tells him from behind the door. "They stole somethin' precious from a rival tribe. A statue of a deer, made from obsidian and wood, supposed to contain the spirits of every animal the tribe had killed. When caught, they put a curse on Red Cloud. They turned him to wood. My father escaped his bonds and stole a horse. They never caught him. Days later, the rival tribe attacked my father's people, massacrin' them for the theft of a sacred statue."

Brody's eyes drift to the wooden Indian. Grim-faced, time-roughened joints creaking, the creature loads another arrow.

"My father spent the rest of his life runnin' from his tribe in their various guises: coyote, hawk, cougar…deer. When he died, the curse was passed on to me. They're punishin' me for his crimes. And they'll punish you if you get in their way."

Brody looks over his shoulder. Incensed, the herd pours over the Dodge on a wave of frantic whispers. The sound of them now is deafening. He scrambles away from the railing, puts his back to the door, wishes he had his knife, or better yet, his gun. He has never felt so vulnerable, and in truth, afraid, as he is at this moment. Sweat trickles into his eyes; he blinks it away. But, *Death by deer*, he thinks, and splutters a laugh. No one will ever believe it. He elbows the door." Let me in, man."

"I can't."

"Then toss me out a weapon or something. *Anything.*"

"You don't need one. In protectin' me, Red Cloud will protect you too."

Helpless to do anything but watch, Brody draws his knees up as the deer that have made it onto the Dodge leap toward the house only to be struck down in mid air by the arrows from the wooden Indian's bow. Red Cloud's feet haven't moved from his small rectangular pedestal; only his arms look alive. They reload the bow, faster and faster, until they become a blur, and above them, the Indian's painted eyes are narrowed, mouth down-turned in a grimace. The wooden points of the arrows cleave the air, thudding into the hides of the seemingly endless ranks. As they fall, the deer turn to clouds of dust, which in turn swirl upward as if caught in a vortex. And in those miniature twisters, there are screaming faces.

Time draws out, and Brody is desperately aware of every second that's lost to him. Any moment now he expects to hear sirens, drowning out the screams of the dying deer. *Should have kept walking. Nothing but bad luck in this goddamn town. Should have just kept on walking.* He imagines the faces on the cops as they jump from their cruisers, pistols trained on him, ready to bring him down, only to find themselves watching a wooden Indian pegging a bunch of homicidal deer.

"Every day it's the same," Blue Moon says wistfully. "And will be until they force me to take my own life, or step outside to meet them, whichever happens first."

"Then why not make a deal with the old man? The guy who makes the deals."

"Because I have no interest in the kind of peace he has to offer."

More arrows tear flying deer from the air, their bodies thumping down hard on the car, making it rock on its wheels, denting the hood, the roof, decorating the pale blue metal with dark blood. Brody watches, mesmerized, until the death of the animals begins to feel monotonous, a tiresome display of a hunter's brawn. He's even starting to feel a bit sorry for those poor bastards. He stands, brushes splinters and dirt from his already ruined suit. "I'm leavin'. I have to. Pissed away too much time already in this freakshow of a town."

"Better wait, boy. Won't be safe till they're gone."

Brody puts his hands on his hips, glances at Red Cloud, who ignores him. "Tell me something, Blue. If you've got your goombah here with his endless supply of arrows, why can't you come out, at least as far as the porch? That tribe of yours don't seem to be bothering me none. Not up here."

To Brody, it's a short forever before he gets an answer, and when it comes, it is in the form of a door easing open and not a voice. Brody peers at the widening crack between door and jamb. It is dark inside. Low to the ground, as if Blue Moon's been sitting on the floor all this time, the old man's hand emerges from around the door. In it is held an old-fashioned revolver, which he sets on the porch. Then the hand withdraws and the door is quickly shut.

Brody stands there, staring at the grooves in the door, at the memory of what he thinks he has just seen.

"Take it. It's loaded."

Brody nods, but doesn't reply. Instead, he stoops, collects the gun and checks to see if the old man is pulling a fast one on him. It's an old Colt, but it's fully loaded and looks serviceable. "Why are you helping me if you know so much about what I've done?" he asks at last.

"Because I'm no judge, boy, and I'm certainly no better. I know there are always two roads, but the right one ain't always necessarily the good one. I've traveled both, and I still can't tell 'em apart."

"All right then," Brody says, feeling dazed as he slips the gun into his waistband and slowly descends the porch steps. Arrows cut the air over his shoulder, but he doesn't flinch. Deer rain down on the Dodge, smack hard against the ground, kick and protest imminent death. The gun is cold against his belly, as cold as he imagines the old man's hand was. *They stole something precious from a rival tribe. A statue of a deer, made from obsidian and wood.*

Obsidian and wood.

He wonders how many nights his sleep will be plagued by what he has seen in this town, how often he'll be dragged out of his dreams by the wooden Indian, the tribe, and the old man's hand. He stops short of the car and ducks low as a deer launches itself up over the hood, watches it jerk back at the behest of Red Cloud's arrow and drop heavily. Blood speckles his cheek. Antlers scratch the bottom of the driver-side door. The dust devils spin away, elongated faces within twisting in torment, and then disappear. The passenger side door is facing him, so this is where he's heading. He expects it to be locked; another trick, another inconvenience, but it isn't and swings open with a labored groan. There are cobwebs on the steering wheel, beer cans and used condoms on the floor. A pine tree freshener spins lazily from the rearview mirror but the interior smells of rotten meat. He's inside, hand on the keys when another deer, eyes wide in fury or panic, Brody can't tell which, and doesn't much care, rams the side of the car, its head colliding with the glass on the driver side, inches away from Brody. It cracks, but doesn't shatter.

With shaking hands, he turns the keys. The engine whines, then catches and roars into life. He yanks back the gearshift. The grinding noise is not encouraging, but then the car bucks once and heaves backward, throwing up dirt that sprays across the porch, where an old wooden Indian is tirelessly defending an old man made of black glass.

He shakes his head, looks back to the path. The deer are crowded there, watching him, blocking his way.

"To hell with this," Brody mumbles and jams his foot down on the accelerator.

20

The pain begins at sundown.

I'm walking, not even a half a mile clear of Winter Street when my guts turn to liquid fire. A gasp and I'm doubled over; another, and I'm on my knees, my shoulder against the graffiti-riddled wall of the long-abandoned Brautigan's Drugstore, my hand splayed on the concrete before me. My vision begins to blur, then it paints everything red, as if I'm wearing crimson shades, or there's blood in my eyes.

Another wave of pain and then I realize the first few rounds were nothing. Nothing compared to the incredible torture that comes with the sensation of my bones narrowing, shifting, bending, poking at the skin in an attempt to reshape me. My muscles protest as they're played like cello strings. My nerves sing in torment, jarring the thoughts from my head. It's as if I've been bound in barbed wire and someone is tightening it, ever so slowly.

I fall forward, both hands flat on the ground. Dark blood leaks from my mouth. In my peripheral vision, I see my arms shrink, grow thin. My gut no longer strains against my belt. It's a deflating balloon.

I throw up and can't face the gruesome sight of what's emerged.

Jesus Christ, I'm dying, is all I can think, because surely this is what death feels like.

My hair falls out; my vision fades.

My throat is burning, but a hand raised to massage it meets cold hard metal. My nails *scritch* against it, then they too fall out.

I scream, or at least try to, but the power of that anguished scream is somehow diminished, robbed of its power by the metal box in my throat, and so emerges as little more than a forced whisper.

I'm afraid, petrified, and shouldn't be because I asked for this. This is the bargain. This is what Cadaver wanted, what I wanted, and now I'm getting it. He's out; I'm in, *let's call the whole thing off!* my thoughts chant cheerfully, and its almost enough to draw a smile from me, but the agony scrubs that notion away in record time.

I glance to my left as tears roll down my sallow cheeks, into the soaped-over plate glass window of Brautigan's Drugstore.

Cadaver is a pale ghost, on his knees, sobbing.

I weep for us both.

Abruptly, the pain in my head that seems intent on cracking it open subsides, and I'm flooded by memories and knowledge not my own. It's almost as bad as the pain. Such an alien feeling, it's as if my brain has become a theater, open to players I've never met. I bring my hands up and clamp them to the sides of my skull in an effort to contain them. When I close my eyes, I see myself as a bird, soaring high above the town, cocking my head occasionally to listen to the pleas that drift in dreams through the roofs of sagging houses. Where I land, is up to me. There is no shortage of time, no quota on the amount of promises I can make, or lives I can alter. Everyone can have whatever they desire most, if they are willing to offer me something in return. It is then I know, as the bird swoops down toward the tavern on the hill that was once burned but is burned no more, that all of us have been, and will continue to be, slaves, not to God or the Devil, but to ourselves, to our innate need to make things right, to attain what our lives tell us we cannot have, and do not deserve. Cadaver—*I*—am a mechanic in the clockwork of man, but I am nothing without the cogs that make it run. But no…I am not Cadaver, not entirely. I am still here, still stumbling around inside. My old self claws at the walls, looking for the exit, just like always.

At last I go numb, pinprick specks of light making my sagging skin glow from the inside, and when finally I trust my legs to lift me, I stand, and let myself lean against the drugstore window.

This is what I wanted, I have to remind myself from the depths of this alien skin. *This is what had to happen. It was the only way.* Every time I blink, I'm somewhere else. Flying, soaring, spying at lovers who have plans to kill each other, gazing into the eyes of elderly folk who have all but given up but would jump at the chance to escape, detecting the scent of long buried bodies in long forgotten plots, reading the minds of the lovelorn, the desperate, the lost. Every house in Milestone is a vault of secrets, but it didn't take for this change for me to know that.

Now behind my closed eyes I'm standing atop a rotten post by a deserted parking lot, peering at the reflection of a raven, and beyond that, at the willowy woman in the gray dress who's praying for my death as she scrubs another man's blood from the floor.

⚬

He awakes in a bathtub, raises his head, and winces in pain. He has been sleeping. This much he knows, but it is all that he knows. His neck hurts from the awkward way he's been lying. Cold water from the showerhead drip-drip-drips down the back of his neck, making him shiver. His joints ache; there's a taste in his mouth that repulses him, makes him want to gag. It's as if he's been sucking on road kill. With no little effort, he manages to sit up, tries to look around and yelps as a bolt of pain shoots from the back of his head down to the base of his spine. "Jesus…" he moans, and reaches a hand back to try and negotiate his comfort with whatever muscle is holding it hostage. As he does so, he jerks his neck a little, the hand bracing the tendons and muscles there should they decide to unravel, and notices the faded flowers on the wall. *Tulips*, he thinks, and remembers the crude joke about them that he composed but never remembered to share with Iris. It doesn't seem funny now, only cruel. He starts to shake his head and flinches as once again pain reminds him he has not yet been cleared for such a move. He moves his hand to his throat, gingerly probes the flesh there. It's raw, tender. It hurts, and the feel of it combined with his discomfort starts to lead him ever so slowly back to the memory of what happened to him.

"I was—" He's not sure where the rest of the thought goes, or what it's supposed to make him see, but now his nostrils are filled with the scent of oil. The creaking of a strained rope resonates in his head and his eyes widen. "I was—"

"Dead."

He turns too quickly and cries out as the muscles contract protectively around a not yet healed break.

"You were dead," Iris says, from the doorway. "And now you ain't."

Her voice is cold, which seems to suit the situation, though he has never heard it from her before.

"What happened?"

"Your daddy saved you. Now get up and get yourself together."

"I can't…I'm—"

"The only law we have around here now." She tosses something at him. It glances off the side of the tub and tumbles into his lap. He recognizes the chipped and grimy gold star as his father's. "And you got work to do."

The sun is down.

On a post in the parking lot at Eddie's, opposite one of the formerly broken windows, stands a raven. He caws and bobs his head at my approach, but I don't know whether the greeting or warning is meant for me, its own reflection in the smoked glass, or if the bird is a familiar of the woman inside. It makes little difference, I suppose.

I open the door and step inside.

The smell of soot and smoke rushes to greet me like the extension of a ghost that can't wait for me to join it. The room looks smaller than it ever has before.

Gracie is on her knees, both hands clamped around a sponge soaked rusty brown by the blood that has gathered in a wide ragged circle beneath a toppled stool.

"Vess," I say, and she looks up. Her face is wan, and sweaty, her eyes narrowed as she tries to focus on my shadowy form. Cadaver, and people like him, like me, I have found, are not friends of the light.

"Come to gloat?" she asks, returning to her labors.

I let the door swing shut behind me. "There'd be little sense in that." I suppress a shudder. It horrifies me every time I speak to hear that grated hollow whisper, though I am not dependant on that ugly little microphone for volume. Eventually, perhaps, but not yet. "It would be as pointless as cleaning up the blood of a man to hide it from me when I'm standing right in front of you." The voice is my own, of that I am sure, but the throat through which it has to pass certainly is not.

Gracie's scrubbing slows, her hair obscuring her face. I am struck by the desire to brush it out of her face, a lingering impulse from not-so-better times, but that brief surge of need is enough to confirm what I already know. I am still here. I am still *me*. Somewhere.

At length, she ceases her cleaning altogether and raises her face, tilts her head a little. Sniffs the air. "How did this happen? What did you do?"

"Fate is a fickle thing," I tell her. "Which is why we are told to never put our faith in it, never to rely or depend on the chips falling where we want them to. It doesn't work that way, and only a very desperate woman would try it."

She smiles, sits back on her haunches, brushes the damp hair from her brow. Her eyes are like beetles nestling in bleached wood. "So you know then?"

"I didn't, until the change. Until I was allowed to know."

"That old bastard," she sneers suddenly, rising to her feet. "He cheated me."

"You're hardly in a position to cry foul." I step further into the room. The light from the hurricane lamp on the bar flutters. Shadows writhe.

"Fuck you."

"Was a time," I start to say and grin.

She stares at me for a long moment, her breasts rising and falling rapidly beneath her sweat and bloodstained dress, and slowly, slowly, a smile begins to crawl across her face. "But you're him now, aren't you?"

she says. "You're not just a pig-fucking Sheriff stuck in a rotten vessel. You're *him*, which means you can do for me what he wouldn't. What he was *supposed* to do."

"Tell me why I should do anything for you."

"Why else are you here? You know who I am and you want rid of me. I understand that, and I even promise not to hold it against you. We can consider the old contract null and void and start anew, what do you say? You give me what I want, and I'll give you what *you* want." She lets the fingers on one hand trail over her breast. An unconvincing look of lasciviousness crosses her face. "What do you say? I remember how you used to look at me, how you studied me."

"Does life mean that little to you?" I ask her, ignoring the proposition. "That you'd sell so much of it for your own gain?"

"Spare me." Contempt overwhelms her face. "Why should I be condemned to stay here because of a mistake, because of one small error I made tryin' to escape that rapin' bastard? Should I have shut my mouth and done nothin'?"

"You killed Gracie. You killed an innocent woman. Sacrificed her to get out."

"I did her a favor." The mention of her crime is apparently sufficient motive for her to drop the act, and so she does, even as the words continue to come. Her hair ripples, shortens, darkens. "She was miserable, just as much Eddie's prisoner as I was. She hated me, and I her. She'd never have trusted me if I told her I'd take her from here, and she'd have been right." Her skin turns stark white, cheekbones pressing against the skin as it tightens to suit the rounder shape of her face. "I would have taken her home to Toyko and sold her to the men who crave such bargains. But it never came to that. There was never much chance to plan anything." Her accent has changed, become clipped, sharper, the lips forming them leaner. "Eddie made his own mistakes, and often. One of them was to accompany me home to meet my family." She smiles proudly. "My family did not take to him. They put on quite a show for my American husband, and when he came home, he was quite mad." Though she's still wearing that drab gray dress, the body inside it has changed. It's thinner, smaller, the breasts mere nubs beneath the material, the arms stick-like.

"Gracie—*you*—said you didn't come home with him."

"Not at first, but neither my family nor I were content to take his mind. They wanted to see him die through my eyes. So a week later, I came back, only something had changed in him, something we hadn't foreseen. Whatever magic we'd done to his mind, it negated *my* magic. I couldn't hurt him, couldn't influence him. I was powerless. He was a raging beast, and he beat and raped me before I could think of a way to stop him. And then he tried to kill me." Lian Su's smile fades. She slowly turns her head to face the window, but her eyes are still on me. "In the moment of death, I left my body, and took the daughter's, trapping her in mine. Too late I realized what I had done. The mark *I had carved* was still on the little bitch's chest, and it was a hex I could not undo from the inside."

"And here you are."

"And here I am."

"While Gracie rots in a freezer on the bank of the Milestone River."

Her smile returns. "She liked the river. And her father took her life. Not me."

"He thought he was killing you."

"I'm hardly to blame for his short-sightedness."

"And what about your family? Why not summon them?"

"Because of what he did to me. His violation was a lot more severe than even he—had he still possessed the faculties required to compose such a thought—even knew. He made me a victim, an unclean one, prone to vengeance of a basic kind: Human violence *without* magic, *without* influence. This is forbidden. I am either a *majo*, or a human, and whichever I choose is the way I must be." Her face wrinkles in disgust. "And I have been forced to play as one of you for long enough."

I approach her, taking my time. "And what if you get what you want. What then?"

"I will leave."

"And go where? It doesn't sound as if you'd be welcome at home."

"Home is a small place. I am not tethered to it. I have survived on my own since I was fourteen. I can do so again."

I walk past her and take a seat at the bar. She follows, a smile on her face that tells me she knows she's going to get exactly what she wants. "One for the road?"

I nod silently.

"You shouldn't look so glum, Sheriff. Is it all right to call you that now that you're…in costume?"

Another nod, but I'm barely listening. What I'm doing as she pours me a tall glass of whiskey, is fingering through someone else's memories, namely my predecessor's seemingly limitless information about everyone in Milestone. It doesn't take me long to summon up Lian Su's callous visage, and in the time it takes her to put the cap back on the bottle after pouring her own drink, I know she's been lying to me again.

"It's a game," I tell her, my fingers moving toward the glass. Old habits die hard, I guess.

I expect her to deny it, though at this stage of our little tête-à-tête, it would be silly. But she doesn't. Instead she takes a long drink, sets her glass down on the bar and raises her hands. "Aren't you the clever one."

I shake my head. "You came here for the specific purpose of ruining this town. Why?"

"Like you said. It was, and still is, a game. When you've had the kind of life I've had, you get bored easily. Trust me. When Eddie came to my land, his talk of this place intrigued me. I had to see it. Had to smell and feel it, and ultimately…"

"Destroy it. And what was Cadaver?"

"A tool, but a powerful one, and I *am* stuck here, I didn't lie about that. I needed him to set me free. Now I need you to do it."

"And if I don't?"

"If you don't, I'll break your son's neck again." She shrugs. "Simple as that."

Of course I'm going to set her free, even without knowing what she'll do once she's no longer tied to this place. Walk outside and raze the town? Take off on her broomstick? It's anyone's guess.

"So tell me," she says, casually, as if we're discussing shoes. "What would you like for your part of the bargain?"

"I want you to leave Milestone."

"I was planning to."

"Well you'll forgive me for not buying that. This way, you won't get what you want unless I get what I want, and what I want is to be rid of you."

She shrugs. "Plenty of other towns. Plenty of livelier places. You have nothing to worry about."

"Good."

"Funny though."

I wait for her continue.

She sighs dramatically. "I would have thought as this town's sworn protector you'd have asked to have your dead friends brought back and to have all the misfortune undone. Above all, I expected you to ask for escape yourself."

I raise my glass in a toast and offer her a sardonic grin. "I *have* escaped."

21

"Why aren't you saying anything?"

Iris is looking out the passenger side window, at the silent houses hurrying past, the deserted streets whizzing by. There should be children playing here, their laughter echoing around the neighborhood. There should be adults standing in the doorways or sitting on the stoops, watching with dreamy eyes the vagaries of a youth they once knew and would kill to know again. There should be smoke from the chimneys, lights in the windows, but there are only houses, and the breeze, and a bruised horizon to suggest the sun has ever visited this town. "There's nothin' to say," she tells Kyle.

"Well…" Kyle, still stiff-necked, but no longer in agony, frowns, struggling to understand how he is here, and why Iris won't talk to him.

"Just drive, ok? We can talk later."

He doesn't respond, knows she doesn't want him to, and that confuses him. He has remembered his meeting with Cadaver, recalls how the confidence he brought with him, its weight similar to the gun in his pocket, fled once he was given the chance to express it before someone who could make it so. Hate persisted, but his determination evaporated as he finally realized the power he held in his hands, the magnitude of what he was planning to do, what he *could* do. In the end, uncertainty stopped him. As Cadaver stood patiently before him, a figure made of dust and shadow, he could not determine whether he was condemning his father to death just so he could get out of Milestone, or because he really believed the old man deserved to die. And that doubt was enough to drain his resolve. Assaulted by memories of life before the hate, he wept and fell to his knees. Cadaver hadn't seem at all surprised, leading Kyle to wonder if he had anything to do with the sudden sequence of sentimental flashbacks. In the end, he hadn't known, but was left alone in the room to mull over the possibilities. He could still sell his father out and get away from Milestone. It wasn't too late, but even as he told himself that, he knew that it was. Once in a man's life is enough to consider betraying his own blood. He could try leaving on his own, a thought that filled him with such inexplicable dread, he quickly dismissed it, and the rational explanation it demanded as to why this was so. The third option was to stay, and die here, and it was as he was imagining this, maybe five or six more decades in a town without life or color, that the fourth and final option began to make itself known.

He could stay and die here now, ending the torment and the confusion, ending a life that seemed frozen in an unhappy moment that might last forever. And it would let his father know that they had both failed each other.

"Faster," Iris tells him, interrupting his thoughts at the perfect time. Any further and they might have claimed him, left him the same gibbering wreck he was when Cadaver impassively handed him the length of rope.

"I'm going as fast as I can. And what the hell is wrong with you anyway?"

"You're what's wrong with me."

"Why?" *Because I'm a dead man walking*, he almost answers for her, to fill the silence where her own response should be. But he swallows his words and concentrates on the road, the lights spearing through the dark. Eddie's, she told him, and that was enough. Without knowing how, and too afraid to attribute it to some sense picked up during his brief walking tour of death, he knows they're supposed to head to Eddie's, and that he will find his father there.

That scares him.

Everyone gets to die. Few get to die and have to answer for it later, at least not to the living.

A twinge of dull pain across his throat makes him lift a hand from the steering wheel. He has already checked for marks and there are none, but the skin there feels stretched and smooth, like a healed burn. He should be dead; he isn't, but something inside him hasn't returned with him. There's a cold empty space where his hate should be, and its absence has left him confused, without identity, as if in dying, he lost the only part of him that knew how to survive, the engine that kept him running.

They pass beneath the dark black rectangle of a set of broken traffic lights, swinging in the strengthening breeze. Beyond it, the street is deathly quiet, a deserted movie set. Vacant, lifeless.

Something dashes out in front of the car. With a hoarse cry of surprise, Kyle jams on the brakes and the car screeches to a halt, smoke from the tires rushing ahead of them, becoming fleeing ghosts in the headlights. But he isn't looking at those ghosts, he's looking at the deer that's standing there, staring in at him, a glimmer in its oily eye.

"Fucking thing," he says, and takes a breath that scratches at his throat. "I didn't even..." He trails off with a shake of his head.

"Look," Iris says, nodding pointedly.

The deer hasn't moved, but beyond it, Kyle sees that it isn't alone. "*Jesus.*" There must be a hundred of them, or more, all of them racing in from the road out of town, stumbling and leaping over each other in their haste. It's an incongruous scene. Deer are not often seen in town unless they're dead, their legs sticking out of the back of some hunter's flatbed. "Looks like they're running from something."

"Or toward somethin'," Iris says.

∽

Brody drives, the night like a dark bubble around the car. He's hunched over the wheel, sweating and waiting, just waiting for *something* to jump out in front of him, maybe a vulture made of razorblades or a clown made of fog, or some other trick the town keeps stashed up its sleeve to torment those desperate to escape it. The car makes clunking noises beneath his feet and there's a barely visible stream of smoke coming from something under the hood, but that's okay, that's all right, he's still moving and that's what counts. A hawk feather suspended from the mirror by a black leather thong flutters toward him, then away, trying to distract him, trying to coax his eyes from the road so he'll crash, maybe end up sinking in a quagmire where the sand sings as it takes you down. This godforsaken place has pushed him about as far as he can go. It's taken his woman and run him through the grinder, and all he wants now is to be gone. Prayers tinged with reluctant promises of reform suggest themselves as a viable way to kill the time until he hits the edge of town, but he's not quite ready for that yet. Him and the Almighty haven't exactly been on speaking terms over the past four years or so, and there's a good reason for that. Brody doesn't like the uncaring sonofabitch, not after losing so many people he loved, and figures if God has any sense, he'll feel the same.

Black tangled trees race past the car in a blur.

Brody blinks sweat from his eyes, wipes a sleeve down his chin where something has tickled him. The interior of the car feels awful small and getting smaller, and a glimpse of his reflection, lit only by the ghoulish green glow from the dash, forces him to keep his eyes on the windshield.

And then…*there*, up ahead, a sign, a big white sign with black letters, and Brody eases his foot off the gas. Hope tenses his muscles. The placard is the only pale sight in a night thick with dark, and as he lets the car coast up to it and stop, a smile splits his face. It reads:

YOU ARE LEAVING MILESTONE! HOPE YOU ENJOYED YOUR STAY!

Underneath, in a childish scrawl, someone has added: IN HELL.

"Amen," Brody says, and closes his eyes, just for a moment, to thank the only thing he truly does believe in: Luck.

It's only when the passenger side door opens with that awful grating shriek and a horribly familiar face pokes in to grin at him that he realizes, not for the first time in his uneven life, that belief is a misguided one.

"No," he moans and begins to hammer his fists on the steering wheel in frustration. "This isn't happening. Goddamn it all, this *isn't* happening!"

The dashboard light makes his passenger's grin a green one as he slides into his seat. A foul smell rolls in with him. "Aw, c'mon now. Don't you go getting yourself all worked up, friend," Dean Martin tells him, eyes wild above sallow skin. "There's nothing wrong here the right number can't fix."

"It's done," I tell her.

"Just like that?"

"Just like that."

She looks doubtful. "Nothing feels different."

"It isn't supposed to. It's still the same jail cell. You won't see the difference until you try to step outside."

She stares hard at me. "If you've tricked me…"

"Then I'll be stuck with you, which wouldn't make much sense, now would it?"

"Oh you'll be stuck with a lot more than that, Sheriff." The hardness doesn't leave her eyes, which stay fixed on mine, as she steps back, slips the straps of her dress down over her narrow shoulders, and lets the drab gray dress fall soundlessly to the floor. Both of us look down. The scar, the angry welts that have kept her here, are gone, and she runs her fingers over the unmarked area, a satisfied smile on her face.

"I know what you thought," she says. "When you saw me do this earlier. When you saw the mark. You had to struggle not to be turned on. You wanted me."

"Seems to me," I reply, "That it's very important to you to believe that. Well, believe what you like as long as you're going."

She looks up, feigns hurt. "Is that any way to talk to a lady?"

"I wouldn't know. I've never been that good at it."

Her fingers glide over her dark erect nipples. "That's too bad. You have no idea what I could—"

"Get going." I have to clasp my hands on the counter to hide their shaking from her. "My part of the bargain is fulfilled. Time to fulfill yours."

"You're no fun at all, Sheriff. It's no wonder everyone hated you."

That's a jab that hurts, and hurts deep, but I do my damndest to make sure she doesn't see it.

"Such a waste. But I guess you're wearing the only costume now that suits you, and that's really all it comes down to, wouldn't you agree?" She gives me a bow, and spits on the dress lying at her feet. "But it will get old," she remarks, with a wink, and slowly makes her way around the bar, moves up close to me. There's a peculiar smell from her, not entirely unpleasant, but strange and offensive all the same. Her pale hand alights on my arm. I repress a shudder. There is no appeal here; her nakedness does nothing but repulse me, and even if it didn't, all I can think of is all she's done, all she's made come to pass in this town, even as I was bumbling around pretending I knew how to protect it.

Lian's right breast brushes against my sleeve. Her fingers find my hair. "I should really kill you," she says in a low voice. "What would what's left of the town say if they heard I'd been hiding here all these years and didn't go out with a bang?"

If that's what she does, and assuming I *can* be killed, I'd consider it a mighty friendly gesture on her part, but of course, she knows that, and it's not in her nature to do anyone any favors, which is why I'm certain she has no intention of leaving Milestone. I'm willing to bet those few copper pennies in my pocket that as soon as she steps outside and gets all the confirmation she needs that she's well and truly free, she'll raze this town and everything in it. Then maybe I'll die, but for now, all I'm hearing is big talk from a small lady.

"But we're friends," she adds, perhaps because she's had her fingers in my mind, and can taste the doubt on them. "And a friend wouldn't do such a thing."

I choose to take that as fear that whatever she thinks I've done for her will be cancelled by my death. Whatever she has in store for me, it won't happen until she's sure she's off the hook. Makes me glad I took precautions.

"For a woman eager to be out of here, you're sure taking your sweet time about it." I draw the bottle toward me, fill up my glass and down it quickly. There's not going to be time for another refill so I guess it's best to get one while the going's good. Too bad I don't feel a damn thing. Might as well be drinking water.

"Then I guess this is sayonara," she says, with another small bow. This time her eyes don't leave mine, and her smile is decidedly unpleasant. She leans close; I try not to flinch. Her lips are like slugs against my cheek, her hair like catgut on my skin. When she draws back, her pupils have filled her eyes, making them look full to bursting with black ink. She moves away, toward the door, the dim light not dim enough to hide the black and blue shapes that are swimming beneath the milky pond of her skin. On the threshold, she hesitates. I can't see her face; her back is to me, and I find myself wondering what might be running through her mind at this moment. Whether to kill me now, or later? Whether or not to trust the promise of an undead salesman? Whatever it is, it passes, and takes the tension from her shoulders with it.

Her hand finds the door, massages the wood grain as if it's become a lover's skin, then slides lower, lower, toward the knob, circling it playfully, letting her fingertips brush against the cold brass. A nail clinks against the metal. She's toying with it, teasing it, as if enough foreplay could draw a reaction from a hunk of old wood. Her sigh too, comes from the mouth of a woman in the throes of passion and a ripple passes through her, but the satisfied chuckle that follows is not at all feminine, and even less human.

She grabs the knob. Giggles with delight.

"See you soon," she says over her shoulder, as thorns begin to poke forth from her skin.

Then the creature that is Lian Su opens the door to the night.

22

Kyle kills the engine at the bottom of the hill. He is quiet as Iris brusquely pins the Sheriff's badge on his breast. Wearing it doesn't feel right, and that's to be expected. But Iris's frosty attitude doesn't feel right either, and he figures maybe he'll get a chance to quiz her about that later. Right now, there isn't time, or the breath required to force those questions out, because what he sees before him reminds him of a painting he once saw in an art magazine at the dentist's office in Saddleback: A bunch of shadowy things flowing up a mountain toward a cabin with a single light shining in the window. He remembers wondering who in their right mind would hang something like that in their home, or even in a museum. It gave him the creeps just like the sight of it happening now in real life makes his heart slow and the hair rise to attention all over his body. But while it was too tough to make out what that dark mass in the painting was, he can see all too clearly what's racing toward Eddie's.

It's the deer, a whole herd of them, the same ones he almost plowed into back at the intersection. But that's not all that's robbed the breath from him. He raises a finger, presses it to the windshield glass. "Isn't that—?"

From the corner of his eye, he sees Iris nod.

Blue Moon Running Bear, the obsidian man, running like the hounds of Hell are snapping at his heels. Three feet behind him, there's someone else, someone who doesn't seem to be moving quite as fast and yet never falls behind. His arms are flapping wildly, at least that's how it seems to Kyle, until he realizes there are pockets appearing in the herd as they scramble to get to him. *Red Cloud.*

"What the hell?"

"Here," Iris says, drawing his attention away from the windshield. He looks down and sees she's put a gun in his hand, still warm from wherever she's kept it hidden. "You'll need this."

He shakes his head, not to deny that he thinks she's right, but because right now, as he looks back out to the chaos on the hill, he can't figure out how a gun, or anything else, is going to give him an advantage over what appears to be a thousand angry deer.

"Go." Iris pokes him in the shoulder.

"Go where? What am I supposed to do?"

"You're the Sheriff now. Go help the people who need one."

He looks at her for a long moment, at how her eyes still manage to sparkle in the gloom, and he wishes just once, that he could read her mind and see what it is he's done wrong, see how to fix it, because it occurs to him that hate, in leaving him, has opened his eyes to a lot of things he has let go to waste, a lot of things he's squandered, and Iris is one of them. He's known her for most of his life, and doesn't know her at all.

"I'm sorry," he whispers.

"Me too," she tells him, only her words don't sound like an apology. "Get movin'. And keep your eyes open up there."

⌒

Lian Su screams and every one of those glasses behind the counter explodes. I don't quite flinch, don't quite duck, but I make damn well sure my head is turned the other way when that blizzard of shards comes toward me. And as the glass needles my back, I see what's become of the woman in the open doorway. Down on her knees, Lian Su is no longer a woman, but a slideshow. There are so many shapes and colors and different forms slouching back into the bar, all of them pushing against her skin in an effort to escape, it's hard to focus on any single one of them without it making my head hurt. Her face is a misshapen blob, mapped with dark veins, her hair more like snakes that rage around her skull as branch-like arms claw at the floor, dragging a body that no longer has the strength to carry it back to safety.

Her mouth, little more than a dark hole leaking worm-like things onto the floor, opens wide, and from that ancient and rotten gullet fly words in a language I don't understand. The force behind them though, makes it clear they are not compliments.

I back away from the bar.

Back on this side of the threshold, Lian Su looks a little more human. The shape of her has settled, even if the activity beneath her skin hasn't. There are still all manner of things pulsating and pushing at her from the inside out, making her seem like a rubber glove filled with cockroaches.

The head she raises to regard me is pitted with dark spots, like a negative image of chicken pox. Dark stuff runs from every hole in it. She convulses, grunts with pain, and I feel something inside me respond in sympathy. "*Youuuuuu,*" she says, grabbing another hand full of floor and pulling. "*Welsshhhhhhed.*"

That's not exactly true. After all, isn't death an escape in itself? And it's not as if she didn't provide me with the means to make this happen. Back here, after the fire, while still in her Gracie costume, she told me something she didn't have to share, and I didn't think I'd ever need to know: *First time I tried stepping over the threshold of this place, it made me sterile and ejected the baby that was busy growin' in my belly,* and then: *I put it down to coincidence and tried again. That one gave me such a pain it dropped me to the floor and left me there for two days, paralyzed and bleedin' from every hole in my body. So I gave up, figurin' if I tried a third time, it might be the last.* She had no reason to tell me all of that, but she did, and I used it.

This will be her third try.

"I'm giving you what you wanted," I explain, moving to the center of the room.

She gurgles something I can't understand, and hauls herself closer until she's lying about two feet from my shoes. If she stretched out her arm, she could touch me.

I trust her injuries to keep her prostrate for a moment and raise my head.

The door to the tavern is wide open. Beyond, I can hear rumbling as Blue Moon's tribe try to run him down, the *thwick-thwick-thwick* sound as Red Cloud's arrows take them out. They're getting closer.

～

Kyle's feet pump the crumbling earth as he races alongside the deer. They move like maddened things, their hooves barely scraping the earth, but much to his relief, they pay him no mind. It's the two Indians they're after, though Kyle can't begin to fathom what they could possibly have done to invoke the rage of a dumb bunch of animals. Then again, neither man is made of flesh and bone, so trying to gauge the severity of their transgressions seems a bit ridiculous. As he runs, gun heavy in his hand, heart heavy in his chest, he realizes he's glad to be alive. There was nothing in death but a vast empty space, now a small dark pocket in his memory, and despite the confusion that clings to him like a shroud, he's *here*, and running, tasting life with a sense of purpose. He doesn't know how long that will last, or if it will at all, but reminds himself that tonight, if nothing else happens in that tavern up ahead (which seems unlikely), he will swallow his bitterness and thank his father, who will no doubt shrug it off with embarrassment. The guy could win the lottery and he'd shrug like he knew it was coming.

A woman's scream drifts down the hill and Kyle falters. Stops dead. He waits, listening for it to come again, and despite the thunderous passage of the deer only a few feet away, does not feel compelled to move.

Up ahead, Red Cloud turns and hurries, his stiff-legged gait carrying him into the tavern.

There is no sign of Blue Moon Running Bear, which suggests to Kyle that he has already made it inside. Then again, the man has been sculpted from the night itself and his eyes are stars, so it could be he's up there somewhere and hidden within the folds of darkness.

Kyle stands alone, the grass damp with dew, crickets sawing their songs around him, birds making unenthusiastic attempts at nightsongs for an unappreciative audience. Some of the deer, heads lowered, antlers like daggers of bone aimed at the wood, assault the door of the tavern. The rest spread out around the long narrow building, encircling it, trapping the men inside. Still Kyle waits. He knows Iris has sent him here to help his father, to repay the personal debt they've established between them, and that time is of the essence, but he finds himself unable and unwilling to move. He waits, tells himself that despite the urgency of the situation and the obvious need for his help, he will continue to stand here until he hears the scream again and is proved wrong in thinking it came from his long dead mother.

～

When Dean gets done crooning some song Brody's never heard, he flashes that famous smile, then, with a deft move like a magician shucking back his sleeve to demonstrate there's nothing concealed inside it, his hand flashes out and he breaks one of Brody's fingers.

Brody cries out with pain and doubles over, hitting his head hard on the steering wheel. Tears flow as he cradles the wounded digit. "Jesus, man. What the *fuck?*"

Dean sits back, admiring the night beyond the windshield. "The problem wasn't so much you killing that guy pretending to be me, sonny. Problem was when you whacked him, you took away another reason for folks to remember me."

His face contorted with pain, damp forehead pressed against the wheel, Brody tells him, "He was trying to rob me, for Chrissakes. Guy had a *knife* to my throat."

Dean nods his understanding and spreads his hands. "Hey, he was a punk. I know that, but it still upset me. After all, no one wants to think about some dumb old dead crooner, now do they?" He purses his lips, then continues. "Oh sure, the old farts play us on their radios, but they don't think about me or Frankie, or any of the old boys. Not any more, even though it don't cost 'em a dime. Not one dime, friend. They just keep us locked away with memories of the first time they got laid." He narrows his eyes at Brody, as if he's worried that it's too complicated for the kid to understand. "The proud moments, y'know? Life's moments. But it don't matter what the music playing in the background was. Oh no. That gets forgotten. We get forgotten." He sighs, looks back out at the road. "Then you have the crazies, the guys who got hit on the head one too many times in the ring, or came back with busted heads from one war or another, and just because I was singing on the radio while they waited to get their brains put back in, they decide I'm God. They decide they're going to be me, and damned if they don't walk around like little mirror images, singing and dancing and reminding people of the good 'ol days. Highballs in one hand; smoke in the other. Reminding people of *Dino*." He rubs his hands together in delight and grins. "So here you have some goddamn yuppie couple who are eating cavier, sipping champagne in the park while Tommy wonders how many deadbolts there are on the woman's underwear and she's wondering when's he gonna stop wondering how many deadbolts there are on her underwear because she's not wearing any, when up the street comes waltzing the ghost of Dino, looking like me right down to the smile and the sparkling eyes, right down to the snazzy shoes. Only he smells like dog shit and old pizza, but hell, the job's already been done, because the girl sees him and starts remembering, and she tells the guy about how she's free next Sunday and maybe he'd like to come over and watch a movie, and its one she remembers seeing as a kid, something about some lecherous but handsome lush, and it sounds like a prime opportunity for Tommy to bang the broad, so he agrees. Cut to Sunday, my friend, and both of those jerks are squatting by the TV watching me do my thing, and they're enjoying it. And I'm getting off on it.

"That, kid, is who you knocked off."

"I didn't know."

Dino lights a cigarette. "Why'd you kill him?"

"I told you."

"Sure. Sure you did. Because he was going to rob you right?"

"Right."

"Well ain't that something. You took the guy's life because he stole from you." He slaps his knee, tipping ash onto the floor. "Just like *you* stole from *me* by killing him and robbing me of the limelight, right?" He laughs loudly. "Life can be a hell of a thing sometimes, can't it?"

"I didn't know. I swear I didn't."

Dean blows out a plume of blue smoke. It flows across the windshield and up Brody's nose. He coughs before he can stop it, looks fearfully at his passenger, then allows himself a sigh when it appears his involuntary protest has gone unnoticed.

"That was some pretty broad you had too."

With no small effort, Brody raises his head. "Yeah, she was."

"Too bad about the drugs."

"Yeah."

"You know her long?"

"Maybe a year."

"Know who she was?"

Brody feels a tightening across his chest. The casual way the man is asking these questions, the way he's not looking at him, makes him fear that Carla might have been someone a lot more important, at least to the ghost of Dean Martin, than he ever suspected. She certainly played the guy's music enough to drive him crazy, so maybe…

"Wanted to be a ballerina," Dean tells him, a wistful smile on his faces. "Like any little girl. Grew up, wanted to be a lawyer because she got hooked on *Matlock*. Got older still and wanted to be a model, even spent some time in L.A. That's where she discovered the shit she kept putting in her veins. Came back, cleaned up, got herself enrolled in a nice community college thing, studied to be a medic. Dated a guy who beat the shit out of her at every available opportunity, so she ended up getting involuntary hands-on training with the medics. She left him and the college, hitchhiked her way to Texas, considered getting into music. First guy she approached told her he'd give her as much time in the studio as she gave him on his couch. The old story. She thought of suicide, but dismissed it in favor of resuming her habit. Why? Because I told her so. I thought her being messed up and alive was better than her being dead any day of the week. And she was helping to keep *me* around, playing my records every time she felt blue, mentioning my name whenever the subject of music came up. And why? Because her grandmother and me had a thing one time, back in the late '50's, right when I was at the top of my game. Showed up backstage on night at a Vegas show, a real country girl, out of her league and well aware of it, but just there to prove she had the guts to come say "hi" to a man she thought she loved because of how I looked and because I could sing real well. I took her to dinner a few nights, and sent her on her way, and that was that. Liked that gal a lot.

"Once I went balls up and they put me in the ground, I figured I'd look in on her from time to time, and kinda got to like it. She always played my records too. After she died, I watched over her daughter, then Carla." He whistles. "What a kid. Helped that she liked my music of course. But I watched her real close, watched her life get worse and worse and not a whole lot I could do about it. Oh sure, I'd help her throw up after a bad night, or put her car keys where she could find them, maybe keep a bad guy she was thinking of dating out of the picture until she forgot about him and he forgot about everything except when to empty his colostomy bag. But she was on the downward slope, friend, and I couldn't do enough to keep that from happening. After she left Texas, I followed her to Gainesburg, where she met you."

Brody remembers. The bank job with Smalls, a low-level thug with dreams of grandeur that ended up splattered all over the wall of the First National. Kyle had kept his share, and spent the first of it at a roadside diner a hundred miles from Gainesburg. That was where he'd met Carla. She'd been sitting alone in a booth, staring into a cup of coffee, looking like she was considering jumping into it and drowning. He'd watched her from his own booth, weighing up the positives and negatives of approaching a girl when he was on the run from the law, when she took the initiative and slid in beside him, started talking about the weather, and music (*Do you like Dean Martin?*), as if they'd been friends forever.

"I didn't mean for her to die," Brody says, grimacing as he inspects his broken finger. "I swear I didn't. I loved her."

"You think you did."

"No, I—"

"The same way you think you loved all those other girls you dragged along on the little crime spree you call your life, all those other girls you turned into mothers because you don't care. Sooner or later they stop becoming your problem. Sooner or later they stop becoming anything at all."

"That's not how it is."

Dean looks at him, grins widely. "Look who you're talking to. There's no sense arguing with me, and why would you want to? You're stressed out enough as it is."

"Please, look…"

"I'm not going to kill you, kid."

Every muscle in Brody's body unclenches, and he allows himself to sit back.

"That's not how I do things. I just wanted you to know who that girl was those guys put in the ground back there. She wasn't just another one of your crack-whores good for a hundred miles only. She was someone, and she was a damn sight more human than you'll ever be."

Brody nods. "I know you don't believe me, but I did care about her."

"Sure you did, kid." Dean cracks open his door, puts one foot out on the road. "Sure you did." He exits the car, brushes dirt from his trousers and leans in the open window. "Do me a favor, will ya?"

Brody looks at him. "Sure."

"When you get on your way, play some of Carla's discs. I don't imagine there'd be a nicer way to sing her to sleep." He winks, "See you soon, kid," thumps a set of gold-ringed fingers down on the door, and walks away whistling a song Brody has heard but can't place. It comes to him by the time he finds the strength to sit up and start the ignition again. It was one of Carla's favorites. 'There's No Tomorrow.'

23

Though Blue Moon's face is made of black glass, I can see the doubt and wariness etched into it, or perhaps I'm seeing those emotions swirling beneath the surface. Can't say I blame him. He has risked everything to be here for a man he has always trusted. Problem is, I'm hiding in the body of a man he doesn't.

He nods that great big hunk of glass, his eyes glimmering jewels in a dark mask. "Sheriff."

"Thanks for coming, Blue. You too Red."

There is nothing about Red Cloud to suggest he's a living thing. He's standing there to the right of the door just as he always stands by Blue's door, motionless, face raised to the sky, painted eyes staring upward, mouth set in a grim line. He's a cigar store Indian, nothing more, but I know he's listening, and his quiver is full.

Something slams against the door.

Blue looks down at the witch. She's on her knees now, head lowered, lank hair hanging almost to the floor. "She goin' to make it?"

"Don't know. Would be better if she didn't."

He sighs and steps closer to me. Seen through him, the flame from the hurricane lamp on the bar is fragmented, the light dulled and trapped in feeble shards inside his chest. "What do you want us to do?"

"She's not going to let this slide," I tell him quietly. "Chances are she's going to make me very sorry I crossed her. If that happens, I want to be sure I've done at least one thing right. I wanted to give you and Red Cloud what you want. I want to set you both free."

Blue glances from Red Cloud to me. "I didn't come because of that."

"I know you didn't."

"And after all this time, I'm not sure I want it."

"Maybe not, but it's no way to live, Blue. You deserve better."

A sigh that sounds like someone blowing air over the top of an empty bottle and he shakes his head slowly. "Sheriff, we've been friends for a long time, but that don't mean you know all there is to know about me. Now I've had plenty of time to think it over and it seems like everyone comes to this town for one reason only, and that's to pay for the bad things they've done. I don't know why it has to be Milestone, or whether or not there are a thousand places like this all over the world, if there even is a world outside this town anymore. All I know is we're here because we brought ourselves here, and I figure if I'm meant to pay for my sins by living out the rest of my days like this, then that's what I'll do."

"What about Red?"

"Hell, Red doesn't know how to do anything else now but use that bow and arrow of his. Truth be told, he was never much of a talker even back when he was flesh and bone, but his company was always good, and company enough for me."

"I'd go crazy stuck in that damn house, Blue."

"You're stuck in a house of your own now, Sheriff, and I don't figure that's much of a way to live either."

A bang and a crack as antlers splinter the door.

As if it's her cue, Lian Su raises her face, looks from Red Cloud to Blue Moon, before settling her gaze on me. Her eyes are gone, the remains of them already hardening on her cheeks. The teeth she bares are bloodstained. "You tricked me," she says, with what might be delight. "You hid the mark, that's all. A simple thing. What a fool I am."

I take a step back. Blue Moon doesn't move.

Thunder slams against the door.

"You don't belong here, Lian, and you've done enough damage."

"I've done enough damage?" She stands without moving, as if invisible hands have jerked her up from the floor. "I haven't even *begun* to do damage."

The light from the hurricane lamp goes out. Automatically, I move away from the queer gray light that seems to cling to Lian like a second skin. Again she looks around, as if counting her adversaries, and then, grinning, starts moving in my direction.

"Don't," I command. It isn't directed at Lian but Blue Moon, who, though the darkness has made him all but invisible, is moving toward her. I can tell by the sound. I can tell…just because I can.

He ignores me, and suddenly the gray light around the witch begins to swim. Fuzzy misshapen shadows clamber up the walls. He's standing before her. She looks up at him, a tall obsidian man, utterly fearless and with nothing to lose, and admiration flickers across her chalk-white face. "If I broke your heart," she asks, almost sweetly. "Would it break the rest of you?" She doesn't wait for an answer, and he doesn't wait for her to hurt him. In an instant, his hands are around her throat, lifting her off the floor, and from the gloom comes the telltale sound of Red Cloud loading his bow.

"My, but you're a strong one," Lian says and brings her arms up between his, her hands grabbing his wrists. As three of Red Cloud's arrows pierce the flesh at the side of her neck, one after the other, *thwick-thwick-thwick*, with barely a second separating them, she screeches. Her hands convulse, shattering Blue Moon's wrists. Glass rains to the floor. He staggers back, stunned, and raises arms that no longer have hands at the end of them.

Thwick-thwick-thwick. Another trio of arrows fly forth from Red Cloud's bow, this time hitting home in the side of Lian's face. She whirls, ducks low, and ends up in a crouch, one leg splayed out, the other folded beneath her, hands like claws on the floor. It could be ballet; it could be martial arts, but either way it means trouble for the wooden Indian.

"Stop…"

She doesn't acknowledge my request, doesn't look over her shoulder at me. Blue Moon, forgetting his newly acquired handicap rushes her. By the door, which continues to deteriorate under the weight of the deer, Red Cloud calmly draws back the string on his bow, his face forever expressionless.

Lian Su raises her hand in the air, palm faced in my direction, as if she's calling a halt to proceedings. But then something swishes by my ear, catches the hazy light and smacks into her palm. It's the bottle we drank from at the bar, still half-full, and before I can begin to guess what she's going to do with it, she brings it to her lips, empties it into her mouth, then almost immediately spits it back out. In Red Cloud's direction.

Before it hits him, it ignites, and abruptly Red Cloud is engulfed in violet fire.

Blue Moon collides with Lian Su, driving her into the door. She laughs and chops her hand against the side of his neck. Dark fragments fly, but he raises his arms and brings them down on her skull. She grunts, but does not fall, and delivers a second chop to Blue's neck. Then another. This time there's a sound like spare change falling to the floor and Blue Moon falls. He does not shatter, but enough of him breaks and scatters across the floor that I know he's not getting up again.

Red Cloud makes not a sound. The fire seeps into the cracks in his hide, vanishing inside him, burning him from the inside out. Smoke seeps from every fissure. The wood begins to blacken. His eyes have become red-hot coals.

He reaches for another arrow.

I've got to get her outside again. I've got to get her over that threshold, weaken her. With this resolution comes self-chastisement for not dealing her a killing blow when the opportunity was there, an error that cost Blue Moon and Red Cloud their lives. But of course, there's a very good reason for that lapse in judgment: I can hurt Lian as much as I like, but I'm not entirely sure I can kill her, or anyone for that matter. I can set it up so they kill themselves, offer them bargains that put them in the line of fire, but pulling the trigger is not something I believe I'm allowed to do.

But I'll do all I can.

As if she senses this, Lian turns to look at me, a smile growing as she gleefully steps on one of Blue Moon's legs, crushing it and scattering glass everywhere. Behind her the door is weakening, barely hanging on its hinges, and I wonder how much of that is her doing, because the weight of those animals out there combined with their infuriated battering, should have brought it down long before now.

"I have to tell you," she says, kicking aside a rough chunk of obsidian. "Although I ache in parts of me I wasn't aware I had, this is turning out to be quite a lot of fun."

There's a whoosh of air, a sickening crack I've mistakenly thought has come from the door, and she stops with a sudden intake of breath, shudders, and looks down at the point of an arrow which is sticking out of her cheek, black blood dripping from the tip.

Red Cloud, still burning, reloads. But his movements have slowed and fresh flame has begun to erupt from those cracks in his body. He's wreathed in smoke and wavering.

There isn't much time.

～

The scream does not come again.

Too much time has passed.

Whatever thrall has held him here ebbs away at last, and Kyle runs. His initial awe and fear at seeing them forgotten, he steps off the path and right into the middle of the herd. They don't so much move to accommodate him, as grudgingly let him infiltrate their number. Flies buzz his face. Warm bodies try to crush him between them. Antlers scratch his cheek, stab his flesh, but he continues on, aware that he still has the gun if one of the deer should decide to take him on. He fights his way through until he is almost there and almost out of breath. His throat aches. Anticipating a struggle with the animals that are busy ramming the door like maddened things, he is surprised when they stop their assault, look back at him, and slowly lope away. The wind seems to whisper, as Kyle moves quickly into the gap they've left for him, cocks back the hammer on the gun, and throws the door open.

～

I watch Lian Su's expression change from hate, to rage, to pleading, as she spins around to greet the boy in the doorway. To greet my son.

～

"They hurt me," his mother tells him, and Kyle feels every ounce of his resolve turn to dust.

"Mom?"

She nods slowly, a creature of ethereal beauty, her hair lustrous, skin pale. She is naked, but he does not register this for now. All he can see are her eyes, which look bloated and black. She reaches out to him in a gesture of pleading. She is asking him to save her. But from what?

He tears his fascinated and heartbroken gaze away from her to the burning Indian in the corner, watches as it topples and falls to the floor. The flames are mirrored a thousand times in the shards of black glass scattered around the floor like frozen puddles of oil. Blue Moon and Red Cloud. Dead. He feels a pang of sadness, but it is no more resonant than a gunshot on a battlefield. There is too much else to see, to understand.

Then he does.

Standing a short distance behind his mother is a gaunt old man dressed in a dark raincoat, one eye milky white in the light from the flames, the other staring at him.

Cadaver. The puppeteer.

Kyle steps into the bar, the gun held out before him, aimed at the old man. "You son of a bitch."

His mother drifts aside, her face filled with pride and pain.

Kyle glances at her. "He brought you back?"

"It's not her," Cadaver tells him.

"You shut the fuck up, all right? I'm talking to *her*."

"Yes," his mother tells him, "but it was a trick. He tricked me. Tricked your father too."

Kyle stops dead. "Where is he?"

"He killed him."

He returns his gaze to the old man, who suddenly looks scared and helpless, and that encourages him. "I asked you a question."

❧

There are no words to make him understand, no way to make him believe me, because all the things I could say about his life, the things only a father would know, are a mystery to me. He stands there, Lian Su watching with malevolent glee, and the fire in his eyes does not come from the blaze that has consumed Red Cloud and is rapidly spreading, licking at the walls. This fire is his and I recognize it immediately. When I brought him back from the dead, it might have been forgotten, replaced by the shock of his resurrection, but it never left him. That same fire has marked the worst times of his life, and I've been there for them all, been the genesis of most of them.

But there is nothing I can say. Instead, I change the focus from me to the grinning witch to my left. "She's not your mother."

"That so?"

"Yes it is so. Her name is Lian Su. She tricked all of us into believing she was Gracie for years, but she isn't. She murdered our friend and now she's trying to destroy everything else. Don't let her fool you."

"Fool me?" He grins crookedly, comes closer, the gun held steady in his grip, the muzzle aimed at my face. "You're the only one who did that. Was it you who brought me back from the dead after I refused your deal?"

"No. Your father did."

"And in return…?"

"It doesn't matter."

"The hell it doesn't." Agony makes a melting mask of his face. In an instant, he has closed the distance between us and the muzzle of the gun is a hard cold circle pressed between my eyes. "Start talking."

"There's nothing to say. If you believe that woman is your mother, then you'll die."

"And what do you suggest I do?"

"Start believing the truth."

There are faces at the door, animal faces, but they're not interested in this little showdown. All their eyes are cast down, toward the remains of Red Cloud and Blue Moon. I guess for them, the hunt is over. Kyle's is too; he just doesn't know it yet.

"Your voice…" he says, frowning.

Maybe he does know; maybe he suspects. I say a silent prayer.

"What about it?" With my good eye, I stare hard at him. *C'mon kid. See it. See what's there in front of you.*

"You're not using the…whatever it was."

"Do you want to know why?"

He shakes his head, swallows. "What was the bargain? Tell me."

"Him for you."

"Did you kill him?"

"No."

"Then…then what happened? Where is he?"

Right here, son. Right here, if you'd only open your eyes.

"You were always a smart kid, Kyle. Figure it out."

At length, he does. The gun lowers just a fraction, but the expression of confusion on his face tells me that somewhere within him, he is trying to understand, considering the possibilities. Like the possibility that his father would trade places with Cadaver to get his son back.

For a long moment nothing is said, but the gun drops another inch lower and the hand holding it is no longer so sure. He closes his eyes, shakes his head as if to deny the suggestion that I am willing him to believe.

"He wouldn't do it. He didn't have the guts."

"Yes I did."

I cannot grant my own wishes, can't make my own world change its axis, but nevertheless I've used every ounce of wishful thinking I've got to summon from my rotten throat those three words, spoken in a voice that is unmistakably mine.

"Pop?"

I allow myself the tiniest of smiles, a mere tug of my lips as I'm lit from the inside by a flare of hope I haven't felt since Reverend Hill's corpse hit the floor. Things will never be the same; they can't be, but if I die or go wherever I'd bound for with the knowledge that my son knew I loved him, it will be enough.

"Welcome back," I tell him, and he lowers his head, a gesture of defeat. For the moment I'm uncertain why, or what it is he's mourning. Perhaps he's finally letting go of the fire. Perhaps he came here hoping to find me dead. I don't know and it doesn't matter.

"Kyle. I'm sorry."

It takes him a while to look at me, and when finally he does, there are tears in his eyes. "Why?"

"You know why, and if you don't, it'll come to you eventually. Right now we—"

I trail off.

Lian Su is no longer by the wall, but my frantic search for her is a short one.

She's standing right behind Kyle, and before I have a chance to call out a warning, her hands are slithering over his shoulders, clamping onto the sides of his face. Fear fills his eyes. "Give your mother a kiss," Lian hisses. Blue veins begin to spread across my son's face. Fog fills his eyes. He shudders. "What's—?" is all he manages to say before his lips turn blue. He begins to sag.

"No!" I step forward, reaching for them both.

With little effort, and a sound like glass crunching beneath a boot heel, Lian Su wrenches his head around to face her.

24

It doesn't matter whether you're God, or the devil, or an agent of one or the other, you always know the consequences of your actions. Even I did, though I chose to ignore them. Lian Su knows too what she has set in motion, and calls upon every trick in her book to evade my fury. She's smoke through my fingers, fire on my skin, ice in my bones; she's a legion of exotic bugs crawling over my flesh; blades cutting me to pieces, but I can't die. All I can do is flail wildly at whatever form she chooses to take.

In the end it's Kyle she becomes, a last-ditch effort to play on my grief, just as she distracted my son by becoming his mother. But I know her. I have stood idly by and watched everyone die and everything burn. I have heard from her own mouth and seen with my own eyes the soul-less evil thing she is behind the succession of masks and costumes. And this costume is my son.

With a cry of rage I should not have the strength to unleash, I tear that costume apart, snap its bones, sunder its face, all the while shutting out his voice lest it shatters me like her hands shattered Blue Moon.

"You won't win; you can't," Lian tells me in Kyle's voice.

Once more, Eddie's is in flames. Smoke fills the bar. The deer at the door have moved away.

I drag Lian to the floor, shove her face into the fire.

She laughs.

I grab fistfuls of charred wooden arrows from Red Cloud's quiver and bury them in her chest.

She taunts me.

I slash her throat with a shard of obsidian.

She grins.

Exhausted, but driven by rage that is almost enough for me to erupt into flames of my own, I grab her hair. She turns to black tar to escape me, spins her limbs into threads that shoot out in all directions, latching onto unstable wood, the floor, the crumbling roof, anything to keep her inside this place. But the place won't hold, and neither will she, not under the opposing weight of my anger.

Head lowered, I run through the flames. Joints and muscles protest in screaming agony. I ignore them, make claws of my hands.

Kyle, I'm so sorry.

Lian Su turns to stone.

I tried.

I barrel into her, breaking my nose, my jaw, my fingers, cracking open my skull.

I love you.

I feel none of it as I force her into the air.

Please forgive me.

And over the threshold.

~

"I'll set you free."

Outside, their faces made a rusty red by the roaring flames, stand the deer. One of them, its antlers more viciously intricate than those of its brethren, moves a little closer, eyes me with caution, inspects the writhing woman at my feet who is a mesmerizing kaleidoscope of colors and forms. Blood and fluids of every shade leak from the gaping hole in her belly. Threats in an alien tongue slither from her mouth.

"And what do you want in return?" the deer whispers, turning its head sharply to silence the sibilant dissension from the herd. "We didn't come here for her."

"Blue Moon and Red Cloud are dead. This…woman…has caused many people great pain, and in killing your quarry, has denied you justice, condemned you to search for something you'll never find. There is no place I can think of to keep her that will stop her from returning. If you take her; if you keep her with you, I'll set you free of the hunt."

"What makes you think the land of the dead can hold her?"

"Because for a long time, this tavern was enough."

Maybe Lian Su will come back, and maybe she won't, but what I'm asking of this creature now is all I can think of and it's better than nothing.

After a moment, the deer takes a step forward and slowly lowers its head, cocks it, and prods Lian Su's wound with one curved tip of its antler. She convulses and shrieks as dark blue light flares, lighting up every nerve and blood vessel in her body.

The deer turns away. The rest of the herd follow suit. They have taken only a few steps when the wind rises and they become dust in its arms, whirling away in eddies. They leave a curious emptiness behind them.

I look down at Lian. The blue light is eating her away. She fights it, screeching, baleful eyes trying to will a slow and painful death on me as she spasms and struggles. White-knuckled hands claw at the earth; her legs kick. Then the struggling subsides. A faint sigh escapes her twisted lips as her hair turns to water and seeps into the ground. A single shiver, then the eyes are gone, draining back into the hollows that held them. Her fingers become trickles, the nails dewdrops, and in what seems like only a couple of seconds, Lian Su is gone, turned to water that quenches the thirst of the earth at my feet.

Behind me, Eddie's collapses.

The fire rages on.

❧

Iris is waiting at the foot of the hill, shivering in the cold breeze, her eyes focused on the blaze. When I reach her she says nothing, just shakes her head and gets into the car. I expect her to leave, to haul ass out of here and never look back, but she waits. Goes right on waiting until I come around to the passenger side and slide in beside her. We sit there in silence, watching the tavern burn for the second time.

At length, she turns to me and studies my face, tentatively touches the already healing wounds. "Did you tell him?"

"Yes." I take a deep breath that feels like sand going down my throat, and wait a moment, debating whether or not the question needs to be asked, then I ask it before I can decide. "Why didn't you?"

"It wouldn't have mattered."

"You don't know that."

She smiles sadly. "I'm afraid I do, Tom. Maybe someday I'll tell you about my life and you'll understand why." She lets her hand fall away, brings it to the ignition and starts the car. "Where should we go?"

I look out the window, my mind already drifting along the road, to the remains of a car with a dead woman still inside.

"I have to bury Cobb's wife. Promised him I would."

"Okay," she says quietly. "Then where?"

I haven't the heart to tell her that whatever the destination is, it won't be one we'll share, so I close my eyes and try to find sleep that, like so many simple things, will forever remain out of reach for people like me.

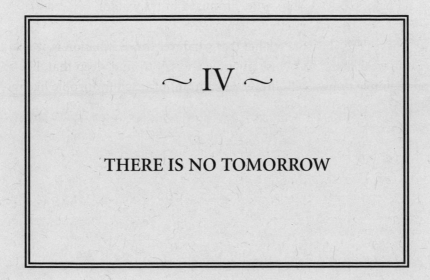

~ IV ~

THERE IS NO TOMORROW

25

The Indian's car gives up the ghost sixty miles past the border and Brody figures that's more luck than he has any right to expect. After all, he's out of that goddamn Twilight Zone and close enough to a normal town to get the junker fixed, or find himself a new one. Hell, if there's time, maybe he'll take a stroll down Main Street, try to find a doctor he can wake up to get a patch-job done on his finger.

Maybe. That clock is still ticking at the back of his mind, and even sixty miles isn't far enough away from that hellhole he just came screaming out of.

Prioritize, kid, he tells himself. *There'll be plenty of time to chill out when I'm clear on the other side of the Mexican border.*

After a perfunctory glance at the corroded innards of the Dodge, he slams the hood down and starts to walk. A few miles back he encountered a—mercifully graffiti-free—sign that told him he was entering Saddleback, and that'll do him just fine. Had it said MILESTONE, then he'd know for sure he'd died and gone to Hell.

Ahead, block-shaped buildings cast jagged shadows across the narrow street. At first glance Saddleback seemed just as desolate and dismal as Milestone, but there are lights on in a lot of those buildings, and laughter echoes hollowly from an alley. Above him, the stars are a welcome sight, and help to light his way until he reaches the amber glow from the houses. Even the air feels different here, lived-in, as if normal people pass through it every day and their words linger long after they've gone home to bed. There is no sense of gloom, of hopelessness.

It's just a town, with regular folks. No glass or wooden Indians, no mad preachers, fire-handed healers, or homicidal deer. Just regular folks.

He walks a bit further, as relieved and calm as the lacerating pain in his broken finger will let him be. A new wave of voices catches his attention.

He follows it, drawn to the sound of normal human conversation, and it brings him to a small bar, with brightly lit mullioned windows and a garishly painted sign above the door that proclaims it THE FALLRIGHT INN. Brody groans silently at the joke, but makes no move to go inside.

It's just a tavern, and a normal looking one, with the animated shadows of customers spread across the drawn blinds beckoning to him to come inside.

He chews his lower lip, regards his broken finger, and sighs deeply.

"To hell with it," he says at last and tugs at the door, which he half-expects to be locked from the inside. It swings open without a sound and a wave of heat welcomes him, chasing the chill from his bones.

As soon as he steps foot into the tavern, he smiles. There is no gloom here, no shadow of death, no lunatics, just a bar with polished brass rails and gleaming glasses stacked in a classy looking row of mahogany shelves on the wall behind the counter. The roof is lofty, and devoid of cobwebs; the walls clean and adorned with pictures of past visitors, winning race-horses, and sports heroes.

But it is the light Kyle notices most of all. It's clean, and bright, and there is more than one. Here, the shadows are flat and unthreatening.

There are more people here too, at least twenty at a guess. They turn to look at him as the door swings shut. Relief overwhelms him. "Name's Brody," he blurts, then immediately hides a wince. *Way to go asshole. Why not say: Hi, I'm Brody, the murderer? You might have seen me on the news?* But if anyone recognizes him, it doesn't show, and the air stays the same. Still, Brody reckons his mouth may have just put paid to the thought of staying for more than one drink. He edges up to the counter, and the barman, a stout man with ruddy cheeks, a bushy gray moustache and a peeling pate, nods in greeting.

"Evenin'."

"Whiskey," Brody tells him. "Make it a double."

"Right," says the barman, and goes to get the bottle. Brody glances at the mirror behind the bar, and nods his satisfaction. Normal folks; normal town.

Except maybe, for one man, who appears to be sobbing over his drink, his face wrinkled up so badly that his eyes have disappeared. No one seems to be paying him much attention though, so Brody feels no guilt in asking the barman about him when he returns with his whiskey.

"What's his story?"

"Who, Kelly?"

"That his name?"

"Yeah. Thad Kelly. He's a regular. Runs the auto shop."

The barman begins to wipe down the counter, a sure sign that there's a story here he loves to tell. Brody takes a sip of whiskey, relaxes a little, and nods his encouragement, but all the man tells him is, "He wasn't supposed to know your name," and walks away.

Brody frowns, and looks back to the mirror.

Only then does he notice the car keys on the man's table, the grief in Kelly's eyes when he finally opens them and looks at Brody's reflection.

Only then does he notice the wild-haired priest sitting in the shadows, and the sad-eyed cop watching him from the corner.

"Oh Jesus…" Heart pounding, he licks his lips. Stands.

Takes in the rest of the "regulars".

Suddenly the lights don't seem so clean, so bright.

And from a small transistor radio set atop the counter between a woman who looks like some silver screen siren whose name he can't remember, and a naked old lady with shriveled breasts and a garishly painted grin, Dean Martin starts to sing.

~∾~

Iris sits on the edge of her bed, a cigarette clamped between her fingers. Through the boards over the window, she can hear Horace and Maggie arguing down on the street, but after a while their raised voices blend in with the natural ambience of the night and she no longer notices.

The Sheriff is gone. Kyle too, and despite what they might have come to realize about their roles in the town, Milestone will die without them. It has no pulse, no reason to go on breathing, to keep pretending, and right now, as she sits here alone with only the shadows for company, the temptation to empathize is strong.

She slides off the bed, the cigarette held at a safe distance from the bedclothes, and drops to her knees. Despite the candles, the darkness beneath her bed is thick. On all fours, she fumbles, fingers outstretched until they touch cold metal. With a satisfied sigh, she tugs, pausing to jam the cigarette between her lips, then, back on her feet, and with both hands clamped around the handle, hauls the heavy object into the light.

There's a fine film of dust on the box, which is roughly the size of a small refrigerator, or a child's coffin. She brushes it away, traces with gentle fingers the initials that have been branded into the lid.

K.V.

A whoop of laughter from Maggie informs Iris that the argument on the street has ended. Either that, or Horace has made a remark in his defense that has proved inadequate. With a faint smile, Iris shakes her head, draws on her cigarette, and scoots back on her knees. There is only one latch on the box, and it looks ancient, but Iris knows it is still functional. Tonight will not be the first time she's opened it.

She snaps the latch, absently wiping the dust on her shirt, and eases open the heavy lid.

Inside, snug in their cotton beds, are a dozen small jars.

Each one bears a label, but they all say the same thing: TIME FLIES.

Trapped within all but one of the Mason jars are insects, miraculously still alive despite the amount of time they've been cooped up in there. Iris has kept this box beneath her bed for years, ever since she discovered it buried beneath a loose concrete slab in the ruin of what passes for the building's back yard.

At first, she'd thought it was exactly what it looked like: a small chest freezer, or a cooler, but then her imagination led her by the hand to more extravagant and exciting possibilities. *Maybe some bank robbers hid their loot in there. Maybe it's packed to the brim with jewelry.* Impatient, and at the mercy of childish excitement, she opened it, only to find it full of nothing but what she assumed were lightning bugs.

The flies press against the glass, as if they know they're in her thoughts. Their bodies begin to glow a queer violet color. Iris smiles. They never fail to cheer her up, even when the weight of her sadness seems too much of a challenge for them.

"Hello my friends." She picks up one of the jars and holds it in front of her face, watches them take flight again inside their little glass prison.

She wonders what would become of these strange little creatures, should she dare to let them out. It is an idea that has occurred to her before, but she has always managed to convince herself to wait. Someday, she has always promised herself, she'll find out what they are, and whether or not it's safe to release them.

Someday.

Her smile disappears.

Always someday, never now.

And now everyone is gone.

With an uncertain smile, she walks her fingers up the glass toward the lid.

The insects follow.